THE FISHER MEN
OF ANTIOCH

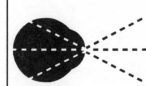

THE FISHER MEN OF ANTIOCH

A 3-IN-1 ANTHOLOGY

MARIANNE EVANS

THORNDIKE PRESS

A part of Gale, a Cengage Company

Farmington Hills, Mich • San Francisco • New York • Waterville, Maine
Meriden, Conn • Mason, Ohio • Chicago

LIBRARY OF CONGRESS CIP DATA ON FILE.
CATALOGUING IN PUBLICATION FOR THIS BOOK
IS AVAILABLE FROM THE LIBRARY OF CONGRESS

ISBN-13: 978-1-4328-6224-4 (hardcover)

Published in 2019 by arrangement with White Rose Publishing, a division of Pelican Ventures, LLC

Printed in the United States of America
1 2 3 4 5 6 7 23 22 21 20 19

THE FISHER MEN
OF ANTIOCH

THE RETURN

To John and Mary Hilger ~ No one could respect the nourishing, loving and Godly lives you lead more than me. Thank you for the inspiration (and research help!) you provided not only for The Return but for the entire Fishermen of Antioch series. The Fisher family is fictional, but the truth of their stories is something you live out day-by-day. Love you!

1

'Quickly bring the finest robe and put it on
him; put a ring on his finger and sandals
on his feet. Take the fattened calf and
slaughter it. Then let us celebrate with a
feast, because this son of mine was
dead, and has come to life again;
he was lost, and has been found.'
~ Luke 15:22–24

Phillip Fisher crouched into a squat and
dug his fingertips into hard, dry earth that
crumbled free against the exerted pressure.
He crushed the soil into his palm and then
opened his hand slow, allowing particles to
whisper, sift, and swirl against an arid —
too arid — gust of air. His gaze moved
across low-lying green leaves burnished to
rich gold by the rays of a setting sun. He
took in the sway and toss of underdeveloped
soybean plants, and his brow furrowed.
Pushing to a stand, he swiped dirty hands

against a pair of well-worn jeans — the only pair he had ever allowed within the stylized, designer-laden wardrobe of his recently vacated condo in Indianapolis. He eyed the family farmhouse.

An ache built deep in his chest as considerations of all he had done wrong barreled through his mind. All the figurative slaps in the face he had delivered to the ones most precious to him — the ones who remained sheltered inside the sturdy, if time-worn, walls of his childhood home.

A curving breeze whispered through the beds of vegetation. Dust skimmed against his face like a stroke from God, and he knew one thing to be true. He needed to come to terms with his life. Fast.

In deference to that goal, Phillip clenched his jaw and rejected further introspection. There was no time for regrets, only action. Reclamation.

Don't travel backwards when you're trying to get to the future.

Isn't that what Pop would say? Probably. The Fisher family patriarch, Jonathan, constantly preached one nugget of wisdom after another. Nowadays, Phillip wondered why he hadn't paid closer attention.

He latched his thumbs in the front pockets of his jeans as more hot air blew, tossing his hair, filling his senses with the pungent aroma of grass, fertilizer, and sunbaked earth. Without question, Pop needed help this season. All it took was a glance to realize the upcoming fall harvest would be rough. Maybe Phillip could help. Maybe he could redeem himself through hard work and dedication. In return, he hoped for nothing but the chance to begin again.

He studied the farm even closer as he crossed a pathway that framed the southern boundary of their four-hundred-acre spread. Cream colored paint peeled slightly in spots. The black shingled roof, worn and patched in a few places, would need replacing sooner rather than later. The wraparound porch remained timeless and welcoming, dotted by his mother's cheery, bright flower plants. Brown wicker chairs were angled toward the west where a flat lay of land had always set the stage for magnificent sunsets.

All the same, times weren't great. A frown pulled at the corners of his mouth, puckered his brow. He saw it all, loved it all, even as his chest swelled, because he sure hadn't shown this farm, or his family, any semblance of that emotion over the past few years.

Almost from birth, the spirit within him

had striven for much more than the tiny, rural community of Antioch, Indiana could provide. A memory dance sent him reeling backwards by three years to the day he graduated college and left Antioch for the rarified, big-city realm of Indianapolis.

He blocked that bitter recollection in its tracks. A resolute stride led him up wooden porch steps that creaked comfortably and then on to a screen door he opened against a protesting squeak.

He stopped short.

Should he push through the closed front door? He already knew it wouldn't be locked. Should he knock? Should he —

The door swept open. Against every ounce of doubt, uncertainty, and pain came the weathered, loving eyes of his father. And all it took was that look to make Phillip dissolve into the boy — the son — he had once been.

"Phillip. Welcome home."

The greeting came out gruff and thick. Without a moment's hesitation, Pop pulled him into a silent bear-hug. Pop was a big man, tall and stocky. Farming — his life's expectation and legacy — had molded him into a rock-solid, formidable life form.

Until now.

Now, the rock-solid countenance showed

fissures. Lines had deepened around his mouth and cut grooves against the corners of tired, though determined, eyes. Big shoulders sagged a bit. Dad was ailing; a former indomitability wavered beneath a heart beginning to slow, and wane. Those facts topped the list of reasons why Phillip knew it had been best to return home to Antioch. So, he enjoined the hug full force, sinking into a moment of reunion and precious affirmation. After that, he was dragged across the threshold.

"Anna! Anna, come in here."

That happy, booming summons vibrated through the air. Scurrying footfalls approached from the rear of the house, and seconds later Mom stood framed in the narrow archway fixed between the kitchen and family room.

"Phillip!" She wiped her hands briskly on the apron always fastened at her waist then dashed forward to claim a hug of her own.

"Mother and I were in the kitchen. Saw you walking up. Could hardly believe our eyes." Dad coughed — cleared his throat in a heavy way, though he smiled with unfettered joy. "Are you in town for a visit, or longer, or . . ."

The leading edge of that question wasn't lost on Phillip. He wrapped his arms around the shoulders of his parents and was led straight to the kitchen table, of course. Where else would they convene but the foundation of nourishment, welcome and gathering?

Since Phillip didn't answer his father's question right away, Pop seemed content to move on. "Have you talked to your brothers?"

"I texted Ben when I landed at the bus station and —"

"The bus station?" Mom's arched brow and wide eyes spoke volumes, telegraphing the silent question: What on earth were you doing at a bus station, and why weren't your brothers charging forward to help?

Phillip shifted uncomfortably. "Yeah. Anyway, he wanted to help out, but he's —"

"He's over at Dunleavy's getting a couple replacement parts for the tractor." Dad chimed in. "Considering repairs for the irrigation system, too. Still, Aaron could have stepped in. I think he's out back in the barn seeing to Dollie and Marcus. Simple maintenance. That could have waited a spell."

Dollie and Marcus, the family's two horses. Regarding Aaron, Phillip hadn't even attempted to reach out. Way too much acrimony simmered beneath the surface of their relationship to enable any kind of request for help.

Once again, Pop plowed on, ever steadfast and unflappable. Except for his health . . . except for a massive, giving heart that grew weaker and weaker. "Do you have any luggage? Plan on spending a few days?"

"I plan to spend a few days and then some. I brought a few things with me, but I'll get 'em later."

Weeks ago, Phillip had opted to either ditch or store his possessions in Indy. Bare necessities had followed him in a large duffle that currently rested in a secured locker at the depot in town. That included the lease he had let expire on a car he'd driven based on name cachet alone. No sense spending money on a designer vehicle that no longer fit his lifestyle or mindset. Besides, Pop had a workhorse of a pickup truck parked in the barn that had logged well over a hundred thousand miles yet remained solid and dependable.

His folks opted not to push on that count, a fact for which Phillip was eternally grateful. How could he explain selling his car, his furniture and all those material trinkets that had overtaken so much of his soul? There'd be time enough for that later — he hoped — if acceptance and forgiveness ran deep enough.

Phillip heard the back door open and close. Heavy, booted footsteps approached at a fast clip and into the kitchen strode his brother, Aaron.

"Hey, Dad, I —" Realizing Phillip's presence, Aaron froze, and stared. A hot silence fell through the atmosphere while a firestorm of hostility and anger sparked along a live wire. "Phillip."

The one-word acknowledgement lacked any pretense at warmth and came across more like an indictment than anything else. Phillip expected no less. Knew he deserved no better.

"You're back," Aaron continued. Acid ate its way through those two simple words.

"Yeah, and I hope I —"

In the millisecond it took Phillip to blink, his brother's fist connected soundly with his jaw. Phillip saw stars, dancing dots; he swayed and nearly toppled before he heard Aaron's bitter growl.

"Welcome home. I've got work to do."

The resounding crack of the slammed front door filled the air like a gunshot.

It was the height of summer; that left *Sundae Afternoon* packed with customers. Mila Thomas's approving gaze captured youngsters laughing with glee, spinning on retro-style chrome and padded stools at the front counter of her sweet-treat shop. She took in teenagers with their heads bent over milkshakes or sodas or the sundaes for which her family's shop was deservedly famous. Every window-side table overlooking Main Street was occupied. There were adults and seniors who reclined against the back of leather booths, appearing to be happily engrossed in conversation and people-watching. Sundae Afternoon was Mila's pride and joy because it carried on a few of what she felt were the more necessary components of living: connection, community, and simple pleasures.

Mila snapped a clean, damp towel from a metal rod beneath the service counter, all set to wipe the surface clean of condensation beads and milk splatters. She focused her attention on Trudy Sellers, a long-time waitress at the shop. Presently, Trudy's focus was fixed on the shop entry. When Mila followed the trajectory of her colleague's gaze, her motions came to a standstill.

A block of sunlight poured through the glass of the wide, double doors. Dead center and perfectly framed, Phillip Fisher stood in the light — all wide-shouldered, six-foot-plus, chestnut hair, and dark-as-night eyes of him.

"Well, I'll be." Mila murmured the words, transfixed. "So, the rumor's true. He's come back." Mila sucked a sharp breath, and the slight gasp she made wasn't lost on her friend.

Trudy shot a wizened gaze in Mila's direction. "Back in town, and handsome as ever."

Mila didn't respond verbally, but she certainly wouldn't argue the point. She raked her childhood friend with a lingering glance while Phillip scoped an empty spot to occupy. Handsome? Absolutely. But life, it seemed, had roughened some of the store-bought polish and preppy-ways she recalled from times gone by. In their stead, lived a visible realism, a depth that intrigued her as he strode to the front counter and folded onto a stool.

Mila got a closer view of his face. She gasped. He sported a big, fresh bruise along the squared line of his jaw. What in the world . . . ?

The front counter server took Phillip's order for a hot fudge sundae with the works.

Mila retrieved the coffee pot from Trudy's grip and gave her colleague a sweet smile. "I've got this one."

Trudy snorted. "Oh, I'm sure you do, missy."

Mila added a touch of sashay to her walk, a little oomph to her smile. "Phillip Alexander Fisher. I guess a hearty welcome back to Antioch is in order. How are you?"

"Mila."

There was smoke and silk in his tone as his gaze lifted from the laminated menu. The stroke of his gaze, the welcoming quirk of his lips, caused her pulse to trip into a pleasant thrum. Trudy wasn't kidding — he was indeed as handsome as ever, with thick waving hair that now curved just past his shirt collar. Mila filled his coffee cup then set aside the steaming, fragrant pot. "I heard you were back."

Phillip replaced the menu in its metal holder. "How on earth?"

"Oh, trust me. The town grapevine is alive and well. Since he was stuck at Dunleavy's, Ben texted Hailey Beth when you asked for a ride home from the bus station."

"Ah, yes, your scholarly and earnest baby sister, Hailey Beth. Never thought to ask HB for help, but, yeah, I suppose she could have been my maiden in shining armor."

"Basically, that's what Ben indicated when he asked her to help, but she couldn't break away. She's managing the grocery store now."

Phillip frowned. "Really? Since when?

Why isn't your dad at the helm?"

"Dad's taken on more of an advisory role since her graduation from college last year. He's letting her stretch her wings a bit."

Quiet fell; discomfort arrived with vengeance as Phillip's sundae was delivered. "So, you'll not ask me the obvious?" He posed the query, appearing dubious.

"You mean like why you hiked it to the farm on foot, without benefit of a ride from one of your brothers? You mean like why you're sporting a bruise on your face that's roughly the size of a fist? Yeah. The thoughts had occurred." Despite the somber topic, Mila kept her attitude light and judgment-free.

"I'll ignore the questions and tell you that I'm a customer today because I made a return to town just now — courtesy of Pop's beat-up old truck — to grab my luggage from a storage locker at the station, I'll settle in temporarily at the farm."

He sounded so defeated, so overwhelmed. Was his voyage home that riddled with strife? Mila softened further. "Aaron could have —"

"He was busy." The three-word snap made her rear back. Seeming to realize his mood was focused in the wrong direction, Phillip's shoulders bent, and he finally dug into his ice cream treat. "Sorry. Aaron's a touchy subject for me right now." He flexed his jaw back and forth. "Literally."

"Do you mean to tell me he's the one who gave you that bruise?"

"His strength has improved since our younger days, that's for sure."

Their younger days. When the three Fishermen — as they were called — seemed tight as could be, united by an unbreakable bond. As such, she could only imagine the way Phillip's arrogant and hasty exit a few years after college had fractured a great deal of loyalty and trust within their close-knit clan. For Aaron, especially. Ever since Mila could remember, the middle Fisher had looked up to and revered his big brother.

"He missed you, Phillip. You get that, right?"

"Sure I do, as evidenced by the blooming purple and brown splotch on my face. After the blowup, Pop stormed after him — I hope to give him the thrashing he deserves — and I escaped on fast feet to let matters settle."

Escape and running. Again. Mila sighed at Phillip's pattern of behavior. "Do I need to explain to you — you of all people — that being left behind has just as much consequence as doing the walk-away?"

The look he delivered just about seared her skin. "And so, with that, I'm in the wrong yet again. Vacating and abusing everyone's expectations. I swear, it's the story of my —"

"Oh, honey, you can go sell that sad tale somewhere else. If he didn't care, if your leaving hadn't affected him, he wouldn't be so hostile, now would he? He'd be able to just let it slide and let it ride. Right?"

Following that decisive interruption, Mila stared him down in a way that succeeded in drawing his complete focus. But the stare-down backfired. She didn't just look at him, she fell into him, absorbed him in all his shades while he raked her with a questing gaze as though seeing her for the very first time. And in many ways, perhaps that was just the case. Times had changed in their handful of years apart; too bad she couldn't cushion him from the blows of that separa-tion . . . and desertion.

Fighting a tingling brush of butterfly wings in her tummy, Mila continued their battle. "You disappeared without a second look back. That hurts. It left a mark on the folks around here who've always cared about you."

He gobbled his sundae, seeming to ponder things for a bit. "Guess I never realized people held me in such great stock. The family, yes. As a unit of the Fishermen, yes, because of my dad and my mom, and my brothers. Beyond that . . ." On a shrug, he let the sentence dangle.

Mila hoped her eye-roll and vigorous head-shake displayed exasperation in no uncertain terms. "Don't be an idiot, Phillip. You're who and what you are because of everyone around you, because of your family and what all of you create together." Remembering her self-assigned task, Mila wiped the counter with hard, circular motions, her thoughts so storm-tossed she had to wonder. Why was she reacting this way? Was she, in some small way, one of the people who had been marked by his leaving?

Evidently so.

Phillip stilled her efforts at needless cleaning by settling his hand over hers. The gentle glide of his fingertips against the back of her hand, the dewy warmth of the cloth, seeped through her skin.

"Do you want to know why I came to your shop, Mila? It's because I knew somehow, some way, you'd understand, and you wouldn't sugarcoat the facts."

Her shoulders eased from taut to relaxed; her lips softened to a smile. "Well, I do try."

Tension gradually evaporated. "I'm touched that Sundae Afternoon was one of the places you wanted to revisit, seeing as how you've only been here a few hours."

Phillip looked up, pinned her with a body-warming gaze. "What can I say? Sometimes a guy just needs a heap of ice cream and a friendly face."

Mila leaned across the slim, chrome lined counter that separated them and gave his cheek a kiss. She wanted to welcome an old friend home — nothing more. It took her by surprise when that simple, natural brush of lips against warm, musk-scented skin galvanized her senses and lifted her heart-beat into a fast rhythm.

"Just for that, your serving is on the house."

"I can pay for dessert, Mila."

Humility, trampled pride, flickered through his eyes the instant before he lowered his head and toyed with the spoon that rested in his serving bowl. He picked at layers of vanilla, chocolate, nuts, and ba-nanas now congealing into a mix of colors, textures, flavors.

"I have no doubt of that. Let's just call it a welcome home treat, friend to friend."

He relaxed a trace; full lips lifted into a

reluctant smile. "You always were a sweet-heart."

"Still am," she sassed, giving him a wink and moving away so she could regroup . . . and focus on a few other folks who crowded her establishment on this bustling, sun-drenched day.

All the same, her pulse continued to skitter and throb. Phillip Fisher was back. Injured physically and emotionally, for sure, but all the same, he was back.

Why in the world did that fact send a thrill down her sensory chain?

2

Phillip climbed into his dad's pickup and pulled away from the curb in front of Sundae Afternoon. During his return trip to the farm, the all-consuming memory of reuniting with Mila Thomas rode shotgun in ways both tempting and irritating. On the tempting side of the coin, she haunted him — with those great big brown eyes and that heart-shaped face framed by long, flirty curls of brunette hair that danced free from the confines of a loose ponytail. She had hardly changed since high school. Her demeanor remained unspoiled and as sweet as any treat to be found within the walls of her famed shop.

On the flip side, he was irritated by that reaction because just like that, she had slipped beneath his skin, and rollercoaster emotions toward Mila were the last thing he needed right now. Right now, he needed to earn back the good graces of his family.

Right now, he needed to find a place to live — preferably in town and far from Aaron's hostility. Beyond those daunting circumstances, the Thomas and Fisher families often found themselves at loggerheads over business matters related to the Antioch farming industry. Nevertheless, her tenderness — something he craved — flooded his senses. The memory of her simple but evocative kiss, the way she had leaned in to brush his cheek with satiny lips, elicited a fresh rush of heated pleasure. The way her peaches-and-cream features softened with affection as they'd chatted stuck to the grooves of his memory and played a sweet, unexpected song.

Dust kicked into a wavering gray and yellow plume as he turned onto the dirt drive leading to the barn of the family farm. Mila was right. He needed to face the turbulence if matters were ever to be resolved with Aaron. The jerk.

Hmm. Not a great start on reconciliation from an attitude perspective. Determined to readjust his thinking and try to understand his middle brother's hostility, Phillip braced an elbow against the open window frame, his touch on the wheel loose and easy.

Aaron walked across the wide entry of the barn, lugging a bale of hay as though God

Himself had orchestrated precisely what Mila suggested Phillip find. An opportunity.

Going tense, Phillip slowed the vehicle to a stop then rested his forearms against the thin black steering wheel. He leaned forward, peering through cloudy glass into a land full of memories — into the moment of his leaving.

Sad but quietly resolute, Pop had stood at the center of the farm's great room, his attention focused hard on Phillip. "Go. I won't stop you, and I won't try to change your mind. Some things life and God need to show you on your own without the safety net of home and family. But know this. We'll always be here. No matter what comes, this is your home. None of that changes. Hear?"

He had, but despite Pop's caring words, Phillip had tasted nothing in the air but antiquity, an endless life-cycle that would mean precisely . . . nothing. What was the point of living and dying for the land? For crops? For never-ending battles with weather cycles, and merchants, and on-again, off-again workers paired with equipment that worked, or didn't work, at its own seeming whim? What about money — or more precisely, the lack thereof, which eradicated any sense of security, and at times, even dignity? No. No way could he do it. There had to be much more to life than struggle and strife.

All the same, splinters lodged in his heart. This wasn't his father's fault. "I know you mean every word, Pop, and truly, I don't mean any disrespect."

"Not directly, no. I realize that."

That piece of gentle acceptance arrived in the form of a laced arrow that pierced the bulls-eye of Phillip's spirit. He'd clenched his jaw to keep from crumbling and vacating a plan that was foolproof, and most of all, *right.* Pop would never understand the drive, the need for fulfillment that nipped at Phillip's heels. He needed to break the chains, and that required a touch of temper. "Could you please have some faith that I can actually make something of myself outside of a farm I never understood? A farm-based existence that would only lead to a life I've never wanted? It's not about money, or acclaim, it's about security. Fulfillment. It's about finding the life *I* want, not a life that's dictated to me."

"I get the conflict, son. I've battled it myself when times go bad, but that's when you bear down. That's when you pray, press on, and find the pathway God intends. Maybe this is it for you. Like I said, nothing's stopping you, but we'll always be here."

Steel-eyed determination and a gruff tone accompanied the statements. As ever, Pop was unflappable. Steady as a compass arrow pointing due north.

Phillip snapped to alert and back to the present as Aaron moved past the threshold again. This time, his sibling caught sight of the truck, and most likely realized who sat behind the wheel because he froze for a second, scowled deep, then returned to hauling hay.

Phillip hopped from the cab and slammed the door closed, boots kicking up dirt clouds as he strode to the barn. He crossed the threshold, surveyed the familiar, musty confines, and searched for a pitchfork. "Hey."

Aaron didn't break stride, didn't offer a glance. "Yeah."

"Can I help?"

Aaron stomped to the wide-toothed implement Phillip required and nabbed it by the wooden handle. "Start spreading." He tossed the tool and Phillip captured the time-worn piece of equipment on the fly and with ready ease. Aaron acknowledged that fact with a surprised glance.

"What's the issue?" Phillip stared him down. "I haven't forgotten everything about being on the farm."

"Except when you have appointments elsewhere." The accusing jab left Phillip wanting to impale the pitchfork straight into the nearest bale and leave his brother to his misconceptions and irritating, hostile simmer. His hand tightened on the wood. Rather than follow through on a reckless impulse, he joined Aaron inside the nearest horse stall and began to spread a layer of fresh hay. Before long, sweat tacked his shirt to his back, and dusty debris coated his jeans, his arms, and even his hair. Yep. He was home again.

"Where do you plan to settle while you're here? Going to spend a few days at the house?"

"I'm not here for a visit, Aaron. I'm here for good. While I was out, I picked up a copy of the Times Gazette. I'm considering renting a place in town."

Aaron harrumphed. "You've always been an urban junkie."

"Meaning downtown Antioch is urban? That's news. When'd that happen?" Hey, he could fight fire with fire. Definitely.

Aaron snickered at the jest, though Phillip could tell his brother had tried hard to stop the reaction and still hadn't spared him a glance. Even so, for an instant, a familiar sense of levity wound around them.

That easing prompted Phillip to take a gamble. "What happened, Aaron? What motivates all the anger you're brewing toward me?"

Aaron's motions went still. His back and shoulders stiffened. "The fact that you need an answer to those questions says more than any answer I could ever give." He returned to pitching hay.

"Oh, I have theories, but I want the truth. I want answers that come straight from you so we can start to deal. We're brothers. We were close —"

Aaron rounded on him and threw his pitchfork against the farthest wall where it banged, clattered, and came to rest. "Oh, forget any kind of trip to the land of nostalgia!" His roar cut the air. "I was the good son."

Phillip pointed at his bruised, still aching face. "Yeah. For sure."

"Joke away, Phillip, but you know exactly what I'm talking about. I stayed. I was the stronghold. I did what I was told. I did what was needed. What was expected. I had no choice in the matter, but I'd do anything for Mom and Dad. Dad's health crashed, and he needed me. I stuck. Never once did I complain. Never once did I turn my back. Can you say the same?"

"No, I can't, and that's my shame to bear."

"Yeah, but through it all, Dad treats you like some kind of a conquering hero. Unreal."

"He'd do the same for you, Aaron, and you know it. Get over yourself and be grateful he didn't have to. Be grateful you were smarter than me and chose the better course. I thought this farm was what you wanted. It's like you were born to this life. You've been here all along and never missed a beat. How could I know you'd build up such a pile of resentment when I left? This dream wasn't mine. Where's the fault? Where's the sin in that?"

"The sin is in the way you spit on everything this family created. You walked off, dreamin' of dollar signs. Meanwhile, Dad had to rely on someone. Well, that someone was me, and that someone was Ben. I, for one, refuse to go kow-towing to the first born just because you've deigned to grace us with your presence again. Dad nearly died, and you didn't even have the decency to —"

"Pull it to a stop, brother, or you'll regret it."

"This farm had to survive! I took that personal. You should have, too. This was your home, too. We were *family*! We needed

35

each other, and you could barely spare the time to visit when our father was in ICU, his heart barely *functioning*!"

Phillip nearly gagged on a serving of shame and remorse.

After grabbing a ragged breath, Aaron stormed on. "The heavy lifting had to be done, but you blasted south down I-69 and left us in the dust. Well played, big bro. Well played. You turned your back on us and everything else when we needed you the most. Dad especially. Rubs against me like sandpaper."

"What rubs you? That I wanted some stability in my life? A sense of order and maybe — just maybe — some small measure of security? You can go ahead and rant on about dollar signs and blasting down I-69, but dollar signs were the least of what propelled me to leave. I wanted a life I could take pride in. A life all my own. A life where I was in control."

"Control?"

Phillip nodded — emphatically.

"Control is an illusion, you idiot! Did nothing at all about this place rub off on you? Impact you? *Teach* you?"

"Yeah, it did. It taught me to cling to what's right. That's why I'm back. My er-roneous expectations about security crash landed. That's why I'm back — because of the wrongs I've done. I know I have no one to blame but myself."

"You left us. Without a backward glance or even a thanks-for-the-memories. Meanwhile, the rest of us fought to manage and just get by while Dad did his best to recover.

"Congratulations. You lived life exactly the way you wanted. Now, you've come back with your tail between your legs because you failed, and all the while the ones you hurt most — Mom and Dad — extend a hallelujah chorus. Well, not here. Not from me. Suffer the consequences. The consequences are I'm angry. I'll tolerate you, but I can't forgive you. Not yet, and maybe not ever. From my point of view, nothing mattered to you except *you*."

Phillip sank, sadness, guilt, and regret all crashed into him like a runaway freight train. "Your fist-plant to my jaw told me your views already, but thanks for removing all doubt. Take it or leave it, but I want you to know I appreciate your honesty." He forsook the hay-spreading chore.

Aaron snorted, his face contorted by an ugly smear of hostility. "Want more? I've got piles of it. Take that bruise with you as a reminder. I'm watching you, Phillip. You're my brother, but I don't trust you anymore.

You're in it for your own gain. You're standing here because you needed a safe place to land when the rug you created got yanked from under your feet. I'll bet you take off all over again, and at the first opportunity if that stinkin' cell phone of yours starts bleeping."

"You're wrong on that count, Aaron. And the rest of the crap you're heaping on me is the mess I have to live with, and atone for. No need for you to carry the load as well."

A wavering took place, a falter in Aaron's self-righteous attitude, but then he blinked hard and his eyes went to stone. "Yeah. You're right. You do have to atone. The kind of trust I'm talking about needs to be earned all over again. You broke it."

"Are you finished?"

"For now. Probably not for long, though."

Aaron's smug retort caused Phillip to growl beneath his breath. His skin prickled hot with repressed rage, and patience evaporated like moisture being baked into the dry air all around them.

"I have a parting thought of my own, little brother." He referred to Aaron as such only to tick him off. "You better be careful of that high and mighty horse you're riding. The fall that's headed your way is gonna be epic."

Aaron's face went beet-red in the instant it took him to rear back and hiss like a garden snake.

Phillip let that reaction roll away like so much crop dust. He had no doubt his sibling was ready to launch into another verbal harangue, so he decided to cut him straight off. "And let me assure you, I don't issue that warning out of arrogance, you sanctimonious jerk. I speak from experience." Phillip clenched his fists to keep from using them in violence. He bit down hard against a snarl. "So, don't forget to tuck and roll on the way down."

Aaron's ripe curse rent the air as Phillip stalked away.

3

Sunday morning, a knock sounded at Phillip's bedroom door, soft at first and then louder, followed by his mother's voice. "Philip, wake up. Time for church."

The traditional call to arms. Phillip groaned, rolling from his stomach to his side, sheets and blankets twisting as he checked the face of the clock on his nightstand. Seven-brutal-o'clock in the blessed morning. Another groan echoed as he lifted to an elbow and glanced outside the window opposite his bed. Sure enough, the sun barely peeked over the horizon. The milky gray of dawn barely gave way to the light of a new day . . . on a Sunday, for heaven's sake . . . a day of rest, right? Yet here he was, transported straight back to his childhood while he bumbled out of bed chasing time to get to eight o'clock services.

Yawning large, his adult self literally ached for a rejuvenating shot of hot, black coffee.

That would come later, during a full-on, hearty breakfast prepared by Mom following services. As far as Phillip was concerned, that piece of joyful anticipation was more than worth the early rise, so he stowed the resentful attitude, showered and dressed.

Before long, he was riding shotgun next to Ben in the old family pickup. He loved hanging with Ben because his youngest sibling embodied the best elements of the strong, silent type. Ben didn't look for, or enjoy, unnecessary chatter. An easy silence fell between them, and felt good. In looks, they were nearly identical, with Ben just an inch or so shorter, but they both bore every bit of their father's features.

That's where the similarities ended, though. Phillip couldn't create, or rescue anything mechanical if his life depended on it. Ben, on the other hand, was a mechanical genius.

"I assume Mom and Pop are ushering today?"

"Yeah, it's their week. They left about fifteen minutes ahead of us to get things set up at church, you know, coffee and bulletins and the like."

One of those steadying, Ben-esque silences fell between them. "So, how're the irrigation repairs coming?"

Ben drummed his fingers on the steering wheel and sighed, eyes going flinty. "Not good. Been studying the manual, and looked up some stuff online, but it's tricky. Hate to spend the money on a professional repair, but we might end up having to go that route. After church and breakfast, I'll camp out in the warehouse and see what I can do."

"My money's on you, wiz kid." They exchanged smirks. "Working on anything cool in the wood shop these days?"

Ben's grin spread fast and real, his generally laidback demeanor took on a definite uptick. "I am. A tractor and trailer combo for the autumn craft sale coming up. Almost finished, and almost hate to give it up."

"Yeah. Might have kids of your own to hand them down to someday soon."

Ben hooted. "Not likely. I've got plenty of time for that."

Ben was always the calm one, deceptively intelligent in that he wasn't so much schooled in the art of book learning; rather, he possessed a keenness of intellect no professor, no college on earth, could ever teach. It always seemed to Phillip that Ben was connected to some form of mysterious, unseen wavelength of knowledge. Ben could revamp wiring systems on tractors, trouble shoot sorting machine jams, and even repair complex irrigation systems. He could fix anything mechanical, but he most enjoyed creating items out of wood, and steel. While dusty miles passed on their way to church, Phillip wondered why he hadn't he given his brother more credit for those attributes.

Silence fell once more, and that was OK. Phillip embraced the peace and quiet as he watched homes and fields blur by his passenger window. Attendance at Sunday services had been sporadic since leaving home. In Indy, he went to church every once in a while, but not with the kind of dedication and sense of community that tied knots of connection around the townspeople of Antioch.

Antioch Christian Church seemed to rise from a rolling swell of farm land. Red bricks, a soaring spire, a massive structure, spoke of a centuries-old acknowledgement and appreciation for God's hand in the land and lives of its parishioners. Low-lying, leafy soybean plants, tall, wavering stalks of corn, and strawberry fields carpeted a terrain that shimmered beneath a gentle, though humid breeze.

Phillip shook his head. If only that humidity would transform itself into some cloud cover and a weather-breaking downpour.

Followed by Ben, he tracked toward the stairs leading to the church entry, already figuring Aaron was either inside or on his way. Ben had informed Phillip last night that Aaron had laid claim to a small two-story place on a couple acres just a mile or so from the farm.

As soon as he crossed the arched entrance, with its wooden double doors thrown open to the summer morning, Phillip heard the choir performing its opening meditation song. Following worshipers down the main aisle, Phillip took a seat and settled in. A reluctant admiration and welcomed time-lessness blossomed for the way attending church and praising God was as deeply ingrained into this town as the roots of its crops.

Mom and Pop had already secured the family's regular station, a pew four rows from the front, left of the altar. Mom paused and nudged Phillip, then Ben, into place. That put Phillip right next to Aaron who was already seated. Aaron flexed his shoulders and jaw and then straightened the lines of his suit coat. Never once did he look Phillip's way. Instead, he stared at the altar.

"G'morning." Undaunted, Phillip keyed in on his brother, deliberately calling him out, intent, and waiting on a response.

"Morning."

What a reluctant flat-liner. Phillip ground his teeth and decided to give up on communication for the time being. Rather, he bowed his head, following Pop's lead by sinking into prayer while the melody of *Great is Thy Faithfulness* wrapped him in a soft quilt of familiarity.

God, he began in silent earnest, *I don't want my relationship with Aaron to be like this. Help. Please help.*

The prayer was simple, but it came from the heart. Phillip knew God wasn't in the retribution or payback business, still, something at the core of him niggled, causing him to wonder how or why his prayers would even be heard.

In that regard, Aaron had made valid points the other day. Phillip had spent an awful lot of time turning his back on things like faith, and tradition, and family. After such a nose-thumb, why should God care about him now? *Why?*

Because my love for you is the love of a father. I love you, Phillip.

His head jerked up on a startled reflex bringing his gaze into direct alignment with a brass cross that showed the patina of age, yet still shone in rays of diffused light. The words of the Spirit came at him in a rush,

45

like wind sailing through stale, closed-off compartments of his heart.

Reverend Taylor, a fixture at Antioch Christian nearing his sixties, stepped to the pulpit and began worship, precluding further inner debate and mystical interactions on Phillip's part.

"I'd like to begin our time together today with a reading from the first book of John, chapters four and five. Here, we read: Beloved, we love God because he first loved us. If anyone says, 'I love God,' but hates his brother, he's a liar; for whoever does not love a brother, whom he has seen, cannot love God whom he has not seen. This is the commandment we have from Him: Whoever loves God must also love his brother."

For the second time in less than mere minutes, Phillip sat, frozen and convicted.

Reverend Taylor continued. "Upon close study, I believe John had a lot to say about family relationships, and that bond of love. The beauty of it. The delicacy of it. Like a bookend to that reading, we have today's Gospel selection. It's one of my favorites — the sermon on the Prodigal. Listen carefully, absorb the familiar with a new perspective, with a fresh spirit, won't you?" He paused to take a sip of water and flip a ribbon in his Bible; Mom and Pop followed along in their own Bibles.

Phillip could hardly breathe as the errant son made his return, as the good son lamented, and as the father welcomed and loved them both in equal measure. Without condition.

Phillip could literally taste those words. *Without condition.* No strings were attached to Pop's acceptance of his return, despite the way Phillip had shunned an entire way of life that had been his family's livelihood and legacy for over a century.

Reverend Taylor continued his sermon. "We must love the fallen, the lost, those who stumble, but rise, and return. We must love our brothers and sisters. And by that I don't mean you should *probably* love, or *think* about loving. No. There are no qualifiers here. Nothing held back. Love must be given, and received, with appreciation, with grace, with mercy, and joy. In the week to come, let's embrace that mission and take the gift of love into the world around us, no matter what the devil throws our way. Amen?"

A chorus of 'Amen' rose from the congregation.

Meanwhile, Phillip's focus darted to Aaron. Aaron caught the gesture and their gazes tagged, held, and then melted away from one another in a unison dip of the head.

Coffee.

Phillip rejoiced, inhaling the fragrance of a fresh-brewed pot resting on a trivet at the center of the dining table. He crossed to an empty seat, taking in the spread of food. When he spotted a heaping bowl of scrambled eggs, his stomach rumbled. The aroma of simmering bacon had filled the kitchen for the past quarter hour; the finished product now welcomed him to the sanctuary of a classic Fisher family Sunday breakfast.

Seated at the linen-covered table, he hefted the meat platter positioned right next to a silver toast rack that had been handed down to his mom from his Grandma Bibler. Hash browns and a carafe of orange juice beading with condensation completed the offering to perfection. Contentment swelled through Phillip's chest while he filled his plate. Right here, right now, it definitely felt good to be home.

Returning his attention to the conversation at hand, he devoured half a slice of bacon then focused on Ben. "When I walked the fields, I noticed the dry condition of the soil around here." Phillip tossed out the observation. "During the drive this morning, I saw the land at the Tenner's place looks pretty decent. Soil was dark and damp."

"The Tenners have state of the art irrigation." Ben shoveled food, intent on his meal. "Our system blew a couple weeks ago. Like we talked about on the way to church, I've been working on it the best I can. Hope to have it up and running in a couple of days. Meanwhile, we're praying for rain in a big way."

"We do need the moisture." Pop buttered a slice of toast. "Ground is drying by the minute. Even when we get it fixed, the irrigation system on its own won't cut it for very long without some help from God."

And there it was — less than a handful of days into his return — the never-ending battle between earth, man, and God that had haunted Phillip since his youth. He stemmed a groan. How could folks live like this? Work so hard? For . . . for what exactly? He pushed those thoughts aside and straightened in his chair. "How can I help?"

Pop stopped eating long enough to spare Phillip a look full of interest, and hope. "Well. We could use you at harvest time, if you plan to stick. Could use some help managing the business end as well — paying the field workers, recording the expenses, negotiating crop sales and such." He shrugged. "I need help refinding center after the heart attack. I need to figure out where we're losing, and where we're gaining. Height of the season is about to hit. We're gonna get real busy real fast."

"I'd be glad to manage the business side for you."

A derisive snort came from Phillip's right. Aaron, of course. Phillip speared his brother with a glower then caught his mother's firm, arched-brow look, an unspoken reprimand to both her sons, which banked the embers of Phillip's temper in a hurry. No one disrespected Anna Fisher's meal table. Ever.

Even Aaron had the good grace to backpedal and shoot Mom a sheepish look. Clearing his throat as if to cover a cough, he muttered a hasty, "Excuse me."

"I ran into Mila Thomas when I went into town the other day." Phillip hoped the topic shift would smooth matters further. "She tells me Hailey Beth is running the market now. I'm surprised Mr. Thomas would surrender control to anyone — even HB. Is he still acting as a produce broker? Heaven knows, he loves wrangling with the local farmers."

"Be fair." Pop cut in. "Byron Thomas and

his family are only trying to make a living, just like the rest of us. Byron's easing back his hold on the store, but to answer your question, he remains a tough, trusted produce broker."

"He's the one who needs to be fair, Pop. Byron Thomas arm wrestles us over every crop sale we've ever produced." Phillip itched to continue that stinging indictment, but bit down the tirade when a look of censure crossed his dad's features.

"Enough."

Cowed, Phillip backed off; Aaron sneered. Ben, meanwhile, shook his head at the two of them and continued to wolf down scrambled eggs.

And so, to the table at large, Phillip decided to conclude — and clarify — matters as best he could. "I intend to be here for you guys. I intend to help fix things, or I wouldn't be sitting here. Let me know what to do. If that means a meeting with Byron Thomas to kick off harvest plans and negotiations, then so be it, and count me in."

Ben guffawed. "That'd be an interesting get-together."

"How so?"

Ben shrugged. "He's already been making noise around town that sale prices for produce are going to be lower than usual.

We had that rainy conclusion to winter, and start to spring. The seed corn maggots went to town after that — right up 'til the coin flipped, and drought set in. Now we're being forced to deal with the opposite end of the spectrum — dry land and underdeveloped crops. He figures his argument is reasonable, considering this year's crops may not be the best."

"Weather could still turn enough to make a difference. I'll do some research and pull together yield projections and some strategy for dealing with the weather patterns." Phillip addressed Pop. "If you don't mind me working the numbers, I'll also get you an overview of expenses and income versus outlay and a budget for what needs to be improved."

Ben stopped chewing and focused. "T'be honest, I wouldn't mind turning the business reins over to Phillip. I'm thinkin' he can analyze matters a lot better than Aaron and I could."

Phillip didn't miss the way Aaron bristled at the verdict, so he decided to step forward in assurance. "It's not about better or worse or anything in between. It's about something of value I can provide." He caught his middle brother's eye and held his gaze solid. "Maybe I can turn all that book work of mine into something useful around here."

Silence beat by before Aaron dipped his head in acknowledgement and surrendered — albeit with reluctance. "Have at it. We all want the same thing. Right?"

The words signaled acceptance, sure, but came wrapped in the layers of a challenging bite.

4

A rare sense of contentment rode through Phillip's psyche as he strolled next to Mila. In unison, they ambled along a sidewalk that framed the nearly empty streets of downtown Antioch.

He had noticed her during services today. Hard to not notice a woman so striking. He noticed the floral print dress that skimmed her knees and floated softly around shapely calves, and feet with red-tipped nails tucked into a pair of those strappy-style sandals women couldn't seem to get enough of in the summertime. And it was hard to not notice the way short sleeves had accentuated tan, supple arms and a neck he already knew would hint at the scents of hyacinth and rose. Then there was that impossible-not-to-notice wavy fall of hair that skimmed against her shoulders . . . and the reaches of his imagination.

So, following breakfast, Phillip had secured her cell phone number through Ben, who received it via a text message from Hailey Beth. Going for broke, Phillip had reached out to Mila, simply hoping to do what they were doing right now — walk quietly, wrapped in the peace-inducing cadence of a small-town Sunday afternoon. Most shop fronts were shuttered, although a few folks meandered past.

The vibe was so different from the frantic hustle and forward charge of the life he left behind in Indianapolis. So appealing.

She glanced his way. "You dashed off after church today."

"Sorry about that. Ben wanted to get back to the fields and whatever technical magic he can work on our watering system."

"Um-hum."

Two syllables, drawn out and voiced low. So, she wasn't convinced. Not surprising since the one element that remained consistent, even after his being away so long, was Mila's ability to read him. The resulting connection still knocked him off center, and far from his comfort zone. Seemed he wouldn't be able to slide easily past the truths of his life — but that was OK — right? Wasn't that what had drawn him back home . . . back to her . . . in the first place?

Phillip cleared his throat, and his mind.

"Also, breakfast called." Awkwardness blooming, he further excused his hasty exit as the sun beat warm on his back. "And I refuse to miss a Sunday breakfast prepared by Anna Fisher."

He joked the matter aside, unwilling to express the ways his mad dash had been a bit of a cop out, a temporary diversion from the battle that mounted when he saw her, admired her, and tried to figure out what to do with that realization. The dining table discussion of their two families had eradicated second-thinking and led him to this warm, sun-drenched moment.

"I can't blame you there." She hesitated a beat or two, their footsteps synchronized in a way that somehow tugged at him. "Aaron seemed a little stiff-necked today."

"Oh, Mila, you don't play around, do you?"

Her answer was a quiet chuckle then a prodding silence, and the lift of a perfectly shaped brow pulled his attention to dark, sparkling eyes.

"And not much gets past you," he said. "Yeah, Aaron and I were pretty much convicted during services."

"Maybe God is just tapping you guys on the shoulders. Keep reaching out." Her gentle advice came to him coated by the balm of an understanding he craved and appreciated.

Mila took hold of his hand, lacing her fingers through his. It was a friendly, caring gesture. Nevertheless, the glide of her skin against his pulled at Phillip's gut and sent a mighty zing through his senses.

"Chances are you'll have to prove yourself. I know that isn't necessarily right, but it's part of the process of winning back trust."

"I get that, Mila, but come on. I'm honestly exhausted by the struggle. See also: completely over it."

There came no ready reply, but for the sympathy and care that lived in the depths of her eyes.

Phillip pulled in a deep breath, forcing himself to steadiness. "Hey, I have an idea."

"I'm all braced."

The shift seemed to relax her at once. Mila beamed a tantalizing smile and he swung their joined hands, smiling as well. Just because. "Let's take a canoe ride out on Zeffman's Pond."

"Avoidance?"

"I prefer the term 'sanity preservation.' "

Mila stopped, drawing their sidewalk voyage to a halt. "I'd love it. You know what? This feels like old times. Remember back in high school when we'd jump straight over the side of the boat and into the water?"

"We always referred to it as 'the murky deep,' remember?"

"I do, even though the water was all of four feet at the most."

"Sure, but, it *was* murky." Phillip led her forward once more, retracing their path to the pickup truck he continued to abscond from the family. He needed to rectify that at some point. That, and establishing a place to live. Roots. "Let's do it."

Stationed within her second-floor apartment at the north end of town, Mila executed yet another outfit change. Upon rising, bed-rumpled PJ's had been replaced by proper church attire — an airy, cotton dress with short sleeves patterned by pastel flowers. Following services, she'd traded formality for black shorts and a comfy white tee. Now, following her walk with Phillip, she shucked the shorts and a simple cotton shirt in favor of a bright yellow swimsuit along with a white, knee-length cover-up.

Reviewing the results in a vanity mirror, she smiled at her reflection, knowing Philip would find a way to dunk her in 'the murky deep.' Best to be prepared. So, rather than question her escalated anticipation level, she stuffed her feet into a pair of flip-flops.

While Mila moved through her bedroom, her sister, Hailey Beth, flopped onto the bed not far behind and continued their conversation. "Wait a minute. You're doing *what*?"

"I'm taking a canoe ride. Now, stop with the tone."

"What tone? I don't have a tone."

Mila skewered her little sister with a hot, disbelieving glance. Ever-so-innocently, HB fluttered her lashes and plucked at the fringes of a pink satin throw pillow propped against the headboard of the bed.

"Oh, yes you do have a tone." Mila fluffed her hair. "And it reeks of inquisition."

"OK. Guilty. I mean, it's pretty interesting to me, and worthy of questioning, that this little scenario between the two of you is ratcheting upward."

"Give me a break."

"I present Exhibit One. That would be the phone call I received from Ben yesterday asking me to give him your cell number so he could pass it on to Phillip." HB trounced right over Mila's objection. "Like I said. Ratcheting upward."

"Oh, the scandal." Deliberately playing the "I'm bored" card, hoping to throw her sister off the scent, Mila studied her own reflection, longing to add the sparkle and pop of a little jewelry to her accessories.

Nothing doing on that count, though. Not when she'd be on the water with a playful mischief-maker like Phillip Fisher . . .

Her eyes went wide. Why would she bother with that kind of fussy little detail anyway? This was Phillip. This was nothing more than the sharing of a friendly afternoon. A frown pulled at her lips while she considered the way thoughts of primping and polishing suddenly careened through her head. Was it possible — heaven forbid — that HB had a point? Was she trying to win his attention? Was she allowing herself to fall for the rebel? The prodigal?

Blithely unaware of Mila's conflict, HB continued. "Furthermore, I present exhibit number two. The blush that's blooming on your cheeks right now. I repeat. Ratcheting upward." HB grinned, creating a visual of supreme satisfaction. She pushed off the bed and joined Mila, who continued to stare at her reflection in the dresser mirror.

Shock morphed fast into a form of guilty conviction. Yeah, she was attracted. Yeah, she was looking forward to a few more hours in his company.

What was the crime? This was no big deal. Right?

Far past time, Mila decided, to set matters straight. For the record. "He's nothing more than a friend who's come back to town for a visit. We're catching up is all. Simple as that."

Hailey Beth swiped Mila's hairbrush and went to work taming the waves of her long brown hair. "You go right ahead and keep telling yourself that. Meanwhile, I'll keep building my pile of exhibits." Retort delivered, her gaze tagged Mila's, punctuated by the dawn of a smug, knowing smirk.

Mila stretched to tiptoe, unlatched a pair of black band restraints from each end of an aged wooden canoe. In tandem with Phillip, she lifted the vessel from the roof of her SUV. Behind her extended the rounded banks of Zeffman's Pond — an expansive body of water dotted by lily pads and marked by waving strands of scrub grass that pushed through the bluish-brown surface. This was the perfect spot to don a pair of aqua socks and cool off with a swim when humidity and temperatures lifted. Zeffman's was a wonderful place to launch a canoe and simply drift with the breeze.

She shaded her eyes and breathed deep before hefting her end of the canoe and helping Phillip carry it to the water's edge. Covering a couple acres past Old Plank Road near the I-69 highway, Zeffman's

Pond took its name from an Antioch farm family that had once harvested its now-dormant fields. The Zeffman family moved south decades ago, not long after the pond came to be — created when supporting land foundations for an overpass and abutment needed to be dug from the flatlands as I-69 continued its southern sprawl, and urbanization tracked closer and closer to rolling farmland. The added infrastructure had left the Zeffmans cash-rich, but eager to flee the onset of bulldozers, metal and cement.

About a half mile away, that highway buzzed with the distant sound of car engines and the deeper rumble of eighteen wheelers; by and large, though, the plot of land remained peaceful, inhabited by nothing more than birds, deep-throated frogs, crickets, and other insects. A couple years before Phillip left, a few families had chipped in to tree-line the edge of the property closest to the highway — his included.

The recollection fell through her mind and landed in her heart while Phillip steadied the canoe and offered an assisting hand to settle her aboard. He had been a mainstay of the project, helping dig holes to plant a noise-buffering, visually appealing rim of trees.

"What are you thinking about?" Phillip tilted his head as she stepped inside the canoe and braced herself with care.

"I was thinking about when this place came to be. You helped polish off this area for our community. You and your family." She held the sides of the teetering craft while Phillip joined her. He lifted a pair of oars and pushed off, launching their canoe away from the shoreline.

"At the time, I had no idea how unhappy you were."

Phillip plowed thick wooden oars through the water, arm muscles flexing. "Unhappy? I wasn't unhappy."

She absorbed his strong, vital image, and fought not to stare, realizing her senses fluttered and swelled like a crushing schoolgirl. "OK, let's try restless. Does restless fit any better?"

"Yeah, I suppose I can own that description."

"You left a few months later, and that took most everyone around here by surprise."

"I didn't mean to hurt people. To tell the truth, I didn't realize my leaving would matter."

"It does. Maybe that's why the reluctance you're sensing comes as such a surprise. Sometimes we don't realize our importance to people until it's too late."

Phillip stopped rowing and rested his arms against the wooden oar handles. "And do you think it's too late for me?"

No, Mila wanted to scream. *No, never.* But she kept quiet, staunching the flow of emotion that formed a fast-riding cascade through her spirit.

Phillip stared into the distance. "Lately, I'm starting to wonder. I look at Aaron, and even the attitude of Ben and my folks to a lesser degree. It's as if they're afraid to trust me again. I'll try not to hurt them — I can't guarantee anything when I'm only human — but I never meant to hurt them in the first place." Phillip raked his fingers through his hair and groaned. He dug in on the oars with a vengeance.

"Trust has been broken, sure, but trust can be restored. Doing so might take more than a visit or two, but all the same —"

"This isn't a visit, Mila." His gaze lifted; his tone sharpened to emphatic. "I'm staying. There's nothing left for me in Indianapolis. I ditched everything when I was laid off. What matters most to me right now is repairing the relationships I damaged. They were . . . and are . . . the most important aspects of my life. I lost sight of that once. I won't do it again."

64

"You're staying. In Antioch. For sure?"

"Yes, I am."

She barely registered his words. Rather, they buzzed, and echoed.

"The first thing I want to do is find a place to live. It's a little cramped for me at the farm right now."

Mila shook her head, willing her attention to proper focus. He needed objectivity, the touch of a friend who cared, and shared his history. So, she planted emotional responses behind strong stone walls before speaking. "Look at it this way, Phillip. Maybe cramped is what you need. Maybe being cramped is God's way of giving you a chance to re-find solid ground, begin again with your family, and deal with that urge you've got to help manage your father's business affairs."

He looked at her anew. "Thank you."

"For what?"

"For understanding my perspective. With the exception of my mom and dad, you're the only one who's extended any authentic degree of caring since I've returned."

Words stalled when he looked deep into her eyes. Mila caught her breath, battled to remain steady.

"Like I said. Thank you." He resumed their cruise along the perimeter of the pond.

Mila trailed her fingertips against the

surface of the water, brushing at lily pads topped by white flowers, the water silky and warm to her touch. "I'm not the only one. You just told me Ben hasn't given you any trouble. The issue is Aaron, and you know it." She cast a quick sigh. "Plus, there are your dad's health concerns. On top of it all, and no surprise here, Aaron's always had a hot streak."

"And he's bringing out mine, which isn't something I want clouding matters."

"I hear that."

"Yeah?"

"Yeah. Speaking of stress and short tempers, my dad's not eager to start negotiations this season. The farming community drives everything in Antioch, and a lack of rain is making everyone itchy. He's as upset about conditions and projections as everyone else. He's not looking forward to being relegated to the role of hard-hearted businessman and merchant this fall once the crops roll in."

"No worries there. His daughter makes up for that shortcoming."

Phillip transformed from somber to playful in the time it took Mila to blink — and breathe. In an instant, she was lifted fast and sure into Phillips arms then dumped overboard — straight into the water.

Refreshed, but refusing to concede defeat, she sputtered and spewed, then grabbed Phillip's arm with all her might, yanking him over the side of the canoe. He gave in, she had no doubt, otherwise she wouldn't have been able to budge him. The spontaneous eruption set her senses on high alert. Water swished and pushed, cascading between them as Phillip dunked her. Mila retaliated by busting through the water and spraying water straight at him. He ducked his head and diverted by diving beneath surface then launched into a breast stroke that took him halfway across the pond; Mila followed in hot pursuit, exhilarated by their interplay.

Their romp ended a short time later, and they reclaimed the boat, pulling it ashore. While Mila dried off, Phillip laid out two towels, and they stretched side-by-side on the cool grass of the southern-most tip of the water.

Summer bloomed, so, nowadays, swimming and picnics were favored past times. Then, once winter arrived, groups of teens shoveled snow and turned the pond's icy surface into a makeshift skating rink. Today those frigid moments seemed far away. Humidity increased; laden, towering clouds tumbled in slow, capturing her attention, along with her hopes for a drenching rain as the day moved toward mid-afternoon.

Mila tucked her hands behind her head and continued to study the sky. The scent of oncoming-rain slid against her senses, carried on a breeze that skimmed against her skin. "The weather is definitely about to change. Maybe that'll help everyone's outlook."

"I heard we're in for a storm system. I won't complain unless it's severe. We need the moisture."

"For sure."

As though in punctuation, a fork of lightning split thin, white lines through the distant sky. Following a weighted pause, thunder rumbled, vibrating through the air beneath a fast-darkening sky.

"I forgot how quickly storms move through the flatlands of Indiana. I suppose we'd better get going." Regret pierced Phillip's words.

While they secured the canoe and tucked supplies into the back of Mila's vehicle, her mind spun. An idea came to life, moving from the back of her mind to the forefront as quickly as the push of oncoming cloud cover.

She just might be able to help him.

5

Late afternoon crept to early evening. Ready to wind down, Phillip pressed the power button of the television remote and immediately hunted down a channel that would provide some form of sports action to fill the quiet. Just as he settled in a recliner to relax and watch a replay — Baltimore versus Chicago — a derisive snort sounded from the entryway just behind.

"Le'me guess." Aaron entered the room. "You've probably gone all turn-coat on the home team. These days I bet you'd be rooting for Chicago, Mr. Big City."

All of Phillip's noble intentions from the afternoon spent in Mila's company bit the dust and flew straight out the picture window to his left. Outside, rain pounded and drummed, pushing through thick atmosphere, blanketing the world with violent moisture.

Phillip kicked down the foot rest of the

recliner and turned to his brother with a look that he hoped shot arrows. He had endured more than enough of Aaron and his pompous attitude. "How does that chip on your shoulder taste? Need some dip to go along with it? Some salsa, or a soda maybe?"

Aaron flopped onto the sofa. "So. You. And Mila Thomas. And Zeffman's Pond. You consorting with the enemy on top of everything else?"

Surprisingly, humor lit the end of his question, not condemnation. In fact, Aaron delivered a slight smile.

Phillip smirked. "Mila's not the enemy, her father is."

"Is not." Mom chimed in from her spot in a chair not far away. The words were gentle, but the warning of her arched brow was expressive enough to halt the line of conversation.

Phillip arrested all hostilities at once. How could he not?

Mom, as always, presented a demure image, calm despite literal and figurative storms. She had barely spared them a glance. Rather, she crocheted, hand motions steady and rhythmic, her mood contemplative. Her lone concession to the present tempest was a subtle shake of her head as she murmured. "It certainly is good to have the nest full."

"I just came by for dinner." Aaron addressed Mom, then Phillip. "I'll leave you to your game watching. Don't want to disturb. I'll be doing some sorting in the warehouse. Some of the early harvest beans need packing and storing." Aaron spoke with quiet respect.

Mom delivered a lingering look before he quietly retreated. Only then did she set her crocheting on her lap. She tilted her head, regarded Phillip. "You could go after him."

"I suppose I could."

She shrugged, resuming her triple stitch. "I wish you would."

"Are you anxious to get rid of me?"

"Never. But I'm anxious for matters to be set right between my boys." She looked up. "When the three of you aren't getting along, it makes my heart ache, and all-in-all, I don't think that's asking for much."

"Sorry to disagree, Mom, but in this case, it just might be."

"Stubborn. My Fisher men have always been a stubborn breed. Haven't quite figured out whether that's a blessing or a curse." She spoke the words with a smile ripened by love of the deepest, most enduring kind.

"I suppose it's a mixture of both." Phillip ignored pre-game analytics and crossed to her chair. He knelt at her side and lifted the nearest edge of her latest creation, a large square of white rimmed by soft pastel shades made of yarn that felt soft as a cloud. "What are you making?"

"An afghan for the town's mom-to-mom sale in a few weeks. The warmth will come in handy soon enough."

True, since temps would soon tumble into the frosty darkness of fall and winter. But for now, in the heat of late summer, such things seemed far off, so much like the hope he held of reestablishing himself smoothly within the tapestry of his family.

"Mom, I'm sorry. About now, and about the way I lipped-off at breakfast, too."

Her eyes softened; her features melted into affection. "I know you are, and I know you've been required to say you're sorry a lot lately. We're not being very welcoming, and that makes it hard for you to return, and to try again. We each have a share in that responsibility."

"I hope you know . . . I mean what I say . . . both about being sorry and about wanting to help. I really do regret acting like a fool."

"Finding your own way is never foolish,

72

Phillip. In fairness, Aaron should be feeling some regret as well. He's deliberately shoving at you, and everyone sees it." She shrugged. "Everyone except him, of course."

"Thank you for that."

Oh, how he loved her. Tender, earnest, possessing such a keenness of spirit, Mom was a treasure he had unwittingly neglected. Taken for granted. Like so much else in his life.

"You know, the reason he shoves at you has nothing to do with anger and everything to do with love. Your leaving wasn't easy on him."

"I'm learning." Thanks to an opening of his heart, and the same kind of keen-hearted and knowing instinct expressed by Mila.

"I figured as much." She resumed her hooks and pulls with a gentle, steady rhythm. "He didn't leave in a fit of rebellion; but toeing the line, obeying a pathway he wasn't even allowed to choose, hasn't been easy for him. Sticking to expectation hasn't made him any more perfect than you were for finding wings and experiencing the world around you. I believe both of you need to come to terms with that truth — and each other."

We're all the lost sheep, and we're all the

found . . . none is better than the other . . . all are equally loved by Christ.

She rested from her crafting to brush gentle fingertips against his cheek, content, it seemed to Phillip, and happy to have avoided the ruckus of a Sunday afternoon football game and a pair of sons at loggerheads. Couldn't much blame her on either count.

She returned to crocheting, and a message rode through his mind, loud and clear: *Grow up, Phillip.*

Phillip wasn't quite ready to attempt another run of the gauntlet with Aaron. That fact left him with nowhere to run and nowhere to hide. He had already seen Mila today, so there was no chance of getting together again without seeming, well, more than obvious in his sudden attraction. Nonetheless, Philip needed her. He craved a conversation sparked by her snappy humor, shared moments punctuated by their playful sparring. Mila pulled no punches, that was for sure. She made him think — and feel.

Best to dodge that development for the time being.

Resolved to make good use of his time, Phillip parked in the squeaky leather chair behind Pop's aged wooden desk, which still shone thanks to meticulous TLC from Mom's dust rag and furniture polish. The subtle aroma of lemon lifted through the atmosphere. Pulling open drawers, extracting files, bills, receipts, stacks of invoicing, he went to work reviewing current financials for the farm.

The news wasn't good. As expected, expenses exceeded income. The problem was that simple — yet also that complicated.

Pressure built between his shoulder blades while Phillip booted his laptop and launched a spreadsheet. Time to get busy finding some form of a tourniquet, because the farm was hemorrhaging money. Pop had a heart of gold and a propensity toward never — ever — seeing good food go to waste. Therefore, he negotiated with brokers like Byron Thomas, trying to keep prices as low as possible in deference to local consumers. Then there were the extra crops, like the ten-acre side fields of pumpkins and strawberries that were picked, for the most part, free of charge, by field workers and lesser-privileged townsfolk once the main harvest was complete. All of this was noble, sure, but . . .

"I'll give as I can, and as I see fit, Phillip." Pop allowed no leeway on the issue of

rampant generosity. *"God'll take care of the details. He hasn't let me down yet, and I don't believe He'll start to do so now."*

"Even if that philosophy ends up killing the farm from a fiscal perspective? How does that make sense? You're giving yourself away. This is your life. Your livelihood."

"No, son. This is my faith."

The words drifted to him on wisps of memory smoke, from an age-old conversation that stirred a longing, a sadness at the core of his chest. "That ideal of yours is all well and good, Pop, until the stress of survival wears you down and leaves you physically and emotionally drained." Phillip muttered those words into the silence of the empty office, but respect for his dad's fortitude and authentic love of neighbor spurred him forward. Clicking keys, compiling numbers, charting potential cut-backs, he lost himself in the familiar world of business alignment, budget structures and growth potential.

If farm-living could ever be referred to as having growth potential.

But wasn't the gift of earth the prize Pop had always received, and given, so freely? The turmoil pushed at Phillip, prompting him to search, to find a way. For hours, he worked; in the end, he groaned, stretching back tiredly. He rubbed his eyes in time to the rock and squeak of his chair. Blast it all, the cursed spreadsheets didn't lie. His formulas, the macros, the extensive computations threading one quarter to the next and one season to the next over the course of a year, spelled nothing but trouble.

Desperation mounting, Phillip pinched the bridge of his nose and squeezed his eyes shut.

A powerful though unexpected prayer came to life, rippling through head and spirit. *God, you sent me here. Show me. Help me. I want to make a difference. I want this to somehow succeed. Please show me how.*

In an instant, Mila's face materialized against closed lids and the beat of his heart, followed by an answer that reverberated through his soul. He needed to talk to Byron Thomas. He needed to start laying groundwork for the harvest to come in a couple of months. Handling negotiations would remove a stress-ridden burden and ease Pop's load. If nothing else, Phillip could play a bit of hard-ball with Byron Thomas and defend his family's hard work.

Just that simple.

Just that complicated.

Monday morning, Phillip drove to town and

parked in front of Sundae Afternoon, more determined than ever to find a place of his own so he could establish some breathing room. He needed to strategize the rest of his life and sort things through without constant family pressure and involvement.

Trotting inside, he slid onto a stool at the main service counter and opened his just-purchased copy of the latest *Times Gazette*. After ordering coffee and a bagel, he twiddled a pen and scratched notes in the margins of the paper, performing edits on a list of available rentals in and around Antioch. He fingered the handle of his freshly delivered cup of java, inhaled the robust, earthy scent that rose from tantalizing curls of steam. His senses perked further when Mila stepped into view across from him and slipped a neatly plated, toasted sesame seed bagel to his right. The sweet, light chocolate of her eyes was a more-than-welcome sight.

"Catching up on all the latest?" With a finger tap, she indicated the paper he perused.

"You bet." Phillip surrendered newsprint long enough to spread cream cheese across the warm surface of his bagel. "Can't afford to be out of touch in a town as bustling as Antioch."

Mila laughed. "And if you don't mind my

asking, are you escaping from the farm? Again?"

The rebuke in her tone was teasing and mild; all the same, it lit the fuse to Phillip's temper. He'd done more than enough agonizing over family, farm, and finances during the last forty-two hours. "Mila, don't ride me. Please. I came here for respite."

"Well if you're nice to me, I just might be able to offer you some."

Contrition washed through him. He never should have barked at the one who was doing her best to lend support and care. "I'm sorry, Mila. Really. I am."

She softened at once. "No problem. I get the confusion. What happened?"

In brief but thorny terms, Phillip laid out the details of Sunday's blowup with his brother, along with his desperate and futile attempts to find any sort of good news when it came to the sustainability of the farm.

Mila leaned against the counter and sighed. Sadness relayed from her spirit to his. "Aaron's not making it easy, and farm life is tough, that's for sure, but you're a smart man, and you have a lot to offer. Don't lose sight of that, OK? Keep pressing on."

He didn't expect answers. The situation was too complicated to resolve in one sitting of coffee, company, and a snack. Phillip re-centered on the most immediate task at hand — finding a place to call home. He eyed Mila, the seeds of an idea springing to life. "Hey, you're connected. You cross paths with most everyone in town." He waved the paper. "You probably know more about this place than any reporter working at the Gazette."

"Yeah, that's me, a regular newshound."

"Seriously. Can you keep an eye and an ear out for me regarding an apartment or a house to rent? Anything would work. Anywhere close by."

She tapped his folded paper, where red marks and stars delineated potential housing options. "I noticed you were shopping. And I meant what I said about being able to offer you respite."

"Really?"

She nodded, deliberately egging him on with a touch of suspenseful silence.

Phillip arched a brow then grinned at her antics. "Spill it."

"Well . . . I . . . suppose I could rent you the space above my shop. It's small, but I just updated it with the idea of renting. It's a one-bedroom, one-bath, but the main area is fairly big, and open. The kitchen is fresh, right down to the ceramic floor and appliances. It might be a nice set up for you."

Phillip went still, wondering why his heart took off at such a fast, staggered beat. Maybe it was her shy overture, or her slight stammering. Charmed . . . and magnetized . . . he struggled to formulate a response. "You . . . you have . . . I mean, I don't need much, but I wouldn't want to intrude or anything, or . . ."

OK, this convo had escalated rapidly toward being plain awkward, all because he had trouble processing her offer.

Mila's skin went from creamy to rosy pink as a blush came to life.

How was he supposed to interpret that?

"No problem. And I promise not to price-gouge."

"Oh, ouch. And would that subtle dig be an ode to the relationship between our fathers?"

She chuckled, breaking the tension. "Maybe . . . maybe not. Who knows? There's always been an intensity between the two of them. Weird, isn't it?"

"I guess." He had to respect that playful, yet no-nonsense attitude of hers, especially when paired with those sparkling eyes and that teasing grin. Phillip let her conjectures fade to the background while Mila studied him. A weird, tumbling sensation hit his

81

stomach. Attraction pushed clear through, taking him by surprise yet again.

Considering what he needed to do regarding crop negotiations with Byron Thomas, Phillip realized he was dancing through a minefield that was cleverly disguised by the low-lying, rippling green leaves of soybean plants.

6

"Well, don't you just beat all?" Hailey Beth gaped at Mila from across the width of a flatbed trolley they wheeled through Thomas's Grocery Store.

Mila halted their forward motion in the middle of aisle four and then proceeded to shelve boxes of cereal. Maybe silence would speak loud and clear, and end any kind of —

"Furthermore," HB continued, "thank you for continuing to build up my exhibit pile. We're up to three now; although, if I wanted to be militant, I could say the fact that you're offering him room and board ups the exhibit count to at least four — maybe even five."

Nope, no such luck. Silence, as usual, wouldn't cut it with HB. "Hailey Beth, I'm serious. Get over it." Mila hoped the use of her sister's full name might demonstrate the depths of her displeasure. Chances ran greater, though, that HB would go straight through her prickly attitude and see it for what it was. Fear. Fear of Phillip's increasing impact — and fear of a budding interest. "I swear, someday I'll get even with you."

"Get even? Get over it? Honey, I haven't *begun* to grill you. He's back in town less than a week and you're ready to rent him the apartment above the shop?" HB turned to the opposite side of the aisle and methodically stashed soup cans.

"Phillip needs a break."

"Yeah, over the head, with a two-by-four."

"Oh, don't you worry about that, honey. Aaron already tried, only with his fist instead of a plank of wood."

HB's righteous tirade softened on a dime, melting to sympathy. Yeah, Mila could totally relate to that level of sensitivity.

"You're kidding me," HB said. "Wow. I wondered about that fading bruise of Phillip's. I knew Aaron was pretty busted up when Phillip took off the way he did, but, man. To flatten him? That takes moxie."

"Along with a strong dose of stupidity." Mila hoisted a bag of rice puffs and waggled the temptation. "Grab us a couple bowls, and the milk from the mini fridge in back. Let's have a snack."

HB lit up like the fir tree at Christmas. "I

do love my breakfast cereal."

"This I've known for well over twenty years."

HB scampered off like an eager puppy.

"Don't forget sugar. Or the spoons," Mila called after her.

"Yes, mother." HB's snarky reply was stifled by distance.

The office space to the right, where Dad — and now HB — ran the coordinates of ship was next to the storage area at the rear of the store. A small kitchenette was to the side with its ancient coffee maker and old, but serviceable duo of dining tables where staff congregated for breaks and meals.

Wooden floorboards creaked comfortably beneath Mila's feet as she finished storing boxes and then sat in wait on the bed of the dolly. She loved this place — knew its every inch by rote. The mercantile was well-run and well-loved. Over a hundred years old, Thomas's Grocery remained a community bedrock. Mila took that fact to heart.

Stability filled her with a solid sense of belonging, of roots — but those roots weren't stifling. Rather, those roots served a purpose, providing her and her family with nourishment and a clear path to the future. Following a pre-ordained destiny didn't bother her as it did Phillip. She found peace along the tree-lined streets, the stately old homes, the time-honored gathering spots, and most of all, the people of Antioch. Phillip, on the other hand, had always pushed against its figurative walls, dreaming of silver-lined clouds and bright blue skies. When a stark harvest season hit his family hard at the mid-point of their high school careers, Phillip had turned ambition — a yen to leave the confines of small-town Indiana — into an all-encompassing mission.

"Here you go."

Hailey Beth's return jarred Mila from her thoughts, and she accepted a bowl and spoon, pulling open the cereal bag and pouring them both a healthy serving. Milk and a load of sugar came next, then companionable silence as Mila indulged in her breakfast snack and returned to the task of sorting her emotions.

"Phillip's not all bad, you know, and he's not entirely in the wrong for trying to find his own way in life. I offered him the apartment because I figure he could use a little support. Besides which, I worked my tail off on that renovation with every intention of renting the space. I figure, why not be there for him? That's all there is to it."

HB giggled her way into a disbelieving

snort while she spooned and chewed. "Yeah. You just keep tellin' yourself that, sister-mine. Just keep tellin' yourself that. From where I sit, we'll be into double-digit exhibits before the week is finished."

The rumble and vibration of the sorting machine called Phillip to the barn. He parked the pickup and made tracks for the interior of the massive structure, painted by Pop in the colors of black and gold in homage to Mom's alma mater, where she had earned her teaching degree. Inside, Aaron stood facing the threshold; Ben stood across, sorting freshly harvested beans.

The sorting machine resembled a conveyer belt, crafted of rolling, vibrating metal cylinders that chugged and spun, spitting beans, leaves, branches and bramble from the back of a harvester nearly as old as Ben. His brothers sorted with expert hands, extracting waste, while beans bounced and rolled down the line into stainless storage bins.

He could help with that — and inform them of his plans with Byron Thomas. He joined them and gave a nod. "Hey."

"Hey." Ben and Aaron answered his greeting in unison, not breaking from the task of using gloved hands to sort the good from the bad. Phillip grabbed a pair of work gloves from a nearby bench and slipped them on, going to work next to Ben.

"How's Mila?"

Phillip regarded Aaron with surprise. He knew about Mila? "What . . . you got a video cam loaded into the dash of the truck or something, Aaron? Cripe!"

"News travels fast in Antioch. Can't sneeze without the next-door neighbor handin' you a hankie."

Phillip held back a spontaneous burst of laughter at that analogy. He wasn't quite ready to give Aaron the satisfaction of a score in the humor department. "I suppose so. Anyway, yeah, I was at Sundae Afternoon. Looks like I might have found a spot to land."

"Land?" Aaron's tone was snide, but he didn't break stride from the task of sorting the small batch of beans.

"Yeah. In town. Above Mila's shop. An apartment."

"Then you're serious about staying here? Staying here for good and for real?" Aaron blinked, giving up sorting and shutting down the machine for the time being. "Seriously?"

"Such a shock, little brother?"

Aaron snarled at Phillip's response, as

expected — and hoped.

Phillip added a grin, just to solidify antagonism. "Maybe you don't believe in me, or my intentions, but you'll learn what's what, just like I've had to learn about the mistakes I've made." He could take ownership, and responsibility for his decisions. But now, as Mom indicated, it was time for Aaron to do the same.

"Whatever."

Nice surrender — not. Phillip bristled, yet refused to give up.

Ben shook his head but kept quiet, picking stubs, leaves, and branches from the still life of vegetation that stretched before them.

"I did more than socialize with Mila while I was in town. I paid a visit to Thomas's Grocery. I'm meeting with Byron Thomas at the end of the week."

"You're *what*?"

"Don't sound so shocked, Aaron, I told you I intend to make progress on the business side of things." A steely impasse followed. "I'm presenting preliminary projections for the crop, and I figure working with Byron first will lay the ground work, and help us all as we deal with the bigger distributors like Swarington Foods and Gordon Wholesalers. Like politics, all things start local, right?"

"True enough, and smart, I'd say."

Thank God for steady-handed Ben. Phillip clapped him on the back and prompted Aaron with a look. "Do we keep sorting or what?"

Aaron fired up the machine. "You sure you're ready for that kind of meeting?"

"Right down to a prior year recap and upcoming crop projections."

"And you're staying? For the time being, I mean."

Why did he keep pushing the point? "For quite a while, I mean, or I wouldn't be signing a lease. I'll need to find gainful employment, but I can get by for a short time, especially since I don't owe much more than rent and don't need much more than the essentials."

"Prudent of you."

"Aaron, you got something on your mind about what I'm trying to do? Something constructive? If so, speak up. But if you're spoiling for a fight, itching to rehash old garbage, I'll be on my way."

"On your way. Like before. Like when you blew into town for a few days when Pop was in critical condition, then blew right back out again before he even had a chance to see you."

Phillip's skin burned, but outwardly he

kept right on sorting beans, leaving the early-birds on the conveyer belt for further processing, tossing unsalvageable produce and waste into a large wicker basket with two metal handles. "At the time, I was in the middle of a make-or-break business deal. I was struggling to keep my job at Millenbech Incorporated, not that I expect you to ever understand the humiliation, the gut-punching, conscience-draining pressure of what I had to face. It was high-stakes finance centered on retirement investing and the market was far from kind."

Aaron struck a sarcastic pose. "Gee. Sounds kind of like what we live right here on the farm. Kind of like what Mom and Dad contended with all their lives. So, tell me, how'd that whole security thing work out for you, Phillip?"

"It crashed and burned. Thanks for celebrating." Bellowing a mighty roar, Phillip hefted then pitched the entire basket of soybean refuse straight into a leaf-riddled, green-and-yellow mass of vegetation across the length of the ground. "I've had it! I'm done! I'm finished being your whipping post! I've done nothing but swallow crow from the minute I crossed through the fields of this farm, and I'm *done*! What does it get me?" Phillip didn't give his brothers time to answer. Rather, he exploded into a deeper fit of emotional pyrotechnics. "My acceptance of your criticism, and your disdain, has gotten me exactly *squat. Nothing.*"

Rounding on Aaron, Phillip pointed a finger straight toward his chest. "I've received nothing but resentment from one of the people I'm trying hardest to make peace with and make understand what I went through. My silence regarding the guilt you're determined to pile my way might seem to indicate I accept your attitude. Let's be clear, here and now. I *don't*! I'm *finished*! You can take your resentment, take your bitterness and anger and shove it, Aaron!

"You're the one I need the most, and you're working twenty-four-seven to make me feel like garbage and push me away. If that's the way this is going to play out, I guess I have to deal; but I say to you here, and now: Give me the respect I deserve, if not your affection, for being here and for making amends. Or, are you too blinded by hatred to see clearly and not man enough to be civil?"

Diatribe delivered, Phillip didn't look left or right. He didn't even attempt or offer to clean the mess he'd created. He'd done enough of that lately. Let Aaron come to terms. Stalking from the barn, he made a straight line for the farm, slammed the back door behind him and took the stairs two at a time. In his room, Phillip flopped onto his bed, hoping he wouldn't catch Mom's heat for rattling a few door hinges. He covered his eyes with his arm as silence — and ramifications — set in. Man, how he needed Mila right now. He needed her with an ache that came to life vividly, and with over-whelming power. He needed a place where he belonged again, and her refrain played straight through him.

Phillip sequestered himself in Pop's office. He completed his notes and accompanying financial analysis for the meeting with Byron day after tomorrow. A knock sounded at the closed door. Assuming it was Mom, he looked up and smiled to himself. Nobody comforted like Mom. "Come on in."

When the knob turned, and Aaron crossed the threshold, Phillip struggled to keep from falling out of his chair. "Ah . . . Mom's in the kitchen, and if you're looking for Pop, he's at the barn, with Ben, and they're —"

"I'm looking for you." Aaron's quiet tone was followed by the door closing and a husky clearing of the throat. "Mind if I sit?"

Phillip's nerve endings sizzled to alert. "That all depends."

Aaron maintained eye contact and sat in the chair opposite. "Phillip, I . . ."

"Phillip? Want some tea? Coffee or anything?" Oh, sure. *Now* Mom arrived, calling from the hallway just beyond.

"I'm good, Mom, but thank you."

"You're welcome, honey."

Her footsteps faded against a tense, gauging silence between Phillip and his brother.

"Phillip," Aaron began again, "I had no idea you had been through the wringer like that."

"Now you know."

Silence followed.

"Do you feel like talking?" Aaron leaned forward, elbows on his knees, eyes shuttered, but Phillip caught a glimpse of something — a vibration of vulnerability.

"As I said, that all depends."

"I'll listen this time, OK?"

Phillip stretched back, took the figurative temperature in the room, and then decided to go for broke. Holding nothing back, he explained the struggle of surviving in the world of finance, of finding a way to maintain ethics, sanity, and a positive attitude while witnessing business dealings that crushed people and their life circumstances like eggshells. All in the name of profit. All in the name of stockholder security rather than the future of people who worked in the trenches day after day.

"I made the mistake of thinking this place was too small to hold my dreams." In the present moment, worlds wiser now, Phillip cringed at the idea. "Me and my idiotic, self-centered, materialistic ideas."

"Materialistic?" Aaron shook his head. "You were never about money grubbing."

"No, I never wanted money for the sake of money. But you convicted me on the whole security thing and craving money as a safety net, as a means by which to build a soft place to land. I wanted stability. You also convicted me on all of that being an illusion."

"Maybe. But, I was rough. Mean-spirited."

"Yeah."

After a heartbeat, they shared a grin, full of knowing, full of history — full of brotherhood.

"I want you to know I'm behind you on the whole Thomas meeting thing. I know you'll get us some good information about what's to come locally and in the Midwest. I appreciate it. You're not just helping Dad, you're helping all of us, and despite my — moods — I realize that fact." Aaron cleared his throat and stood. Looked at floorboards rather than meeting Phillip's eyes. "I love

95

you for that, and more. I'm your brother, and I know it's about time I started acting like it again."

Phillip didn't answer with words. Rather, he stood and took hold of Aaron's arm, tugging him into a chest bump, then a long, hard hug that was returned full force. "Thank you, Aaron. For that, and more."

Pop had returned from the barn and settled into an easy chair in the living room for a quiet reading session.

Phillip gave his father's shoulder an affectionate squeeze in passing. He was headed outside — to Ben. Talking with Aaron had given him hope that normalcy — a new normalcy, anyway — might come to them all. Phillip paused at the doorframe of the barn, watching.

Ben crouched beneath the open, narrow front hood of the tractor. Tinkering. Finessing. Always patiently fixing and manipulating. He grumbled something Phillip couldn't quite make out. A smooth ascent and subsequent hop onto the seat led to Ben cranking the engine. The rust-dotted antique shimmied, burbled, and expelled a stream of blackish-gray diesel smoke. The tractor backfired once, then revved to smooth, solid life.

"Well done." Phillip stepped out of shadow and joined his sibling.

Ben grunted, revved the engine again, nodded in response to the sounds — whatever they meant.

"I came back wondering if I needed to help with clean-up around here. I didn't mean to explode the way I did."

"Aaron and I made do."

Phillip looked around. Sure enough, the floor of the barn had been swept into order. "Thanks for —"

"Make amends." As usual, Ben didn't favor extra verbiage.

"Excuse me?"

He sighed deep. "Oh, don't cop some kinda professional, polished, citified attitude with me. I'm sick of it. You've been here, what, just over a week or so, and you still can't find even ground with Aaron?"

"But I've —"

"But nothing. I'll say the same thing to him I'm saying to you. I'm sick and tired of watching my brothers go at it like a pair of barn cats. You're the leader, Phillip. You're the oldest. The first born. Act like it."

Among other attributes, Ben harbored a well-masked, oceans-deep sensitivity to the people he loved.

"I'm already there."

"Meaning?"

"Meaning Aaron and I have reached a truce. A pretty friendly one, in fact."

"You . . . you did? How did that hap—"

"Hey, Phillip. Hey, Ben."

Hailey Beth Thomas stood framed in silhouette against the sunlit entryway of the barn. Silence descended. HB chewed on her lower lip, watching Ben, clutching the rounded handle of a wicker basket so tight her knuckles turned white.

Ben kept a steady eye on their visitor. Quick and agile, he leapt to the ground and nabbed his t-shirt from the top of a nearby hay bale. In the sticky silence that followed, he mopped his face with his shirt before yanking it on. "Hey," he murmured as he brushed past HB.

Phillip took note of the way she stared after Ben wordless and transfixed. And she swallowed hard.

Clearing his throat, Phillip sidled up to her. "Is it just me, or is the atmosphere in here a little humid today?"

She spun toward him and glared. "I heard the engine firing back here . . . so . . . I . . . I figured I'd find you . . . your dad . . . mom. Somebody."

"Mm-hmm." Phillip grinned, enjoying the fact that she was tongue-tied. Over his little brother. Wild.

She shoved the kerchief-wrapped basket into Phillip's gut, and he expelled a *woof* of surprise. She had always been feisty and sassy — yet beneath it all, a sweet little marshmallow.

"This is from my folks, with their regards and good wishes, for your dad's continuing recovery."

The basket nearly overflowed with home-made goodies. Now he felt like a heel for giving her the business. "Thanks, HB. We appreciate it." He made sure his gentle tone reflected that truth.

Right on cue, the hardness in her eyes went soft. An echo of Mila doing just the same thing resounded through his system.

"Mom stocked it. Fresh baked banana bread and her homemade apple jelly. There's some strawberry preserves as well. Hope you all enjoy it."

"I know we will. If you head to the farm you can deliver it to them in person. I think they're in the front room, and they'd love to see you."

She looked over her shoulder, seeming to trace the general trajectory of Ben's leaving. She chewed on her lower lip for a second but didn't leave right away. "I hear you're taking a look at the space above Mila's shop tomorrow morning."

Seeing the apartment was incidental. What he couldn't wait to do was see Mila. He couldn't wait to move to a spot where he'd be in even closer proximity. "I'm sure it'll be great. Hopefully I'll ink a lease."

"And hopefully you're aware of that fact that I'll be watching your every move. If you end up" — she made a pair of air quotes — "inking a lease, know this. I'm her little sister, but I'm big enough to take you on if you step out of line or hurt her."

Where was this coming from? "You warning me off, HB?"

"No, not at all. More like making you a promise."

She turned away then, haughty and lovely and resembling her big sister just close enough that their exchange made Phillip realize his emotions were crazily out of whack. And he had another fleeting thought as he watched her stride across gravel, kicking up dust plumes as she made tracks for her car: Her unsteadiness regarding Ben left Phillip intrigued. Since he still held the treats basket, it seemed she wasn't paying a visit to his folks. Was she afraid of running into Ben again? Sure seemed that way. Interesting.

Ben, you better stay on your toes with that one.

7

Phillip stood in the middle of the great room in a sun-drenched, top-floor apartment above Sundae Afternoon. Framed in the expansive center window, Mila turned toward him, smiled.

So simple a gesture, really, yet his heartbeat quickened. He could feel its vibration, and couldn't stop wondering. What was with this overpowering need? This attraction? Where did this yearning come from? The emotions were foreign to him, and as unexpected as an afternoon snow squall in late August.

"So?" She tilted her head, waiting.

"I'll take it." He spoke fast, and he spoke of the apartment, but his focus remained trained on Mila like a beacon finding home.

"Oh, c'mon. You barely even toured the place."

She drew back a gauzy set of white sheers, flooding the room with additional sunlight.

The sky was cobalt; through the open window, trees rustled against a soft but arid breeze — curse the stubborn, stinking drought. An occasional car engine split the silence, along with voices that carried from the sidewalk not far below.

"I don't need an extensive tour." Phillip joined her at the window and took in the view, enjoying the restful ambiance of Antioch. "You were right; it's perfect."

And that was the truth. The subtle aroma of fresh paint permeated the air. With creamy gray walls, white crown molding and dark-wood floors, this space was an empty canvas Phillip knew he could happily make his own. Especially since Mila would be a constant presence in the shop that stretched just beneath his feet.

The living area came alive with a micro-fiber couch, a love seat and a couple of end tables. The additions helped, since he had stored precious few items of furniture. Autumnal oranges, reds and yellows popped color against the walls in the form of abstract canvases. A quartet of throw pillows, and some glass-encased candles completed the room. The colorful show of vitality probably came straight from Mila's hand. All he needed to do was install an entertainment unit, a television, and some stereo equipment. The eat-in kitchen was equipped with a small dinette which rested upon sandy-colored ceramic tile and held shiny-new appliances. There was just one bedroom — unfurnished — but it was sizeable, with an en suite bath. Items he presently stored in Indy would do a nice job of seeing to the empty spots. Phillip was prepared to discuss rent terms and the finer aspects of striking a deal.

Mila stood stock still, sunlight and shadow pouring around her in blocks of gold, transforming her profile into a gorgeous, if surreal, kind of halo.

Phillip frowned. "Have you changed your mind about offering the apartment?"

That was about the only thing he could think of that might prompt such a potent — yet unreadable — regard.

"No, not at all. I'm just wondering if . . . I'm wondering how . . . I mean . . ." She huffed and thrust fisted hands on her slim hips. "I hate having to ask questions like this, but how do you see yourself affording the rent?" Her chest rose and fell on what seemed to be a fast grab for air. "I mean, I'm not trying to be a jerk, I just need to know if —"

Phillip's tension eased. He stepped just close enough to take hold of her hands, to capture her gaze. "Mila. I'm solvent. Sure, I need to find a job, and some solid income, but I'm able to provide for a good, long while thanks to a few deals I won and a severance package. My bank can verify those facts. So, no worries, OK?"

She fought his hold for a few seconds, looked beseechingly into his eyes, then went all soft and easy. Phillip experienced a melting of his own, and maintained their connection.

"Well, OK then. Let's head to my office and finalize matters."

"Sounds good."

He followed Mila down a wide metal stairwell and to the entrance of her private office. He plopped into a chair across from her desk while she sat and shuffled papers. Uncovering a manila folder, she opened the flap and pushed toward him a sheaf of papers that would initiate the legalese of an apartment lease.

Phillip went to work filling in the blanks.

"I hear you're meeting with my dad the day after tomorrow."

"Yep." Phillip opted to play poker-face and kept on writing.

"Do you have a particular topic in mind?"

Pause, pen scratch, scribble. Pause. "That's for him and me to discuss."

Phillip stopped writing. *Current position, and length of tenure.* Hmm. He reread the sentence and tapped his pen against the top of the paper, thinking of how best to —

"He's not the only voice in the market, Phillip. You know that, right?"

"I know that, Mila." *Would* to-be-determined *work?* He shrugged, filled in the information about his most recent job along with the requisite end date of his employment. "He's not the only voice, and he's not even the most powerful voice, but his negotiations have always set the tone for local producers — which you know, because you're a smart, well-versed lady." He lifted his head, speared her with an unflinching look. "Byron Thomas has always established precedent in Antioch, and that's always governed my family's bargaining point when it comes to crop prices. I need to know what's to come this October when the harvest is in full swing. I'm doing everything I can to stabilize the farm. Nothing more and nothing less."

"Which is wonderful, and it seems I'm about to have you on the hook for a minimum of six months as leaseholder, but all of that leads to another question I want to ask you."

"Which is?"

"What happens if everything turns? What happens to you if the world of big-business comes calling again? Where will you go? Will you stay? Have you even considered such a thing? After all, it could greatly impact me as a landlord —"

Mila's mini-rant came to a stop just as Phillip finished his paperwork and slid it across the top of the desk toward his lovely new landlord. He forced himself to a point of calm. "I guess I'll have to figure that out when and if it happens. And since I'm officially on the hook, I want you to know one more thing." He focused on full lips, pressed a bit taut by tension, but touched by a tempting shimmer of pink gloss. He could imagine the softness — the sweet taste — the give and take of a supple kiss. "I'm here, rock-solid, to see after the people I care about." He focused on her eyes. "All of them."

"I appreciate your time, Mr. Thomas. Thanks for seeing me."

"My pleasure, Phillip."

A handshake ensued. Phillip followed Byron into his office at the back of Thomas's Grocery and settled in for their meeting. An appealingly musty, aged atmosphere permeated the space, an atmosphere that spoke of history. Over a century's worth of Antioch citizens had wandered the floorboards; in that time, the establishment had weathered more than its share of culture change and shifts in the patterns of the world. Nonetheless, for Phillip, it remained a cozy, welcome constant.

"Must admit, I've been curious, and I've wanted to touch base ever since you returned to Antioch. Never seemed a comfortable time or place to do so, though."

"Until now."

"Now indeed."

They shared grins and Phillip studied the man from across the expanse of Byron's dark-wood desk. "I'm happy to have the chance to talk, and catch up."

"Which I'm sure is only part of the reason for our meeting today."

"You've always been astute. Sure, I have questions and thoughts about the harvest to come. You and your company are the starting point for Antioch's farm families. From there, we stretch out to the local wholesalers, then the regional distributors. That's all well and good, but rather than saying the buck stops here, I'm inclined say the buck starts here." Phillip gestured wide to encompass the Thomas mercantile.

Byron nodded, his regard one of visible

respect, and shifted more comfortably into his chair. He was a tall man, muscular, but a touch angular. Sharp green eyes promptly reflected his emotions, along with a keen intellect. Not many fast-balls flew by this man. He was smart, and Mom and Pop had always said Byron possessed depth of heart. As far as Phillip was concerned, that depth of heart was sometimes at odds with the reality of money making and corporate survival.

Survival. Security through business. Phillip could relate to the man.

"Mr. Thomas —"

"Phillip, by now I think you're entitled to call me Byron."

OK, that was a nice gesture. Phillip softened — and accepted — but inwardly remained on guard. "Old habits, and my childhood, die hard, Byron. Thank you for leveling matters."

"No problem, and understood."

"The thing is, my family has given the first fruits of every harvest to your store and the people of this community. During the depths of the harvest season, when my family gathered at table for dinner, or when my brothers and I helped work the fields, I always heard my father tell us to show thanks by returning our blessings, and giving to those around us. That's why, every year, he opens his fields to those who are less fortunate. He's never asked for much, or tried to price gouge, or beg for more than he felt was due. For better or worse, from a business standpoint, he always makes sure he feeds his neighbors first. That's how he's always operated and always will. Again, for better or worse."

"Nothing wrong with generosity, Phillip."

"Correct, and mark my words, I admire and support his commitment. But it's killing him, Byron. Slow, but sure." Phillip hadn't meant to reveal such vulnerability. He pulled in an enriching breath and straightened, going steady, sure of purpose. "I'm counting on you for a return of that generosity. He needs a break. He needs rest. He needs the kind of leeway he's given to others all his life."

"In what way can I help? Surely you're not asking for special treatment."

"Not at all. However, I'd appreciate the mutual, and timely exchange of market information and growth opportunities that can benefit not just you, but Antioch's farming community as a whole. I've been learning fast, and learning a lot. I want to help you by being transparent and above board about what our farm can provide. Meanwhile, you're privy to information that can benefit everyone, and this year has been brutal. I saw that plain when I reviewed my family's revenue statistics. Since I'm sure you'd agree that mutual survival is in everyone's best interests, what I'm here to ask for is continued openness. I'll be handling negotiations for our family this season, and I think you and I can form a determined — relentless — synergy. We need to team up and push for the best prices, the best relay of product, that we can. Not just for us, but for the other farm families as well."

"With that, I'd caution you by saying you're preaching to the choir. I've never been anything but above board."

The elder man's tone edged toward bristling. Antagonizing Byron Thomas wasn't Phillip's goal, but a frank discussion was the only way to navigate the tricky financial waters to come. "That's very true, as well as appreciated."

"I'm a business man, but never — ever — mistake my business interests for a lack of caring, or engaged behavior within my community."

"I know that, and I'm saying all of this only because I want to be clear and direct. I want to lift an annual weight from my dad's shoulders. In so doing, maybe a beneficial road can be paved for you, and for the farming families counting as always on a sustaining harvest. We have one of the bigger farms in the area, so we know our production influences the bottom line for you as a broker. We want to work with you, and I assure you, we want everyone to come out on the successful end of this year's harvest."

Silence held sway, a holding pattern of sorts, after which Phillip continued. "We need to find a way through, Byron. Excess rain and maggot infestations at the start of the season — a drought at the end — we need to work together. And, believe me, I'll do whatever it takes. Everything that's been poured into our fields for generations isn't going to die. Not yet, anyway."

"Interesting you use that term."

"Which?"

"*Our* fields. As in yours."

"Yes, mine. The farm may not be my passion, like it is for Ben, or Aaron, or most especially my mother and father, but make no mistake. Those acres of soybeans are part of who I am. They're part of my family — my legacy. Just like your businesses are to you and yours. Right?" Into his mind dawned the image of Mila, with her straightforward sweetness, her unencumbered faith, those big, dark eyes and that fall of hair that went on forever.

"Right, and fair enough. I'll work with you side-by-side as market data comes to life. That's a promise. Now, tell me about your return." Byron arched a brow. His scrutiny intensified and his lips quirked into a form of knowing that stopped Phillip short. "More specifically, talk to me about whatever designs you might have on my girl, Mila."

Formidable and strong-spirited, Byron Thomas hadn't gotten to where he was in their tight-knit community by burying his head in the sand, nor by being ill-informed. Therefore, Phillip wasn't unprepared for the line of questioning. "You pull no punches. I respect that."

"Return the favor and we'll have that in common."

Touché. Phillip nodded. "We've enjoyed spending time together, getting re-acquainted. Seems to be no secret there."

"And?"

"And, for now, I reserve comment and expectation. Although, I promise, if that changes, you'll be the second to know."

"The second?"

Phillip nodded. "With all due respect, sir, Mila should be, and will be, the first."

■ ■ ■ ■

Rejuvenation and a sense of purpose chased Phillip's heels clear across town. What did he have to lose? If Byron was keen enough to detect nuance, it was past time to move forward. Phillip wanted to test those deep, azure waters that rippled between him and Mila — state his case, so to speak. Charged by adrenaline, pumped by the idea of working proactively with the town's largest merchant to help the farm and his family, Phillip stormed the figurative gates of Sundae Afternoon, ready, now, to take on the matters of his heart. He caught Mila's eye right away, and a rush of warmth crested fast and hard. Somehow, mysteriously, they attuned to one another. Amazing.

He parked on a stool at the front counter and braced his feet on the metal rail, twisting from side to side just a bit while he watched Mila engage her customers. She was as sweet as sunshine, dispensing smiles, winks, laughter and a pat on the shoulder. She loved working the front of the shop as much as she loved ciphering profits and expenses. Such an interesting blend of left brain/right brain. And he wanted to know more.

"What's your pleasure today, Mr. Fisher?"

"Been looking at her, actually." As expected, the reference to his blatant regard caused her to go still, and sharpen her focus on him. Beautiful eyes. Just beautiful.

"Well, aren't you just turning on the charm today."

Phillip didn't look away, not even for a second. "Have dinner with me, Mila. Somewhere out of town, somewhere that's just for us. Fort Wayne isn't too far. We could have a nice evening together."

She peered at him, pulling an oblong bowl from the stacked stash beneath the counter. She started to craft a banana split he knew without saying would be to die for. "You trying to get me to knock a few bucks off your monthly rent or something?"

Phillip laughed hard. "I'm shocked you hold my motives in such low esteem. C'mon. I'm serious. I want to date you. I want to share dinners, and movies, and walks, and maybe even the occasional visit to Zeffman's pond before the air turns cold." To his delight, her cheeks went pink.

"You're wily as a fox, Phillip Fisher."

"I am?"

"You are. In fact, it might be one of your defining characteristics."

"You sassing me?"

"Mm-hmm. Not to mention keeping a list."

"You have a list? About me? That's cool. My ego thanks you. A lot."

She smirked at him. Gave her hair a toss. "Don't let that ego inflate too far. Only half of it is complimentary."

"No problem. I'll help you fix that error. How about the rest?"

"The rest is . . . shall we say . . . up for exploration."

"Then let's give it a go." He slid his hand over hers, soft and gentle, keeping her from dolloping whipped cream on top of the confection. "Seriously."

She nipped that full, plump lower lip and stared at him, visibly considering. "Couldn't hurt."

"You're too kind."

"Not yet, but I might be willing to learn."

Hope took off like a rocket through his chest. This unexpected attraction and relationship development knocked him for a loop, but Mila called to him. "That's all I ask. I'll pick a spot in the Fort. What's your favorite kind of food?"

"Fort Wayne, eh?" Her eyes sparkled, her lips curved. Anticipation rolled off her, pushing toward him, encouraging him. "You are on a mission."

"You've always been perceptive, Mila. Smart, too." He used a thumb to caress the back of her hand. "Let's get together Saturday night. I'll pick you up at five. Leave the restaurant to me. That way, it'll be a surprise for you." Phillip stood to leave.

"Like most everything else these days." She winked, and his knees about gave way. "Tell me about it."

8

In the end, like everything else about Phillip's return, he took Mila by surprise. He didn't opt for Italian, or French, or even the whimsy of Mexican or Oriental fare for their dinner date. Rather, he stuck to the basics of her life . . . of *their* lives . . . and opted for meat and potatoes of the highest standard at Baker Street Steakhouse.

With a warm, guiding hand settled against the small of her back, Phillip led the way to a corner table for two lit by candles, covered by supple linens and decorated by sparkling china and crystal.

"Very nicely done, Phillip. I appreciate this."

"And I'm glad you approve."

"How could I not? This spot is perfect."

He wore a gray silk suit, a deep blue tie. His shoulders were wide, strong, and she could sense now, in his sureness of self and understated confidence, the ways he might command a boardroom — or any set of circumstances.

The idea of his family, of his return — and its tenure — the myriad ways he fought for his family's livelihood, gave her significant pause while they were seated by a hostess. Phillip held her chair, tucking her carefully into place.

He took his seat across, admiration flashing through his eyes. "Green lace becomes you."

"I was just thinking we both clean up pretty well."

"We do at that."

Girlish pleasure coursed the length of her arms, tingling, raising goose flesh. She spread a napkin across her lap. Short sleeves, a long, double-wound strand of pearls, black leather heels — Mila considered her ensemble, thinking she didn't fuss over her appearance very often. The spark in Phillip's gaze made her glad she extended the effort, especially since he had greeted her at the front door of her home bearing a handful of tissue paper wrapped daisies in vibrant shades of yellow, orange, and white.

"I can't get over the changes in you, Phillip."

"The fact that I showered, or the fact that I'm in a suit?"

"It was kind of a tossup. Then, the tie and pocket square came into play. That duo tipped the scales for me." Following a moment of shared laughter, Mila tried to continue, but they were interrupted by the arrival of their waitress. With Mila's enthusiastic approval, Phillip placed an order for spinach artichoke dip with crackers as an appetizer. He was in no rush. That fact danced feather strokes against her senses. "Jokes aside, what I was trying to say is that I admire your change of heart, and your ability to see matters here in Antioch through a clearer lens. With an appreciative spirit, and a lot less fear."

Phillip's expression turned somber. "Well . . . when you get your knees chopped, you learn to roll with the punches. I thought I could somehow make myself immune to strife. Joke was on me, eh?"

He had yet to unfold his dinner napkin. When he picked restlessly at a corner of the fabric, Mila reached out to cover his hand. "You needed to grow up, just as we all do. No shame there. Sometimes life smacks us over the head to accomplish the task."

Phillip shrugged, not meeting her eyes.

"The smack, the chop at the knees, isn't the end of the story. Another thing? It's sure not the whole story. It's only a chapter."

Phillip looked into her eyes so long — so hard — she drew up short. All at once his shoulders sagged, as though relieved of a tremendous weight. "Lord above, but you're easy on me, Mila." He heaved a breath. "And for that, I'm grateful."

His earnest tone, his vulnerability, cut her to the quick. She floundered, but not for long. "I like where you're at now. You've become what I caught glimpses of as we grew up — a good guy with solid character and a lot more love to share than he ever let on."

"Have you been talking to my Pop?"

She chuckled. "No, why?"

"Because you sound just like him."

She brightened even further. "Thank you."

"You're welcome." The repartee dimmed when he stilled and focused on a spot just over her shoulder. "All the same, Pop had a heart attack that nearly killed him and I was cavalier about how it would affect the family. I came home for a few days, I sat at his bedside, but in all that time, while I checked my e-mail, scrambled for coverage at work, tried to execute deals, I didn't absorb the deeper meaning of what was happening. I was too busy building that safety net of mine to pay close attention to the struggles he faced, and the way it drained him, and

121

my mom. My brothers mopped clean up while I lived large in the big city. Serves me right for falling so hard, and so fast."

"A valid point, but as I said, it's just a paragraph."

"I should have been there."

"Phillip, you're here now. You're working hard to do everything in your power to get matters back on track. The rest will come . . . in time."

"If I can build a strong set of projections, craft a business plan that'll align those projections into a solid set of —"

"Phillip, you're looking at the situation all wrong." Mila halted his litany. "Farming . . . the lay of the land . . . the vibrations of the earth . . . are governed by God. They have nothing at all to do with crop reports, agriculture journals, or any kind of ancient almanac. Farming is about the way the soil regenerates. It's about the way nourishment is fostered, acknowledged, and tended to. Seeds coming to life, pushing for soil, and sunlight. Farming can't be read, or calculated, or quantified. There's too much of God's hand, and mystery in the process." Mila went quiet, considering her diatribe. After all, such intangibles were most likely the reasons why Phillip had left the family business, and placed his family firmly in his rearview mirror.

"True enough," Phillip answered at last. "My failure to recognize that truth doesn't taste too good right now."

"Then keep pressing on."

In a sudden, unexpected way, his gaze latched onto hers. "Know what I did, first thing after returning home? I gauged the fields. I dug my hands into the dirt and come up . . . dry." A visible blanket of shame seemed to fall across him, further darkening his mood. Then, just as fast, hope arose, sparking light to his eyes. "Mila, it shocks me, now, to realize everything I left behind. Everything I turned my back on."

"And?"

"And now? Now what I want most to do is preserve, protect, and defend."

"Have you let your dad know that? Have you made that intention clear to him? To your family?"

"I think Aaron is finally coming around, but —"

Mila shook her head. "No, Phillip. There are no 'buts.' Not now. Let your dad know. Make yourself known. Trust me. Nothing will bring peace, and understanding, like being open with the one who needs it most — and that's not Aaron. It's your dad. You exited Antioch as though the fires of hell were nipping at your heels; you had no problem leaving the dust of a small town behind, but all of that changed."

"It did." He pulled in, as though staring toward a spot far removed from the present. "I guess you *can* come home again."

"Yes, you can, and you can find yourself right where you least expected. After all, look where you landed. Home is the beginning. Home is where you belong. Antioch is where you belong, Phillip." A flash of insight struck; Mila realized those wise words might well be turned around and directed toward her. Home.

Now, more than ever, that small, single word resounded through a heart beating fast and furious for all that might come.

Wind whistled through the tips of thick, leafy green vegetation. That same breeze caressed Phillip's face, calling to mind the loose curls of Mila's hair, her full, soft lips. Surrounded by soybean plants, he stood stock still, eyes closing while his mind's-eye drew pictures of Mila — her peaches and cream skin, her sky-blue eyes as they'd talked and laughed and shared with one another at dinner last night.

Prompted to look up, Phillip opened his eyes and followed the path of a quartet of circling and diving birds. Their plaintive caws cut the air while he pondered what to do next. He looked over his shoulder, at the weathered though sturdy farm that had housed the Fisher family for generations.

Be open.

Mila's advice rang clear. Protecting the farm, helping his family, weren't the only elements of his return that kept him pushing forward, and hoping for a more fulfilling path to the future. He could picture Mila here — framed by rolling, green fields and golden sunlight — more to the point, he could picture his life at her side, in promising, tempting glimpses. Together they could make a life, a family, a continuation of both their treasured legacies.

The recognition provided Phillip with a jarring, yet compelling, reason to put down roots and stay in Antioch. Resolved, he turned toward the farm once more, and made his way to the living room, where he knew he'd find Pop.

As expected, he came upon his father seated comfortably in a recliner that had forever been stationed in a far corner of the room, near a picture window that overlooked a spread of land that most likely lent peace and calm to his daily meditations. Old or not, the solid piece of furniture was Pop's favorite. As such, its tenure was assured, faded fabric, sunken cushions and all.

Pop shifted in his chair, gaze steady as he glanced up from reading his time-worn Bible. "Phillip."

"Hey, Pop."

There was such warmth to his eyes. Lines grew ever deeper at the corners, but life had given him many a cause to laugh, to squint into bright sunlight, to weep over water-logged crops, or rejoice over thick, green shoots of well-nourished plant life. Unconditional love, however, never changed. Nor did Pop's loving vibration.

How had he failed to fall to his knees with gratitude for being the recipient of such a gift?

Following an elongated silence, Pop puzzled. "You OK?"

"Yeah. Actually . . . yeah . . . I am."

Sensing authenticity, Pop's warmth increased. "Good. You just back from town?"

"No, I was checking the fields, taking a walk to clear my head."

"You've been working the numbers pretty hard lately."

"I have. And the news isn't great, but it isn't all bad, either. There are ways we can get this farm back to solid ground."

"Your meeting with Byron helped. Harvest

time is about community. We're not alone in this."

Phillip folded onto the couch, its contours comforting and inviting — right down to the smells that surrounded him — the lingering but subtle aroma of tobacco from the use of a pipe, the lemony tang of the furniture polish Mom used to gloss the wooden tables to a shine.

"It's not just Byron who says —"

"Byron, is it?"

Phillip traded joshing smirks with Pop. "I've approached representatives of the Indiana Farm Service Agency. According to Marvin Hilger, the FSA has been helping a number of farms in our area that were hit by that bout of early season flooding —"

"Then the drought that followed. Yeah."

Phillip nodded. "Since the weather shows signs of evening out, a late season growth spurt leaves Hilger to believe fields might yield up to seventy bushels per acre. That BPA forecast is enabling the FSA to issue low interest rate loans. We could enlist their aid, pay back the loan, and still turn a profit in the end."

Pop laid a dark red ribbon carefully into place between onionskin pages punctuated by notes and highlights that had been added to the Bible over the years. He closed the book and set it on the end table next to his chair. "Fine work, Son. I appreciate it."

"No problem."

Pop waited patiently. Knowingly. "Now. Would you care to tell me what else is on your mind?"

Yep. Nothing got past Pop. Phillip leaned forward, propping his elbows on his knees. "The delivery of a long overdue apology."

"For what?"

"For vacating when you needed me most. For running out on the most important people in my life." Phillip paused, gauged.

Pop simply sat — and listened.

"I was arrogant. I betrayed you, and Mom, and my brothers." Phillip hung his head. "I want you to know, I'm sorry for that."

"The fault isn't entirely yours, Phillip. In addition to taking responsibility for your actions, which is always a good thing, I believe that truth is something you need to accept, and realize." Pop reached into the right pocket of his trousers and pulled an item free. He moved a small, smooth stone across his thick, calloused fingertips, caressing it with his thumb. The stone, was unblemished. Pure white.

"What'cha got?"

"A reminder. For you. Something I came

upon in the field, of all places, a week or so after you left. Once I found it, I kinda felt as if it belongs to you." Pop handed over the stone.

It was remarkable. Slightly elongated, yet perfectly rounded, it shimmered to a soft, perfect glow.

Phillip had never seen anything like it — and Pop had somehow found it in the dirt of hundreds of acres of vegetation? Remarkable. "Why would it belong to me? What's it for?"

Pop shrugged; Phillip worked the stone. "At first, I thought it was for me. The image of it comforted me after you left. For a time, it's been a reminder that God makes all things new, and good. Now, I think it needs to go to you."

"Why's that?"

"Because when I found it, I did some research on the significance of pure white stones and came upon an interesting story — you and Aaron aren't the only ones who know how to use the search engine on a computer — and the story I found gave me hope."

Phillip edged toward his dad, piqued and focused. "What's the story?"

Pop drew a long breath. "Well, it seems in ancient times, when a Roman slave was set free, they were given a white stone to carry with them. It was a form of protection — a verification of their status and clean slate. It symbolized freedom, and the dignity of each man's life, no matter their station. That's what you've got here, son. So, keep it. Let that stone be a reminder. Keep it close. As you re-find your life, and your heart here in Antioch, maybe it'll help you stay centered on the fact that you're redeemed. You're forgiven. Most of all, you're loved."

Phillip's throat went tight. He manipulated the stone much like his father had, enjoying its smooth texture and shimmering radiance.

"Sometimes God writes you straight using a crooked line. What's past is past, and backward isn't where you're headed, so focus on what's ahead. Focus on moving forward. Make good use of that clean slate. You're free — with a chance to create whatever it is you want from this life."

Just as when he had stood in the rippling field of green, leafy crop plants, Phillip couldn't help but think of Mila, and her impact. He pondered that fact.

Pop gave another broad shrug and re-opened his Bible. "Guess I don't need to say much more beyond that."

9

Phillip delved deeper and deeper into the intricacies of running the farm. August cooled into a fiery explosion of autumnal color as September chased its way to early October and harvest season began in earnest. The fields of the Fisher farm hummed with the steady cadence of combines pushing through vegetation. Field workers came and went. Ag students from Antioch High School's co-op program showed up. Students and representatives from a few nearby colleges paid visits to the field and conducted soil/produce studies. They were joined by government officials who tracked and recorded crop yields as every attempt was made to build statewide production data.

Through it all, Phillip saw Mila almost every day and discovered an unexpected yet pleasing rhythm to being in Antioch. A sense of equilibrium sprang to life within

the formerly strained roots of his relationships with Aaron and Ben. Slowly — like
shoots pushing through soil — the ease of
their youth patterned into a new, more
dynamic connection. His brothers didn't
seem to mind his efforts to run the business
side of the farm, but operations were a team
effort, governed by consensus.

Mindful of that truth, Phillip figured
tonight's family dinner would provide an
opportunity to include everyone in some
important strategies and plans he wanted to
set in motion before much more time
passed.

Phillip took his seat, savoring the spread
of food stretched across the length of the
dining room table. He breathed deep. Pot
roast. The aroma of simmering meat had
filled the house all day, coming from a slow-
cooker that had to be older than him. Now,
the finished product welcomed him to the
pleasure of a classic Fisher family supper.
Draping a linen napkin across his lap, he
hefted the meat platter positioned in promi-
nence at the center of a feast that included
potatoes, fresh corn, and bread.

After devouring a few forkfuls of smoky,
melt-in-his-mouth roast accompanied by
onion and sweet peppers, Phillip continued
the thread of a general conversation focused

on the salvage operations to be executed. "The way I see it when I study the numbers, crop insurance and low-interest loans from the USDA Service Agency will help see us through. I've got the paperwork and approvals in motion. We'll have to pay the loans back, of course, but not until after harvest."

"As in . . . right now."

Phillip nodded at Aaron. "Exactly. When I built the forecast, I figured we can hit about fifty-five bushels an acre, maybe a little more. At just over ten dollars per bushel, we can have a solid harvest despite the weather rollercoasters we've battled this year." Phillip munched on a perfectly buttered and seasoned potato chunk.

Mom paid close attention and nodded.

"With numbers like that, we could turn a profit," Pop said. "Small, but certainly enough to sustain."

Phillip felt a glow of pride — of ownership and responsibility to those he loved. The feeling had been absent from his life for so long it took him by warm surprise. "Yeah, we could. That's my goal, and I think it's achievable."

"It'd be a blessing, for sure." Pop issued a satisfied nod.

"It'll provide for the future." Phillip eyed his family. "Might even allow for some restoration of the house, some equipment upgrades. If we manage our income smart, we can invest in the future. I'll keep building on the plan." But the plan, Phillip came to realize more clearly, encompassed much more than just projections and agriculture. The plan involved much more than just redemption and a return to the core foundations of his life and upbringing.

The plan involved Mila Thomas.

Thoughts of her followed him home that night, to his apartment. As he drove the few miles to town, he considered the few remaining details left to polish the place to perfection.

His phone chirped to life, flashing with a number that jarred Phillip because it was as familiar to him as it was unexpected. Someone from Millenbech, Incorporated was reaching out.

But why?

Since he was driving — and since he wasn't particularly eager to speak to anyone affiliated with his former employer — he temporarily ignored the summons. Nonetheless, Phillip's nerve endings prickled and curiosity built.

After he climbed the outer stars and unlocked the front door, after he tried and failed to focus on a few meaningless pieces of junk mail he had retrieved from the floor beneath the mail slot, Phillip surrendered pretense. He yanked his phone from the pocket of his slacks and reviewed the home screen. Whoever had called left voicemail. Phillip tapped into his messages and tucked the phone to his ear, already bracing himself for . . . whatever.

Phil, it's Matt Hobbs. Need to talk to you right away. There's an opportunity opening on my team — we had a big win with Symbiotic Technologies and we need you, man. This job would be perfect for you — and you're my first and only call until I hear back from you. Let's talk it over and get you back here. You're missed, man. Big time. So, call me.

Phillip gulped. He stared ahead, unseeing, unfeeling, submerged within a world of shock-absorbing silence.

A knock at the door jarred him so hard he fumbled his phone. Phillip yelped when the device hit the floor; he retrieved it with a swooping grab and headed to the entryway. He opened the door to Mila, who smiled bright.

She carried a colorful basket wrapped in clear cellophane and topped by a rainbow of curly ribbons.

"Hey." Phillip greeted her, but on the inside, he froze.

135

Her arrival struck him with a sledgehammer of guilt. A chill slithered against the length of his spine, but he hadn't done a single thing wrong. Yes, he had to return the call. Yes, he would have to face the tempting pull of returning to a life he had built on his own terms, and to his own strengths, but still —

Mila's prediction was coming true — the very scenario she had posed when he'd executed the lease on her apartment: *What happens if everything turns? What happens to you if the world of big-business comes calling again? Where will you go? Will you stay? Have you even considered such a thing?*

"Can a girl get an invitation to enter when she arrives at your doorstep bearing gifts?"

Phillip regrouped, trembled while he sucked a deep breath. "Ah, yeah, sure. Sorry. I'm a little . . . off. Preoccupied by business." Phillip dodged an outright lie, knowing she'd assume he meant the farm. Guilt, however, grew exponentially. "Come on in."

Breezy and visibly enthused, Mila entered the great room and spun toward him, offering the beautifully packaged basket of fruit and candy shaped into the form of a floral bouquet.

"I know my visit might seem a bit stalker-esque, but forgive me. I've been waiting for you to arrive. I couldn't wait to tell you — I'm celebrating. Sundae Afternoon has been named as a vendor for a national delivery company to help create edible arrangements just like this one. I wanted you to get a first taste of our offerings." She kissed his cheek, her aura sparkling as their gazes connected. "I thought this might be a nice variation on the ice cream sundaes you like to indulge in at my shop every once in a while."

Phillip smiled but knew the gesture lacked ease and a responsive spark. "Thanks. This is great. It looks wonderful — congrats, Mila — that's a huge commission. Much deserved as well."

"You're welcome. I hope you enjoy it." Sure enough, Mila's brows pulled. She tilted her head, silent and watchful. Waiting. "Are you OK?"

"Yeah, sure. I just got home from the farm and a pot roast dinner. I'm well fed and focused. Processed a lot of numbers and did some plotting and planning with the family." And again, that was no lie, just a slight evasion.

"I like that you're calling this home." She set the basket aside; Phillip cursed himself for not possessing the temerity to take custody of her offering and place it in the

137

kitchen or something.

The arrangement was beautiful, with strawberry and pineapple chunks shaped into roses and flowers and held in place by small wooden spikes. There were also chocolates in the shapes of butterflies and birds which were tucked against bedding of green fluff. The sweet optimism of her gift was at complete odds with her unexpected arrival and his sudden bout of turmoil.

"You've landed well, Phillip. I like the way you've pulled everything together. It *does* feel like home, doesn't it?"

Phillip wrestled with uncertainty and anxiety all over again, and wondered promptly why that would be the case. He hadn't even made a return call to Millenbech yet. He had no information to build on regarding matters that had come to life in Indianapolis, and nothing had been discussed. Why was he allowing himself to get so keyed up? Why did he feel bad? Why, even though he had done nothing wrong, did he feel like some type of betrayer?

"Phillip — Phillip, did you hear me?"

"Sorry." Lost again. He needed to straighten up, pronto. "I missed what you said."

Mila firmed her lips for a moment, then assumed a mild, accepting posture. "I was asking about your interview with Maddox Ag Industries. Fort Wayne is a bit of a commute, but the opportunity sounded solid. How was yesterday's interview?"

Oh, Lord. Help me. Please. Phillip shuffled his feet, stuffed his hands deep into the pockets of his slacks. "They're a great organization. They liked what I brought to the table."

"How could they not?"

He stroked Mila's chin with a lone fingertip, hoping to somehow telegraph some measure of the appreciation that swelled through him at her unencumbered encouragement and support. He pulled her close by tugging gently against her waist. "Jason Longbourne, the one I told you about who heads operations, said I'd hear back in a week or so. I met a few members of his analytics and forecasting team — and it's an impressive company."

"Dovetails right into the work you're doing with your family at the farm. You'd be a natural."

"And you're a believer."

"In many ways. Yes, I am."

Phillip dipped his head, claimed her lips without warning, without pretense, without apology. He craved her desperately. He drank from their kiss like a parched man, drawing his fingers softly through her hair, sinking, spinning, allowing the flood of rightness . . . of completeness . . . to overwhelm and connect. Within the moment, Phillip tasted the promise of the future, the contentment to be found in the arms, and care, of someone who loved him, shared his life, and filled his spirit.

The distance between this moment and everything else in his life became meaningless debris blowing away against the love that flooded his senses and unlocked the depths of his heart.

At last they tempered the moment, drawing apart by slow, steady increments that banked the flames rather than burying them.

Phillip came to rest in the steadiness of her gaze, cradled her face between his hands like precious treasure.

Mila slipped her hands against his forearms, never flinching from the intensity of the moment. "I believe in *you,* Phillip."

Don't do it. Don't. Do. It. Sneaking off is wrong.
The refrain played repeatedly through Phillip's mind, forming a repeat cycle he tried — and failed — to ignore.

He wasn't sneaking off. Attending a meeting with his former employer in Indianapolis today was nothing more than a case of exploration. Besides, there was something poetic about having a chance to traverse a road he had thought broken and irreparable. No question he was a different man now. Changed from the core. All the same, he wanted — no, he *needed* — to explore the opportunity at Millenbech, Incorporated.

After Mila left his apartment the other day, he had promptly called Matt Hobbs and discussed the details of a job offering that would put him back in charge of a business portfolio for a tech firm headquartered in Indy the likes of which he had dreamed of for years. Meanwhile, the time in Antioch had helped him grow up. He had learned from the mistakes of the past. Perhaps he could convince Mila to pursue a life in Indianapolis? Wouldn't she be just the type to embrace a new opportunity in an opportunity-driven city like Indianapolis?

He prepared for the two-hour drive south, knotting his blue silk tie, arranging the collar of his white dress shirt and double checking the fall of his suit coat. All the while, doubts slid into place with the neat, expert precision of chess pieces being maneuvered across a board. There wasn't a chance she'd move to Indianapolis. Not after she had scored a major account for Sundae Afternoon.

But that was part of the point. Didn't he deserve the same chance to explore a growth opportunity of his own? To Phillip's mind, chances hovered at the fifty-fifty mark as to whether this day trip would amount to much more than a swan song to his former life. No harm, no foul.

Don't do it without telling her — or telling them. Pop and Aaron especially.

The voice of truth niggled, prodding at him, and Phillip battled. This meeting carried with it all the undercurrents of clandestine intrigue, and from his perspective, there was no reason for that to be the case.

No reason at all.

"Phil!"

Phillip looked up from the current edition of a popular money magazine he held and then tossed it smoothly onto the glass reception table. Standing, he greeted the arrival of Matt Hobbs with a smile and a nod.

"It's great to see you, man, come on back." Matt whapped Phillip on the back and offered an enthusiastic handshake before leading the way to his office not far beyond. "So, it looks as though the sabbatical agreed with you. You've even got a tan going."

Phillip blanched. The tan Matt alluded to

dawned as the result of hard work, sweat, and toil. "The sabbatical? Matt, I wasn't on any kind of sabbatical. I was let go."

Matt crossed the threshold of a glassed in eight by ten room that was so typical a space for the up-and-comers at Millenbech. Phil's business residence had been just a few doors down. Easy come, easy go . . .

"OK, OK. You were let go, but you were never far from mind. We knew we'd be pulling you back in before long." Matt gestured toward a nearby chair. "Have a seat. We simply needed to let the dust settle as that whole 'right sizing' episode played out and economic conditions stabilized."

Economic conditions, weather conditions, soil conditions, what was the difference, really, between this world and that of the farm? The flood of insight left Phillip silent for a moment. The difference was love, and heart. He sat, crossed his legs, and opted not to offer a comment on corporate machinations, and politically correct descriptives.

Matt continued. "So, let's make this short and sweet. As I explained to you the other day, we need your strengths at market reads and strategy. The portfolio we landed from Symbiotic Tech is tailor-made for you because the last thing on their radar is what you can handle for them — financial structuring, debt, and income strategy. It's a slam dunk."

"I've been interviewing elsewhere and unearthed a few opportunities that are just as appealing, closer to home and my family."

Matt stretched back in his chair, swiveling slightly. A Cheshire-cat smile bloomed. "My cue to discuss salary —"

"Ah, no. Not at all."

"We want you back at a ten-percent pay increase with bonus options based on revenue savings to Symbiotic Tech."

Phillip moved to interrupt. A disagreeable flavor bloomed against his spirit.

Matt, however, plowed ahead. "Additionally, there'll be no more chasing your tail riding out month after month of going after sales and accounts. You'll be head of strategic development for their investment portfolio, and we're contracted for a five-year term. Your strength has always been reading trends, market fluctuations. You never signed on for business development, and it was unfair of the firm to expect it of you and add so much pressure."

An epiphany didn't just occur, it dazzled and overwhelmed in a conclusive silence that built and then crowded the air. The life he had vacated, with its frantic do-or-die-right-this-very-second vibrations left him empty and cold — longing for green earth and slow, steady nourishment.

Longing for Mila.

"Matt, I appreciate the vote of confidence." And Phillip meant it. This meeting, this chance, gave him clear definition, closure, and more confidence than ever in a future built around the woman he loved, in the town he loved, in concert with the family he'd never again forsake. Phillip leaned forward. "I'll be equally frank and tell you I'm not sure this is what I want anymore. Your interest, our history, warranted this meeting, and I'll admit beyond that I was curious to hear the details of your plan and see if I was authentically finished with the world I inhabited here."

Matt frowned, openly puzzling. "And?"

"And my answer is: Thank you. Thank you, but no thank you. I don't think this" — Phillip encompassed the office they occupied, the wide-open desk spaces and floor to ceiling windows of the bull pen just beyond that hummed with the buzz and conversation of young lions at work — "is what I want any longer."

"You can say that after only a couple months away?"

"Yeah. Yeah, I can."

10

Mila closed the door and turned the locks on another day at Sundae Afternoon, chiding herself soundly for checking the darkened outer stairwell leading to the upper floor apartment. Sure, Phillip lived just above her store. Sure, Phillip was a paid tenant of the property owned and operated by her and her family. Those facts didn't allow her to check up on him, though. Those truths didn't give her license to be a . . . what was the best word? Watchdog? Beyond-interested-bystander? She chuckled under her breath and pocketed her keys. She had joked with Phillip about being a quasi-stalker. Maybe that comparison wasn't too far off the mark.

Still . . . where was he? The farm? Another interview? Mila checked her watch. It was getting late, past six o'clock actually, and he hadn't mentioned any new job ops since the promising exploration that took place last week with Maddox Ag. Mila stared at the darkened kitchen window that over-looked the stairwell, nibbled at the corner of her lip.

Phillip. In Antioch. For good.

The flood of pleasure no longer took her by surprise. The attraction had also become as familiar as the touch of his fingertips against her cheeks, the underside of her jaw, the slide of his lips against hers. Fighting a quiver, Mila turned, resolute now about walking away from her shop . . . and his empty apartment.

"Ooof!"

Mila absorbed the exclamation and shock of running smack-dab into the broad chest and steadying hold of Aaron Fisher.

"Aaron — I'm so sorry."

"No worries. Sorry for startling you." They exchanged sheepish grins.

"I was distracted. You here to see Phillip?"

"I was hoping to, yeah. Some reps from the USDA stopped by the farm and met with Dad. I've tried reaching him with no luck. Starting to wonder where he is."

"He wasn't at the farm today?"

"No." Aaron shrugged. "Not to be my brother's keeper or anything, but I'm get-ting a little concern—"

"Not to worry. Your brother is both present and accounted for, Aaron."

Mila and Aaron whirled in unison toward the sound of Phillip's voice.

He had stepped toward them from behind, on a sidewalk in front of the shop just now glazed by the pearly grays and rich shadows of sundown. Unheard and unannounced, with his suit coat draped neatly across his arm, Phillip presented a polished and very business-like image. His tie was fixed precisely in a splash of royal blue color against a crisp, white shirt. Gray silk slacks, dress shoes and a vibration of easy confidence left Mila to catch her breath. He looked amazing — dressed to impress. In addition, the quick grin he flashed at his brother — so full of teasing and affection — caused her pulse to react. Phillip was such a gorgeous, charming specimen.

But just as quickly as that thought bloomed, questions mounted. Silence stretched, all but demanding the question that burned through Mila's mind. "You were missed today, it seems. Everything OK?"

"You bet." Phillip's expression went from easy to guarded, but still he smiled.

Mila, however, had not mistaken the veil that crossed his features.

"So, you two were looking for me. Want

to come up for a few?"

Aaron seemed to sniff something in the air; Mila watched in silence as he scowled, and agreed to Phillip's offer with a nod. "Yeah. Sure."

She followed the two men, marching up the stairwell to Phillip's apartment entrance.

Once inside, the conversation resumed in earnest, starting with Aaron.

"Reps from the USDA stopped by the farm today and we were —"

"Looking for me?" Phillip interrupted with smooth ease. "Yeah. I got the voice-mails and saw the half-dozen missed calls. I had no idea there was an appointment."

"It was impromptu. Doug Godfreid and Jeff Thomas from the local office stopped by to talk about the harvest. We spent the better part of the day comparing notes and sharing insights from neighboring farms to get a handle on crop forecasts."

"I was in Indy." Only then did his glance ping from Aaron to Mila . . . and back again.

"Indy." Suspicion coated those two syllables; Aaron visibly awakened to past hurt — doubts — pain. "That's unexpected. What's going on in Indy that you stopped and dropped?"

"A job op."

"A job op?" Mila spoke in a hushed,

hoarse tone while Aaron stared.

"That's not impromptu," Aaron quipped at last, his eyes narrow, nose flared. "You failed to mention it." He gestured toward Mila. "To anyone, it seems."

"Why would I?"

"Maybe because people care about you, Phillip." Mila took over, shocked. He had been at a job interview today? In Indianapolis? Without telling anyone? What kind of covert operation was Phillip running? Judging by Aaron's carefully banked expression of anger, her attitude was matched verse-for-verse. "Maybe because you need to start learning to let people into your life when it comes to matters that are important — life changing."

"Kinda feels like history repeating itself." Aaron had composed himself. His quiet decree, although void of anger and hostility, revealed something much deeper. Hurt. Pain. As a result, his words bore twice the impact.

Sadness entered the room like the press of ocean waves — pervasive, and obliterating all the goodness that had come before. All that had been accomplished in the months since Phillip's return to Antioch. Forward motion had been eradicated as the result of a stinking 'job op.'

Mila wanted to weep, crumple to the ground, and rail at her weakness of heart and spirit. How on earth had she allowed herself to fall? To believe?

To love?

"Don't write me off just yet, brother. You either, Mila." Phillip's quiet statement rang with an undercurrent of decisiveness.

Silence fell and tension built.

He remained carefully composed, his focus moving between her and Aaron while the heat index shot upward. Mila wanted to understand. In desperate measure, she longed to believe in Phillip, but internal struggles came to life. Why had he scurried to Indy without so much as a word of explanation or warning? Why hadn't he discussed this unexpected and sudden 'job op' with those closest to him unless he felt consumed by guilt?

Talk about incriminating evidence.

Heavy hearted and confused, Mila turned toward the door, rested her hand on the knob before taking that last step over the threshold, toward a hasty and broken exit. "I need to get going, but we can talk in the morning if you'd like, Phillip. I want to hear all about it. Aaron, I'll talk to you later."

Although she laced her words with genuine care and interest, inwardly Mila shattered. She left his apartment on swift feet, mindless to everything but the pound of her heart, the prospect of loss, the bone-deep ache of sorrow.

Once the door clicked closed behind Mila, Phillip puffed air through pursed lips. He closed his eyes while rocking back on his heels. On the inside, he awaited that fateful second shoe drop; he braced for the explosion of Aaron's temper, counting it as more than justified.

Hadn't Spirit prompts warned him repeatedly not to skulk away from Antioch? Hadn't he — as though never learning a thing since his return — ignored that rush of wisdom in favor of reestablished pride and, best of all, vindication? Hadn't he — just like before — dropped the ball on those he cared for the most?

Instead of all that, and much To Phillip's shock, Aaron studied him in a posture both steady and calm.

"Phillip?" Aaron heaved a deep breath. "Tell me what happened. Talk to me. Really talk to me about this, OK? I'll listen. I promise."

Aaron seemed sincere, earnest. Phillip opted to take the risk and believe him, launching into a detailed explanation of the phone call from Matt, the agony of indecision as to which path to follow, the resurrection of his professional life at Millenbech, and the interview that had ended with his flat rejection of the job offer, no matter how lucrative. And the upper echelon of Millenbech had made sure it was lucrative.

But nothing could sway Phillip now. He poured free to Arron, like the old days, revealing the sense of finality he needed, the affirmation of the life he had found — the life he now loved on many levels — in Antioch, Indiana, of all places.

Aaron listened without comment or interruption, without the sneers or patterns of judgment that had black-marked so much of Phillips early days back on the farm.

The loosening of restraint allowed Phillip the freedom of exploring himself, pinpointing his motives and goals, revealing the depth of his heart toward Mila.

Nothing on earth could have helped him more.

"I'm through being angry," Aaron concluded. "Too much wasted time and effort."

"And trust me when I say, I'm through running. I'm here for good. If the interview I had in Fort Wayne last week doesn't pan out, I'll just keep looking."

"It's good to have you back, Phillip. Really

good." Aaron's slow-spreading smile curved without reservation and worked on Phillip's soul like a tonic — especially since he knew he had messed up big time with Mila. "Sounds to me as if there's just one thing left to do."

"Which is?"

Aaron laughed deep and free, in a way Phillip hadn't heard near often enough during his return. Aaron shook his head, banging against Phillip's shoulder in passing as he prepared to take his leave. "Get things straight with Mila. You're gone on that girl, Phillip, and I can just about guarantee the feeling is more than mutual. Don't wait, and don't second guess."

"Maybe you're right."

Aaron snickered. *"Maybe?"*

Phillip stared blankly at the floor while thoughts tossed, while nerves came alive, skittering in time to an uneven pulse. He reached into his slacks pocket for his cell phone and punched through recent calls until he found the number he needed. "I'll see her, but there's something I need to do first."

11

Mila's sleepless night led to a morning punctuated by grouchiness and a near-constant urge to surrender to stinging eyes and a sadness that saturated clear to the bones. The morning after Phillip's revelation of a surprise interview with his previous employer, Millenbech, she entered the sunny environment of Sundae Afternoon, looking forward to burying herself in work.

Phillip was leaving. The jerk.

That five-word refrain appeased her anger — slightly — but did nothing to eliminate the pain.

How could he turn his back? How could he walk away? Again? How could he have not told her what was going on? Talk about the pain of a knife jab. They had found their way into a relationship as unexpected as it was beautiful. How could he simply take a drive, have an interview, and then decide to walk away?

Tears built, infuriating Mila to no end. Fierce and determined, she blinked them away. OK. He was leaving. Fine. Let him. Obviously, he hadn't learned a thing about the power of the heart versus a quest for 'more.'

Good riddance.

Her chin quaked all over again, because she was only kidding herself. The leaving of Phillip Fisher was definitely not 'good riddance.'

For the first two hours of her day she scrubbed tables until they shone beneath blocks of cheery sunlight that flowed through the windows. Wretched bands of happy gold. She arranged table vases with fresh flowers, fussing them to perfection when all she wanted to do was wilt, and sulk.

Determined to beat her funk, Mila baked a batch of yellow cupcakes topped by delicate swirls of white crème frosting flavored by vanilla and cinnamon. She piped each creation by hand, then sprinkled the tops with additional cinnamon for both color and flavor. That cheered her a bit. The sweet treats were headed to the sixteenth birthday party celebration of Laura Lake. Laura's mom would be stopping by around lunch time to pick them up.

Starting to hum, sinking into the rhythm of her task, Mila dusted her fingertips against the flower-specked front of her dark blue apron. Rolling her neck, she sighed as pressure eased . . .

And when a pair of strong, wide hands began to gently knead taut shoulder muscles, she jumped . . . then melted.

Phillip.

She could nearly taste him in the air.

"Hey, Mila."

"Hey, traitor." She kept her voice light and teasing, but there were shades of truth in humor.

"Traitor?"

"Just kidding. How'd the family take your news flash? Everything OK?"

"Well, things sure did happen quicker than I thought they would."

Meaning Millenbech. Meaning Indy. Meaning Phillip Fisher, gone. Mila stiffened, pasted an accepting, friendly expression into place. All she could do now was wish him well, and swipe some form of anesthetic lotion against the broken pieces of her heart and piece it back together again.

She surrendered Phillip's magical shoulder rub and turned to face him fully. Mila swallowed a sigh of feminine pleasure. He looked so relaxed and confident — so compelling and self-assured. Dressed casual, in blue jeans, a plaid shirt splayed open over a crisp white tee. She wanted to rest her head on that broad, perfectly muscled chest, sink into his warmth, and live there forever. But fate was a cruel mistress. She maintained eye contact by dent of stubborn will. He wouldn't see her crack. Period. "Congratulations on the new job."

His smile went wide — in a Cheshire-cat-I've-swallowed-the-canary kind of way. "Thanks. Fort Wayne isn't in our backyard, but it's close enough, and the job is amaz—"

"Fort Wayne?" That didn't compute. Mila shook her head. Hard. "You were in Indy. What about Indy?"

Phillip shook his head. "Indy is a dead point. Gone. Off the map. Closed. I belong in Antioch. I belong with my family. I belong with you." He went silent, looking deep into her eyes, as if letting the statement sink in. "I received an offer from Millenbech, but when that happened, once the dust settled yesterday evening, I e-mailed Jason Longbourne at Maddox Ag Industries. Turns out the firm was ready with an offer of their own. An offer he e-mailed me this morning. An offer I've signed and accepted."

Oh, heaven help her, her knees were about

to give way. Joy, love, hope, and relief performed an almighty flood through her body. "You're . . . staying . . . ? You're sure . . . you're . . . you're staying . . . ?" The babbling response was about all she could manage.

Phillip nodded. "Um-hum. But, in all good conscience, I couldn't do so until I made a promise to your dad."

"A promise? To my dad?" For the life of her, Mila struggled to track the pattern of this conversation. She couldn't quite wrap herself around the emotions and reality of what played out between them. Roots curved eager and strong, slipping into place through her spirit, pushing to life.

"You remember, don't you? From one of our first dates? I had met with your dad, and I told you the ways he was looking out for you, like any good father tends to do. When we met, he asked me about my intentions toward you."

She gulped. "I remember."

"I promised him that when something of importance happened between the two of us, he'd be the second one to know about it."

"Second? Because?"

"Because you'd be the first. Thing is? I was wrong."

"I can't even follow this conversation, Phillip. My mind and my heart are spinning all over the place, and I can't even —"

"As it turns out," he interjected smoothly, stepping forward to claim her hands — and help her remain grounded, steady. "He was the first to know."

"To know what?"

Phillip lifted her hands, kissed the tips of her fingers.

Mila tingled, yearned.

"Last night, I told him my intentions toward you end in one place. Marriage. I've asked him for your hand, and the funny thing is, he didn't seem the least bit surprised."

Mila clutched his hands like a drowning woman searching for purchase in overwhelming seas.

Phillip continued. "He knew our feelings are strong, and he gave me his blessing."

All over again Mila wanted to fold against him and collapse, but she remained steady and even, wanting to savor every second of being the recipient of a God-touched blessing.

"Mila, I don't have a ring for you yet; I want to start my job with Maddox Ag and see my family through the rest of the harvest season first, but I want to know exactly where I stand — if you'll have me." He paused, took a deep, meaningful breath of air. "Mila, will you marry me?"

Undone, Mila covered her lips with a hand that trembled. His question, tenderly spoken, crashed into the dam wall she had constructed with swift surety around the perimeter of her heart. Granite crumbled to dust, releasing itself in a flow of tears that began — and ended — on a melody of joy. Pure, unmitigated joy. "Phillip, do you mean this? Are you sure? Are you —"

She got no farther than that in her quest for reason and understanding. Phillip tugged her close and held her tight, safe and secure, just seconds before his head dipped and he feasted on her mouth. Her tears salted their lips, but she laughed — oh, how she laughed — with happiness unbridled, released from her depths as he lifted her and spun in a fast, dizzying circle.

"Mila, I've never been more sure of anything in my life. I love you."

"Then all I can say is yes. Yes, yes, yes!"

And so, he spun her once more, her squeal of delight blending with the rich cascade of his laughter. Chains stretched, burst free.

Once on her feet, she wove her fingers through his hair, drew him down for a long, hard kiss.

"Mila . . ." He gasped and murmured between breaks for air. "You taste like cinnamon."

Kisses poured like rain. "Yeah. So?"

He laughed against her lips, the vibration carrying through to her tummy, to the tips of her toes.

"I love it, but . . ."

"But?" She reared back in his arms, sassing him with a narrow-eyed stare.

"But do you want to know what I really, really want right now?"

"Yeah, I do."

"I want one of your world famous hot fudge sundaes. Think you can hook me up?"

At longest, sweetest last, she laid her head on his chest, snuggled against him in perfect alignment. "I think that can be arranged, Phillip. I think that can be arranged."

THE STRONGHOLD

In loving memory of Ruth Evans
My time with you was cut far too short,
but remains so precious. As an RN, you
healed bodies and spirits. As a mother,
you raised an incredible family.
Your legacy lives on!

1

'My son,' the Father said, 'you are always with me, and everything I have is yours.'
~ Luke 15:31

Aaron Fisher twisted the knob on the radio, cranking the volume on the oldies station. His lips curved as the Byrd's version of *Turn, Turn, Turn* played. The poignant melody filled the air with nostalgia as the words of Ecclesiastes rang out through flawless harmonies . . .

A time to every purpose under heaven . . .

Aaron and his older brother, Phillip, had always joked that the classic song resonated across generations because the lyrics came straight from The Great Author, God Himself, through the biblical verses.

A flood of gratitude covered his spirit. Tides had turned between him and Phillip. Resentment, anger, bitterness had been torn away in recent months, exposing a new-found closeness and affection. Before his sibling's return to their hometown of Antioch, Indiana, Aaron would never have dreamed of resuming strong bonds with Phillip. Aaron had stored too much pain after Phillip's leaving to believe in new beginnings; that emotion had barreled straight to the surface of his soul, and their relationship, when Phillip came back and replanted roots in their hometown.

Antioch was rural, a farm community governed by a slow pace, deep faith, and the kind of small town atmosphere folks craved without even realizing it — until they spent time within its borders, falling into its slow pace and vibrations of peace. Phillip had learned that lesson the hard way, and Aaron had learned to forgive and move forward with his brother all over again.

Praise God.

Aaron smiled once more at the lyrics, then focused on the road.

Members of the Antioch High School marching band high-stepped across the practice field. Aaron rolled down the driver's side window of his vehicle, ignoring the chill of air spiced by wood smoke transforming to the very essence of autumn. Preps for Friday night football were in full swing.

Tonight, the Antioch Tigers would be taking on their arch rivals from Arcola. He tapped his fingertips in time to the school anthem then lifted his hand in greeting to Scott Pepperfield, who drove past in the opposite direction. He needed to stop by Pepperfield Farm Supply and pick up a gear case replacement kit for Ben. Now that harvest season neared its end, youngest sibling Ben would have time to work his mechanical magic on the family's aged but still serviceable tractor.

First things first, though. Aaron checked the clock on the dash of his truck and accelerated slightly. He had about ten minutes to spare. Right now, he had to attend Dad's appointment at Briar Medical Center. His parents wanted him to be another set of eyes and ears as Dr. Skogee diagnosed issues Dad had following a heart attack six months earlier. The cause seemed to be related to his medications, and had reached a point that required attention. Flicking on the turn signal, Aaron executed a left onto Second Street, passing through the outskirts of Antioch's three-block town center.

The medical facility stood just ahead. Aaron shifted restlessly as he neared the end of his drive and Dad's health issues claimed priority focus.

■ ■ ■ ■

Emma Briggs strode down the corridor of Briar Medical Center and stopped at Exam Room C. The door was slightly ajar. Emma retrieved the folder tucked into a storage bin tacked to the wall outside and consulted the top page. Patient name: Jonathan Fisher. From within she heard quiet voices, intent and tender. As she focused on the words, she paused.

"The blasted light-headedness comes at me out of nowhere, Anna-love. I don't mean to scare you." Vulnerability was paired with rich affection.

"I know, and I'm not trying to be a reactionary by hauling you here time and again so you can get checked. The thing is" — the reply of a woman — "I want more seasons with you, Jonathan Fisher. Understand? *Many* more seasons."

A gentle laugh followed. "Understood, and that path curves both ways. We're not that old yet. We both have a lot of livin' to do." A sigh followed. "Good Lord knows how I hate feeling this way."

"He does. And, I do, too. But for now, let that all go. Let's just focus on getting you better."

Shaking free, assuming her professional demeanor as an RN, Emma rapped on the door and pushed it open. "Good morning."

Dual smiles came from a late-fiftyish couple. They struck her as genial and warm, but anxiety coated the air.

"I'm Emma Briggs, Dr. Skogee's new RN, so we haven't met yet. How are you today, Mr. Fisher?"

"Well, it's nice to meet you, Emma Briggs. Tell you what — we'll let you and Doc be the judge of how I am today." The feisty, charming man possessed sparkling eyes and a killer grin.

"I'm his wife, Anna." Anna squeezed her husband's hand in a gesture that appeared instinctive. "Welcome to Antioch. We heard Ruth Carrol retired a few weeks back."

"She did. Off to warmer climates in Phoenix and a son who's eager to have her back in the family fold."

A few more pleasantries were exchanged, a brief bout of familiarity meant to break the ice rather than place instant focus on health-related uncertainties.

Emma settled on a stool and rested Jonathan's chart on her lap as she rolled forward. "So, talk to me about the symptoms you're having. How's the angina?"

"Am I late? I was told I could come in." A

man came through the door who promptly filled the smallish exam space — both physically and figuratively. He was well over six-feet, intense and vital, carved from a foundation of strength and a rugged, naturally honed masculinity. Dark brown hair crested above his brow, curled against the collar of his button-down. Jeans sculpted long, lean legs and a muscular build.

His image stole Emma's focus, and the capacity for sound reasoning.

He extended his hand. "Hello. I'm Aaron Fisher. I'm Jonathan Fisher's son. You must be the new nurse Doc's been telling us about."

"Emma Briggs, yes, and it's nice to meet you." The gentle slide of a rough, calloused palm against hers electrified her senses. That edgy, compelling gaze drew an admiring silence that stretched.

He released their handshake and turned toward his father. "How're you doing, Dad?"

"I suppose we'll be finding that out soon enough."

Emma regained propriety enough to cover awkwardness. "We're about to start the pre-screening of you father. Doctor will see you shortly and he'll ask a few more questions, I'm sure. After that, we'll consider the best ways to move forward."

"Fair enough, and thank you for that, ma'am." Aaron's smile was wide.

Manners and gentility still mattered in this town. Discovering that softened the harder spots of her soul that had built, scabbed, and nearly overwhelmed during the past year.

"You asked about the angina." Jonathan's statement prompted Emma back to the present, and away from a perfectly hewn man who embodied an aura of protectiveness and strength . . .

"Yes, I did."

"Ma'am, I'll be honest with you. The pain isn't nearly as concerning to me as the light-headedness. The occasional bouts of dizziness and the way my chest goes all tight when I try to do the simplest things — things I could do before without a second thought or any kind of problem."

Emma reviewed his chart, but took note of the way Aaron's posture went taut, his eyes narrow with concern. Loving care. Nice, she thought. "I see you're on a regimen of ACE inhibitors. That can contribute to the symptoms you describe."

Jonathan cleared his throat, studied the floor. "Then, there's the cough."

"Cough?"

"Yeah."

When words stalled, his wife took over. "We go to bed. A short time after we settle in for the night, he starts to cough."

Emma nodded. Common. Most likely the result of the blood pressure medication he had been prescribed.

Jonathan shifted on the exam table.

His action pulled her back to the moment at hand.

"All I know is, I want to get to the other side of this thing."

Emma's focus was Jonathan, but her gaze strayed to Aaron. His lips, full and tempting, quirked into a lush curve, distracting Emma all over again. She straightened, embracing the streak of nursing determination that lifted to the surface. "We'll do our best to get you to that goal."

"My farm's in decent shape following the harvest," Jonathan continued. "My family's coming back together like it should. Life is good. I want to be around to enjoy it."

Emma gave his arm a squeeze. "Then let's see to it, Mr. Fisher. The doctor will be right with you."

"Nurse Briggs, thank you. You've been wonderful."

"It's Emma, please." She smiled at all of them. "And we're here to help you manage the meds and how best to cope with the health issues you're facing."

"Emma?" Anna's quiet summons regained Emma's full attention.

"Yes?"

"I promise we'll take what you and the doctor say to heart. Jonathan means the world to me. The world, and then some."

Emma blinked, a little shaken by their obvious love for each other. Thank God for Antioch, Indiana, and the affirmation that good, strong people still existed in this mixed-up world. Was Aaron the same? She wondered, her intrigue toward him continuing to build. Protected by the armor of professionalism, Emma didn't dare explore the sudden and unexpected swirl of emotions that centered on Aaron Fisher. Time to walk away from an emotional time bomb.

2

A strange, unexpected push of yearning worked through Aaron. Emma Briggs, RN, was gorgeous with that wavy tumble of blonde hair, those warm, chocolate eyes, and that petite, temptingly curved figure. He wanted to wrap her in his arms and protect her. Sure, part of that reaction came from curiosity. She was new in town. An unknown, intriguing entity. Aaron's verdict hit fast and hard. She was real sweet, with a caring attitude that came across as genuine. She wasn't polite or cordial out of expectation, but out of authenticity. If she had been around these parts for long, he would have known about it . . . and maybe even pursued —

"Jonathan, Anna, how's my Fisher team?"

Dr. Skogee stepped into the exam room, placing an end to Aaron's conjectures. After greetings, Doc sat on the roller chair and moved closer to the exam table, consulting the paper file while performing a more detailed inquisition regarding medication levels and analysis. Testing options were discussed as well.

Aaron keyed in on the conversation as it turned to reoccurring dizziness, and Dad's episodes of lightheadedness.

"The blood pressure medication you're on might need adjustment." Dr. Skogee stood and pulled out a stethoscope. "Let's take a listen. Lay back on the table and let's do a cursory check."

Dad wheezed a bit, but seemed to do OK.

A tech entered the exam room and wheeled an EKG machine.

Soon, Dad was strapped and monitored. A few minutes later, Dad lifted to a sitting position. In an instant, the blood drained from his face. His eyes glazed and he sank, trying to brace against the table. "Not good." He fell back to the table, barely conscious.

Dr. Skogee nudged Aaron and Anna to the side, stationing himself next to Dad. "Aaron, go get Emma."

Aaron's grip on his cell phone tightened as he brought Phillip up to speed on Dad's medical episode. "I thought he was getting better!" Phillip's panicked tone cut through their cell phone connection.

"He is, Phillip, that's part of the problem. Well, sort of."

"Fill me in."

Aaron continued his account of the way Emma and Dr. Skogee had calmed the situation. "According to the most recent round of tests and blood monitoring, it seems like his overall health is improving, but the medication levels need to be reduced."

"OK, that sounds fair and simple enough. Why did he end up in a crisis? I don't understand."

"It was his blood pressure medication. High BP isn't as much of an issue these days, but his medication is still working to reduce his numbers. They've almost gotten too low. That's why, when he moves too quickly, especially from a seated or prone position, he gets dizzy." Aaron used Emma's descriptives, envisioning her even as he conversed with his older brother. "So, it's good news. But . . ."

"I hate 'but.' "

"Dad's heart valves have gone narrow. Lack of space is making it tough for oxygen and blood to flow the way they should through his body. Doc wants to figure out the best way to solve that problem."

Emma pushed through the door to the

waiting area where Aaron slouched in a chair. She took a seat, holding a thick manila folder. Probably Dad's medical history.

"Phillip, I gotta go. The nurse just walked in."

"Call me on your way back to the farm."

"Yep." Aaron disengaged the call. "Hey, Emma."

"Hey." She paused. "Your dad is doing just fine right now. Dr. Skogee wants to review what comes next."

"Which is?"

"We'll adjust his medication levels, as we discussed. That should give him an immediate boost, but we recommend further testing."

"More tests?" Aaron straightened, his alarm on the rise all over again.

"I'm afraid so. We're referring your dad to a cardiologist in Fort Wayne."

"He needs a specialist."

"Yes. One who can determine if the insertion of coronary stents is indicated."

"Stents mean surgery." Aaron leaned forward, raking back a tumble of hair. "He's already been through so much."

"I understand that, Aaron, but this is for the best. Further diagnosis might help him get back to the life he's longing for."

"True."

A telling silence ensued.

Aaron stopped at Pepperfield's, picked up the gear case kit for the tractor and drove to the farm, eager to bring Phillip and Ben up to date. A flurry of text exchanges indicated they were waiting for his arrival. Phillip's fiancée, Mila Thomas, was at the farm as well, helping with lunch preparations. Gathered family and a nourishing meal would give Mom and Dad less to worry about when they returned home after getting new prescriptions from the pharmacy.

Lulled by the rise and fall of barren land, by the familiar dips and turns of Rural Route Three, his mind drifted. Slowly, perfectly, the image of Emma coalesced. He absorbed the impact of big brown eyes, that wide smile framed by soft, full lips.

What was her story? Certainly, that intrigued him. But there was something more to his reaction. Something about her pulled at him — that misty layer of vulnerability, perhaps? She had revealed such warmth during the session with Dad, then she seemed to retreat behind a demeanor of well-cultivated professionalism. Something about her put Aaron in mind of a wounded, trapped farm animal, fearful of a stranger's approach, but filled with longing and hope, as evidenced by the way she'd reacted to Mom's praise and encouragement.

He hopped from the truck. Turning up the collar of his corduroy coat, Aaron dashed up the porch steps, shivering as those first chilling winds of autumn-headed-into-winter gusted across the open fields and clear through to his bones. He glanced up at gray-cast skies and pushed the door open, wrapped by instant warmth after he banged it closed and stuffed his coat on a nearby peg. "Phillip? Ben?" He strode to the kitchen.

"Sorry, just me." Mila turned from sandwich making and gave him a welcoming grin. "Ben and Phillip are in the barn."

Aaron joined her at the kitchen counter.

She stacked multi-grain bread with fresh sliced turkey, lettuce and tomato. "Today's other selections are tuna and chicken." She wiped her hands on a towel and gestured toward the fridge. "Got veggies and low-fat dip stashed in there, too."

"Nice." Aaron pecked her cheek, appreciating her thoughtfulness. Most of this spread, he was sure, came courtesy of the Thomas's grocery store. "If things don't work out with Phillip, give me a chance, OK?"

She laughed and gave him a shove in the stomach. "You're trouble."

"I've heard tell."

"How's your dad holding up?"

"We'll know more once they get here and give us the full report. Scared the life out of me watching him fall down."

Mila shot him a sympathetic look then resumed lunch detail, slicing triangle cuts through the sandwiches she had already assembled. "He's tough, Aaron."

"Yeah. Still, even the toughest people wear out. That's what scares me."

Ben banged through the side door, entering the kitchen with a fast step and an unwelcome blast of chilly air, ending a bout of melancholy.

Phillip followed close behind and homed in on Mila like a magnet seeking north, tucking against her from behind and stirring a squeal when his cold cheek pressed against hers.

"Hey, Aaron," Ben called, "I saw the gear case in the back of your truck. Thanks for that."

"No problem." He smirked, eager to needle his baby brother with a bit of intel from downtown Antioch. "By the way, Lindsey Pepperfield asked me to tell you hey."

"Mm-hmm."

Ben gave away nothing at all. Typical. The guy could be holding a royal flush during a high-end poker game and the world would never know it. So, naturally, Aaron pushed. "She likes you."

Ben slid off his black leather work boots — it was a universally acknowledged truth that Mom would kill her sons otherwise. "Le'me put these in the mudroom before I'm exiled from the family."

Mila arched a brow with censure. Only when Ben was out of earshot did she pronounce: "You're a clod."

"I am? Why's that? An interested woman would have to take out a billboard on I-69 to ever get Ben's attention. Why not help him along?"

"Because —" Mila fumed. "— Because Ben should find his way to the person whom he's meant to be with without interference."

Aaron swiped a pickle spear. "Interference like what?"

"You're meddling."

"No, I'm prompting things along. Your baby sister has always been interested in him, hence those porcupine quills of yours that are currently digging into my skin. You might tell Hailey Beth to get a move on before it's too late."

"Getting a move on is up to Ben," Philip said. "HB won't make the first move. Nor should she."

"Fair enough. I'll quit."

Mom and Dad arrived and everyone gathered for saying grace and digging into lunch.

"As Aaron probably told you all, we need to consult with the cardiologist in Fort Wayne." Mom's opening words cast a pall. "It seems surgery is indicated. They think placing a stent will increase the flow of blood and oxygen to Dad's heart."

"It's called something like cardiac catheterization or angioplasty." Dad piped up. "The best part is, after I heal, Doc says I'll be feeling a whole lot better, and that the surgery will help me avoid a full-on bypass."

Aaron exchanged glances with his brothers, wondering.

3

Emma found herself pondering Aaron Fisher that evening on her way home. Aaron, the son she already pictured as the family's stronghold. During a point of crisis, he had remained steadfast, calm in the storm. He had tracked her down, directed her to the exam room, then stayed silent, but narrow-eyed and protective, jaw clenched, not missing a thing that took place while she and Dr. Skogee stabilized Jonathan Fisher. Only then did his taut, broad shoulders relax. Only then did he leave the room while a deeper diagnosis took place. The idea of Aaron's strength and attractiveness filled an empty void in her spirit.

Emma considered crisis containment to be a necessary component of her job. But then had come the tribulation of last year. Happy, confident, and fulfilled by her practice at a hospital ER in suburban

Detroit, Emma had tumbled hard and unwittingly into a professional nightmare while attempting to assist with an emergency Cesarean birth. Even now, horrific images flashed through her mind — memories she tried hard to keep buried.

With smooth practice, she turned her back on the past as she unlocked the front door of her apartment. Home was a brownstone just one block east of Main Street. She loved the central location because there was a daily sense of gathering, of lively purpose, and community. Even now, at close to six o'clock, folks hustled past, drawing up coat collars, their conversations a pleasant buzz. Emma hung her coat in the nearby closet, toeing off her sneakers. She rolled her shoulders, issuing a blissful sigh as muscles eased and relaxed. After setting her computer satchel on the floor beneath a small oak table, she tossed her keys into a dark blue bowl. The hand-crafted piece, created from clay, was a gift from her mom and dad. The day's allotment of junk mail followed. After that, Emma ignored the world at large and padded to the kitchen on a quest for dinner.

A yen for Mexican cuisine prompted her to root through the fridge and pantry to create chicken quesadillas. While she chopped, shredded, mixed, and simmered, her thoughts trailed to Aaron Fisher, pushing warmth through her body. There was something mysterious and intriguing about the Fisher son. Edgy, yet soft, his contradictions pulled at her. Emma tore roughly into a package of fajita seasoning, and then some tortillas.

What would a man like Aaron — a close family like the Fishers' — think of her if they knew her history? Bad decisions, escalating moments of emotional weakness had toppled into one another, ending one phase of her career and thrusting her life to a point of ruin. Once upon a time, she had followed her heart and had paid dearly for the mistake. Maintaining distance from those who suffered was the toughest part of nursing; compassion, a trait so intrinsic to her personality, had burned her badly and left her scurrying into a new life in Antioch.

"But Aaron's not the patient." Emma muttered as she lent a few aggressive sauté moves to her chicken. "He's a family member. It's not as though I'd be getting tangled up in my emotions for a patient then watching their lives unravel before my very eyes, watching them die while I'm powerless to — Ugh!" Her hunt for sour cream yielded nothing.

Thomas's Grocery was just across the street. Dinner would keep for five minutes. She stuffed food into the pre-warmed oven and grabbed her purse.

Stomach rumbling, she headed for the dairy aisle and then went to the express check out aisle.

Aaron waited in line with carried a six pack of root beer and a package wrapped in white deli-paper.

"Hey there." She got in line. He was tall, powerfully built. Very attractive . . .

Aaron turned and a welcoming smile crossed his features. "Wonder Nurse. How are you doing, Emma?"

She burst out laughing. "I'm hardly a wonder nurse, but thanks for the ego boost."

"After what you did for my dad today, you're Wonder Nurse. End of story." He glanced at her food and arched a brow.

"I made quesadillas. Totally blanked on the most important component. I'm a sour cream snob."

"As you should be, and as if I didn't like you enough already, that totally clinches the deal."

A blush warmed her cheeks; a tingle of awareness skirted her arms, skimmed to her neck. "And what have you got going on?"

"I was asked to pick up pork chops. My

contribution to dinner with my brothers tonight."

"Nice."

"Dinner and Thursday night football seemed a good antidote to today's excitement."

"Good for you. They live close by, then? Your brothers?"

"Ben's at the farm with my folks. Phillip lives in town. Right above the sweets shop, *Sundae Afternoon.* That's where we're meeting up."

"Oh, my goodness — I'm addicted to their strawberry shakes. They're the first thing I discovered when I landed in Antioch."

"Emma Briggs, Wonder Nurse, your stock keeps soaring. Mila Thomas, the owner, is Phillip's fiancée, and I feel the same way about her chocolate shakes. Indoctrinated from the time I was, what, maybe four or five years old. Back then, the shop was run by her mother."

Aaron lingered after paying, waiting while Emma checked out. They fell into step after exiting the store.

Aaron continued their conversation. "So, Dad heads to Fort Wayne on Monday morning for an initial consult. The specialist was able to fit him in pretty quick."

"That's good. When it comes to specialists, that's not always the case."

"I just hope everything works in our favor. If Dad has to endure this, I hope the surgery will give him more good years."

"That's my wish as well. He strikes me as a special man."

"He is." A touching degree of conviction and humility colored the way he spoke. Then there was the shy, charming way he smiled at the compliment and dipped his head in deflection. When he sidled a glance in her direction, Emma's breath caught. That whipcord of intensity, that heat and longing she'd sensed poured from him in a wave that quickly enveloped. "I hope you don't mind me admitting I wish you were the one helping to manage it all. You and Dr. Skogee, I mean. Having you — and Doc — at the consult would be assuring. It's tough to make sense of medical jargon, and putting Dad's life in the hands of someone we don't even know, in a situation we don't understand, is scary. You're new to us as well, from a professional standpoint, but you stepped up big time helping Mom and Dad through that episode."

Trust. Faith. Confidence. Hope. Emma craved each of those precious intangibles almost as much as she craved the touch of his gaze once more, and that connection of spirit that both startled and intrigued her.

Silence stretched.

Aaron cleared his throat. "Hey, I'm sorry. I didn't mean to put you on the spot. Just an idea I had. I didn't mean to make you uncomfortable. It's just" — he stopped talking, stopped walking, and looked deep into her eyes — "you were incredible today. You were caring toward my parents. You were great, and you're appreciated."

"Thank you, Aaron, and you didn't make me uncomfortable. I'm honored to be able to help. That's what nursing is all about." For better or worse, she added in silence. She shifted her bag while fighting taut nerves and the onslaught of bitter memories — painful emotions.

"Well. Have a good night, now, and enjoy your dinner."

"You, too." He walked down the street.

She hated to see him leave. A battle ensued so powerful she had to fight to keep still. "Hey, Aaron?"

He turned.

"I . . . ah . . . have Mondays off." She covered the short distance between them, but her legs trembled with every step. "If your parents want me to be a second set of eyes and ears, I'd be glad to join you."

He gripped the handles of his grocery

sack. "You'd be a whole lot more than another set of ears, Emma. You're a professional. Are you sure you wouldn't mind? I want to clear it with the folks first, and I don't want to take you away on your day off."

"If they want me there, it would be no problem, Aaron. That's why I offered." She reached into her purse and jotted her phone number on a scrap paper, handing it to him. "Let me know what you need, OK?"

"Fair enough. Le'me have your phone." He input his contact information then his gaze tagged hers, and his lips curved. "See you later, Wonder Nurse."

Wonder Nurse. Emma brushed aside the familiar build-up of nasty memories. Instead, she pocketed her phone. "You really need to come up with a new title for me, Aaron."

"If you insist, Dynamo."

She'd never win this battle. Emma turned away, loving the way their shared laughter mixed on the rapidly chilling air. They headed in separate directions, but Emma's heart took flight in ways she had never dreamed possible again.

4

Emma gathered with the Fisher family around a conference table at Parkview Hospital. Aaron had assured her on the phone last night that, not only was she welcome at the appointment, his parents had expressed appreciation for her expertise.

Dr. Rhodan launched into a detailed explanation of the procedure to come, then concluded. "Jonathan, you should be completely recovered in just over a week. I have every expectation that we'll achieve the results we're after and hopefully avoid the need for bypass surgery."

"Then that gives us plenty of hope to hold on to. Thank you, Dr. Rhodan." Anna's expression assumed a calm, accepting demeanor.

Anna's depth of faith struck chords in Emma's spirit. She wanted to know this woman better, to somehow absorb her surety and confidence. If only she could blot out the past and the song of defeat that troubled her soul because of a death for which she felt responsible. Especially when she considered the tangled web that led to the end of an innocent, unsuspecting life. Emma pushed the clamor away. Sadness, however, lingered, a dangerous ghost that accompanied her on the return drive to Antioch with Aaron.

"Are you hungry? Would you like to have lunch?" His offer cut the silence.

Emma closed her mind from further introspection. The mention of food triggered a subtle tummy growl and welcome distraction. "Sure, that'd be great."

Within Antioch's city limits, they landed at a table toward the rear of Steward's Café.

Aaron highly recommended their tuna melt sandwiches and crème of broccoli soup. He placed their orders and they sipped in unison from freshly delivered glasses of soda.

"Way to go, Super Nurse."

Emma's laughter busted free — a delicious, unexpected, most welcome sensation. "What on earth do you mean?"

"Dr. Rhodan was impressed by the questions you asked about Dad. The way you presented his case so he could answer our concerns was amazing to watch."

Emma shrugged off the compliment. Still, she was human. A flow of appreciative, savoring energy couldn't be helped. "I didn't do much. The more Dr. Rhodan knew, the better equipped he'd be to enlighten everyone involved."

Aaron took hold of her hands, squeezed. "Yeah — right up to the point where the two of you exchanged business cards and entered into that brief but layman-staggering discussion about whatever it was you were speaking of —"

"Oh, please!" Emma laughed again, delighted by the idea of being seen as competent again. Respected. A tentative ripple of confidence came alive in her soul.

"Beyond all that, here's what else I know about Emma Briggs, registered nurse." He set his glass aside and leaned forward, focusing on her with a warm intensity that made her nerve endings dance. "You're compassionate. You're giving. You're new in town, and you like Mexican food. What else are you willing to share? How in the world did you end up in Antioch?"

His interest caused protective walls to quake.

"I enjoy classic TV reruns. Does that help you any?"

"I'll take it. What's your favorite?"

She named a once popular medical series. "The writing, the acting, it's superlative."

Aaron tapped his plastic tumbler against hers. "Here's to good writing of medical characters."

"There was an incredible nurse in the series, too."

"Hmm. Sounds kind of like this other incredible nurse I'm getting to know."

"Charmer. Your turn. Fill me in on the life and times of Aaron Fisher."

"Slick turnaround."

"I'm sneaky like that. Seriously. Tell me about you."

"I'm the middle Fisher son. I'm Antioch born and raised, and I've been a farmer all my life. About all there is to it, really. Enthralled?"

"Completely. So, you're stepping into a legacy created by your family. There's nobility in that. Honor."

"To a degree. It's a necessity as well. An expectation." Aaron shrugged. "I've been counted on to execute the life I was born to. The path God gave me to walk."

Emma studied him. "You certainly don't fit the mold of a stereotypically rebellious middle child."

Aaron hooted a short laugh. "Ask my older brother Phillip about my rebellions.

He'll be glad to let you know I've been far from easy to handle when it comes to my family, and the farm we run."

"Meaning what, exactly?"

"Meaning it's tough to embrace rebellion when your dad falls ill and he's counting on you to maintain the farm that's been a part of our family for generations. Phillip left for the big city after he graduated from college. I had to stay behind to take care of business. We've come around, Phillip and I, but I was ticked off when he left and I was ticked off when he returned. Made sure everyone knew it, too."

Their waitress approached, carrying a tray.

"I had some growing up to do." Aaron's tone was touched by a trace of resentment and a heavier layer of emotion — surrender, perhaps — that caused her to wonder what kind of history, or circumstance, rode beneath his carefully controlled surface.

Emma dug into her food, hungry, but eager to continue their conversation. "I admire your conviction, Aaron. It speaks well of your character."

"Don't put me on a pedestal. Conviction is a hard-won process with quite a learning curve along the way."

They resumed eating for a bit.

Aaron shot her a disarming grin. "OK, it's

your turn at bat. Where did you live before you showed up here in Antioch? What led you here?"

Safer ground. Emma sipped her soda then answered. "My family is from Michigan. I lived and worked in the Detroit area."

"Now there's a life-shift worth discussing. What led you from the Motor City to small-town Indiana?"

The question was innocent — nothing more than caring interest. Aaron's motives were pure. The recognition didn't quell a rolling flame of fear, of failure and shame, from igniting in her psyche. "I wanted a change. I wanted small town rather than urbanism. I have some friends here from college who are stationed near Fort Wayne. I've re-connected with them, and Antioch is close enough to home that I'm just a quick drive away. I've found it to be a nice change of pace. I like it here." Her answer was truthful, though thoroughly rehearsed. She'd delivered an identical reply to Dr. Skogee and the staff at Briar when she'd interviewed. All the same, subterfuge took effort. Then, like now, she struggled to spin her life into as positive a light as possible because the underlying truth was ugly . . . and it hurt.

Emma's acting job didn't seem to fool

Aaron. His brows pulled. His lips — those full, tempting lips — dipped into a slight frown, but he remained blessedly silent, and didn't press.

Their waitress approached and Aaron waved her off with a smile. Emma was pleased to discover the food at Steward's was as good as Aaron promised.

"Do you go to church?"

His straightforward, personal question caught Emma by surprise. "That came out of nowhere."

"Seemed we needed to change topics." He shrugged, spooning his soup. "I don't mean to be intrusive by asking. I attend Antioch Christian with the rest of my family."

"I go to church most weekends, but I haven't found a home yet."

Her emotions ran deep for Christ; she longed for a connection to Spirit. Now, she felt unworthy. She looked downward in regret, pain, and shame, cowering beneath a sense of inadequacy. She felt powerless to change . . . so she bluffed, and put on the armor of an easygoing demeanor. Doing so these days came automatically.

Aaron continued, oblivious to her struggle. "I have to usher this weekend, so I'll be in and out of the pew, but I'd love for you to join me. Our paths keep crossing, after all.

It'd be nice to spend some time together outside of the medical world. I think you'll enjoy Antioch Christian."

What did she have to lose? The idea of an hour of peace, of worship, with Aaron lit a warm path through her soul. "Sure. That sounds great."

"We go to nine o'clock services. Afterward, family breakfast is a tradition. You're welcome to join us back at the farm if you don't have plans."

"Are you sure?"

"I'm sure my mom will insist. Regardless, I'd love to have you there."

"Then I accept. Thank you for including me."

"I'm already looking forward to Sunday." He extracted his wallet from a back pocket. "Lunch today is my treat, Dynamo. I really appreciate you being with us."

"I didn't do anything, Aaron. I just listened. As I said earlier, I agree with everything the doctor recommended, and —"

"Emma? Please, stop." His lips curved. He stroked her cheek. "I want you to do me a favor, OK?"

"What's that?"

"Stop selling yourself short. Your presence was assuring — to all of us. You don't need to speak a lot of words around some stuffy, stilted consultation table to make that statement true. You're a comfort, and a blessing." He paused. "Clear?"

Clear. Her pulse performed a fast crescendo, compelled by his unwavering support . . . and belief.

Aaron drove home, thinking about his time with Emma. Some prideful, bitter memories had risen to the surface for a moment or two when it came to Phillip, but thanks be to God he had learned to defeat his anger and recrimination. Everyone had treated Philip's return home as if he were a rock star — a hero — for simply returning to Antioch with his tail between his legs. Meanwhile, Aaron had been the son of loyalty and reliability. No glory, no praise, only the quiet acknowledgement that he had done what he was supposed to do.

He entered his parents' home and strolled the narrow back hallway. The office door to his right was closed. That meant Phillip was around — good. Aaron knocked twice then opened the door, stepping inside.

Phillip sat behind a large wooden desk rubbing his chin while he studied a few pages. He looked up and greeted Aaron with a nod.

"How goes it?"

"Oh, you know, just another day of trying to figure out how to spend all the money we're bringing in."

"Sarcasm?"

"Just a touch."

"Hey, it's a tough gig, but somebody's got to do it."

"Truth. So, what's going on?"

"Just came from town. Had lunch with Emma to thank her for joining us at the appointment today."

Phillip homed in on Aaron, who made sure to reflect nothing but a casual sense of cool. Phillip saw right through him, though. His lips tipped upward; a vibration of knowing moved through the air. "Emma. Lunch. Nice."

Aaron plopped onto the chair next to the desk. "She's sassy. Pretty. Not afraid to speak her mind."

Phillip gave a rumbling laugh. "Sounds like somebody else I know." He gestured toward a nearby credenza where Dad stashed a bottle of brandy next to a set of crystal snifters. "Want one?"

"Ah . . . sure. Any particular reason?"

"Maybe."

"OK, then. Do I need to brace myself?"

"I have a favor to ask." Phillip was being cagey, uncharacteristically reserved. His big brother seemed hesitant and unsettled.

"Lay it on me. What's the favor?"

"Well, I was talking to Mila today." He handed a half-full snifter of dark amber liquid to Aaron.

"Let me guess. She's wised up and called off the wedding?"

A few short months ago, the comment would have led to a blow-up. Now, the words were blanketed in the tone of an affectionate tease.

"No, go figure, she's still willing to take me on." Phillip swirled the brandy. "She's starting to press me for info. Like, you know, how many attendants we need to plan for. That kind of thing. All the detail stuff."

"Mm-hmm."

"I, ah, wondered. Would you be my best man?"

Aaron understood. This was meant to be a toast, a moment to strengthen bonds, to further eradicate past pain and misunderstandings. Without hesitation, Aaron lifted his glass. "I'd be honored." His voice went rough, so he cleared his throat. "Of course, I will."

"Aaron, that means a lot to me." Phillip relaxed, his smile dawning as they chinked glasses and drank to the future. "We've come a long way."

"And there's lots more of the good to come, I'm hoping. Especially once we get Pop's health issues squared away."

"Amen to that." Phillip tipped back a second sip then gave Aaron a knowing smirk. "So. About Emma. Talk to me."

"Hey, one female-related event at a time, bro." Aaron gave him a salute with his snifter. "Honestly, right now I'm just trying to figure things out, but she's something special. I can feel it."

"Hmm. Well. After you *figure things out,* don't be afraid to come to me, OK? I'm here for you. Two ears. No waiting."

"What, you all about brotherly razzing today?"

"Not if brotherly razzing deters you from taking me up on the offer." Phillip propped his forearms against that old, scarred wooden desk. "Seriously. I want to be there for you. That's all I'm saying."

"And, seriously, I appreciate it."

Aaron was comforted by his brother's assurance, But instinct kicked in, warning him that the road ahead wouldn't be easy. Growing familiarity with Emma's personality and character led him to believe that a deep-reaching sadness resided in her soul.

5

Emma was used to the comfort of scrubs and sneakers. She'd dressed casually for church before, but now she stood in front of her closet, staring at her meager wardrobe. She wanted to make a good impression. She wanted to make more of an effort to look good.

Because of Aaron.

Emma ignored the implication. She fussed over her makeup and hair. She fastened silver hoop earrings into place, smoothed the lines of a slim silver chain and floral pendant that rested at her throat. Nerves stretched. She agonized over shoes. The clock ticked mercilessly toward quarter to nine. Emma muttered and mumbled and strove to be appealing.

She didn't take lightly the invitation to attend church services, but was she ready for the idea of a "relationship?" Was she ready to bear small-town scrutiny and curiosity?

Was she ready to be seen as part of a family that was an Antioch institution?

Way to psych yourself out. Emma studied her reflection in a mirror on the back of the bedroom door.

A solid knock echoed. Aaron had arrived.

She dashed toward the entrance, and yanked the door open. Heavens. What a handsome man. Awareness launched like a heated missile while she continued to absorb the sight of a tall, strong-muscled man dressed in a blue suit coat, tie, and crisply pressed, tan dress slacks.

"Morning." His whisky-smoke voice was mellow.

Just — wow. Blinking, Emma pulled the door open a bit wider and stood aside so he could enter. She mumbled what she hoped would pass as an appropriate greeting.

"You look pretty, Emma. Real pretty."

"So do you." OK, that was a breathless, and completely ludicrous, reply. "Look good, I mean." Emma spun away from his steady regard to nab her purse. "I'm ready to go."

After pulling into a parking spot at church, Aaron rounded the rear of his truck and assisted her from the cab, lacing his fingers through hers as they entered. The gesture was gentlemanly, it felt natural. Emma luxuriated in the sensation of being cared for . . . yet the sensation terrified her. She worked much better when her heart wasn't in the way.

Emma took her seat and Aaron followed suit, positioned at the aisle so he could assist during the service. Filing into place with the Fisher clan, Emma took in the gleaming, dark-wood pews, the old, but well-tended statues, vibrant panels of radiant stained glass, the lines of a stark but eloquent wooden cross. There was a sense of familiarity that spread welcome through the atmosphere while folks murmured greetings, shook hands, exchanged hugs. These were people connected by affection, logistics, farm life, and most of all, faith. If only she could achieve that same level of peace in her own life.

Emma battled futility and her past. Her life was far away from this solid foundation. She had experienced way too much to ever be innocent and trusting again.

The opening hymn concluded. A preacher moved forward, turning toward the congregation. He smiled at the assembly.

Aaron leaned close. Emma became so keenly aware of his warmth, of his subtle, woodsy scent, that her world spun to a sensory stop and her body hyper-focused.

"That's Reverend Taylor. The kids all call him Mr. Max," Aaron whispered.

His breath tickled her skin. She turned slightly and when she caught sight of his grin, tension and fear dissolved.

"Max Taylor has been our minister for almost twenty years now."

Aaron's presence overwhelmed and enticed her. What was happening to her sense of logic these days? She was in *church,* for goodness sake. That delicious sense of haziness faded as the pastor spoke.

"Brothers and sisters, Christian witness has become a daunting task these days." Reverend Taylor stuffed his hands in his pockets and paced. "In the light of our present world, where and how do we find Jesus's conquering army? There's so much pain, so much sorrow. Disasters strike. Innocents are hurt with no rhyme or reason. How do we rise above it all on the hope and goodness promised by God's Word? We need to look beyond worldly chaos. Let's find Jesus in the doctors, nurses, first responders — each one of them desperate to save a life."

Reverend Taylor's words filled the sanctuary, sinking into her spirit.

He continued. "Let's find Jesus in the arms of a comforter, a caregiver, mentor or spiritual champion. Let's find Jesus in the help that comes to those who most need it. That's where His hand, His grace, touches lives in the here and now. *We* are Jesus's conquering army. Take on that mission with conviction and a solid, prayer-filled strength of purpose."

A second hymn followed while the collection took place. Aaron left the pew and executed his duties.

Emma was relieved to have a few moments of solitude to compose herself. Life crashed into her via circumstances that kept her from believing in such lofty hopes and expectations. Despite her inner turmoil, the sermon poured through her, full of nobility and honor. She possessed faith, yet a steel shell encased her heart. Secrets and shame scratched against her soul.

From Emma's point of view, realizations like this marked the problem she faced regarding church. At times, the Word hit too close to home. At times, Scripture informed, prodded and convicted in ways that left her to squirm. Moments like this placed a spotlight on every reason why she had fought against finding a regular place of worship. She was well-versed in hiding her deepest feelings.

And failures.

When services concluded, Emma found

herself engulfed within a sea of Fisher family friends.

"I hope you enjoyed church today, Emma." A middle-aged woman smiled at her. "Might you consider becoming a regular?"

"I enjoyed it very much, thank you." Emma opted to ignore the secondary question. "Everyone has been very kind and welcoming."

The lady — Emma temporarily blanked on her name — had met them before services began. She'd questioned Emma with a busy-body's interest. Though church had ended, she seemed in no rush to leave. Emma's shoulders and neck tightened exponentially, but she smiled, and waited.

"We *are* a caring community. I've gone to Dr. Skogee for ages now — since I was a child, really. You just started at Briar a few months ago, right? Taking over for Ruth Carroll?"

"Yes, that's right. She's a legend."

"I'm thrilled for Ruthie. She's been a dear friend of mine since grade school. I miss her, but no one deserves the chance to love on grandbabies more than her. I see Doc next week for some routine blood work. He monitors my underactive thyroid."

"I'm sure I'll see you then, and I look

forward to it, Jayne." The woman's name came just in time for smooth insertion, and hopefully a gentle farewell.

Jayne preened. "I look forward to it as well, my dear. You know, I hope you'll forgive me for this, but you just seem so sweet, and Aaron here is *such* a fine man. I've known him forever, too. Taught him and his brothers in Sunday school."

Aaron laughed. "Be careful of sharing too much of my bad-boy history, Jayne. What happened in Sunday school can just stay in Sunday school, right?"

The woman chortled and blushed — *blushed* — in the wake of Aaron's charming response. "Oh, now Aaron, you three were just fine." She leaned in to whisper, "You're a lucky lady. The Fisher men are just wonderful, and Aaron's not one to move lightly when it comes to female friends."

"Well . . . I . . ." Taken aback by the woman's unapologetic analysis, Emma stumbled.

Aaron stepped into the breach. "It's always good to see you, Jayne. I think your husband is trying to get your attention. He's just over there."

Emma offered a final smile. She didn't want to be an object of speculation or gossip. In the past eight months, she had contended with enough innuendo to last a few dozen lifetimes. The blessing and curse of small town do-overs was that one received a clean slate where townspeople didn't know the past — but sooner or later, one became embedded within the fabric of the community. From there, well-meaning people would push, prod, or in the absence of clear background, insinuate. Like dear, speculative Jayne.

Emma turned toward the entrance and made a swift departure. No big thing, just a response to a mild bout of self-doubt and claustrophobia.

"Hey . . . hey, Emma?" Aaron trotted up beside her.

Goodness — had she been walking *that* fast? *Keep it together, Briggs. Keep it together.* Emma pasted on a carefree expression. Aaron frowned. Nope. He wasn't buying it. Not surprising.

"You OK?"

"Sure." She refused to elaborate.

Aaron stood stock still wearing a skeptical expression. "Forget Jayne's assumptions, OK? When new people arrive, and new circumstances develop, people tend to dig. Harmless, overall. Keeps 'em occupied. New is interesting. New intrigues . . . and inspires."

She loved the subtle emphasis he placed on the last word, loved the way he looked at her soft and long. Enticing. Antioch was the kind of town that epitomized strong community threads, tightly woven. Here, folks watched out for — and readily discussed — their friends and neighbors. Such was a blessing, and a curse. Emma longed to be open, to share herself and her own points of view. But then, right on cue, fears crowded in, squelching that noble impulse. "Jayne's assumptions don't bother me. Being seen at your side is an honor to me. Flattering. I enjoyed services. Please don't think otherwise."

"Thank you for that. I feel just the same." His grin was so beautiful and compelling. "Now, I'm waiting for the rest of the story."

The rest of the story. She blinked, gazed at him. He offered a perfect segue to reveal herself. An opportunity to come clean about her past . . .

Time to deflect. Pronto.

"Tell you what." Emma rested her hand on his arm. If he didn't care about public appearances, then neither did she. She gathered a small slice of bravery. "I'd like to share stories. Not today, though. Today let's just relax and enjoy brunch with your family."

"Is your history that bad?" The quip came blanketed in a layer of humor that covered Aaron's concern and curiosity.

"Bad or good isn't important right now." Emma winked, assuming the non-troubled, airy persona she had perfected over the past year. "Food is what counts. I'm starved. I can almost hear the coffee perking and the bacon sizzling."

"Fair enough, Dynamo." Aaron laughed, opening the passenger door, gracious about moving toward new territory.

But Emma's efforts at evading the past existed on borrowed time.

6

By the time Emma and Aaron arrived at the farm, the entire family had already gathered. There was something comforting about seeing the table set with plates, juice glasses, and coffee cups. The air was wreathed by the aromas of seared bacon and toasted bread and the buttery sizzle of fresh-cooked eggs.

"Dad's the egg pro. Mom handles toast and bacon." Aaron's breath skimmed against Emma's skin, tickled her ear. "Been this way since the time I could walk."

Aaron's deep, fierce affection for his family left her gaze centered on full, curved lips, strong features and that familiar whipcord of intensity he possessed which both intrigued and excited. The dark wood table was already attended by Ben and Phillip, seated in quiet wait, linen napkins extended across their laps. The Fisher men knew the rules of proper dining etiquette. Impressive.

Following Jonathan's benediction, conversational lines ran along minimal threads. Anna and Jonathan kept quiet and enjoyed their boys. Hundreds of Sundays must have passed in just such a way. These moments came alive with tradition, of special times shared by a family wrapped in the world around them, with purpose, solid convictions, and an impressive strength.

Emma wished she knew such moments of her own. Being the only child of a driven, ambitious business man and wife born and raised in suburban Detroit, Emma soaked in this loving atmosphere with a sense of absolute wonder . . . and longing.

"I'm sorry Mila couldn't join us today." Anna took a delicate sip of coffee. "I invited her to come by when I saw her after church, but she said she had to attend a committee meeting to finalize the details of the quarterly social."

Phillip eyed Ben. "Hey, Ben, HB missed you after services. She wanted me to ask if you could help her set up and install some type of lighting scheme for the social next weekend. She says you know the layout of the community center better than anyone, and —"

"Yeah, OK. I'll help her out." Ben didn't look up.

Aaron and Phillip grinned and exchanged mischievous looks.

Endearment toward the family bloomed deeper. An altogether heart-entrenching and dangerous proposition.

Very dangerous, indeed.

The dream came at her in an overpowering storm of memory, regret, and eerie gray haze. Emma's pounding heart punctuated the nightmare. She was rendered a powerless, paralyzed onlooker.

Mom-to-be Gabriella Peterson complained of annoying symptoms. From a clinical perspective, it was an easy case. Death should have never — ever — touched their world.

Nothing had gone wrong until Gabriella — Gabby — settled onto a gurney in a curtained cubicle with her husband Tom holding her hand, watching over her protectively. Gabby reported symptoms of what sounded like an intense bladder infection.

But an electric wire of foreboding, an instinct, sparked hot. Something told Emma that Gabby's bladder infection wasn't the main issue.

The woman's blood pressure had shot up and she was anxious. Gabriella hadn't presented anything previously to her general physician. Anomalies, therefore, became easy to write off. She was thirty-eight weeks pregnant. A rise in blood pressure wasn't unexpected. Elevated proteins could be written off to a simple infection, or some form of internal reaction.

But swelling in Gabby's feet and legs tipped the medical scales in Emma's mind. When matched to the rest of Gabby's symptoms, it led to one very dangerous precipice. Preeclampsia. Emma had brought her disquieting observations to the attention of attending physician, Oliver Brandich, who was ready to send Gabriella home with a script for antibiotics.

Doctor Brandich appeared unconcerned. These were all standard-issue end of pregnancy factors.

Emma was in no position to argue the point. Especially to the man she loved, to whom she was engaged, whose judgment she respected and admired.

Detailed memory faded to chaotic static, to a blur of noise, blips, beeps, alarms. Gabby's condition deteriorated fast and furious. Oliver and a team of ER personnel went to work, spending the next couple of hours scrambling to plug holes in a medical dam while delicate physical walls crumbled and gave way.

And regret rode in with the crashing impact of an onrushing locomotive.

"I should have pushed!" Emma worked next to Oliver, muttering the words, regretting them as soon as they were spoken.

"I don't want — or *need* an *RN* to second guess my diagnosis." Oliver's anger reached out, snapping. "Work with me, or get out of my way. I need to save this patient, and her baby, not justify my actions before a committee of one!"

The talons of Oliver's temper scratched deep grooves against her mind, her heart. How could those belittling words have possibly come from his mouth? This was the man she loved. This was the man with whom she shared her life and soul outside the walls of their workplace.

"OK. Doctor, just tell me what you need. You can do this." Ignoring emotional lacerations, Emma rasped words of support. *Could* he do this? Rebuking doubts, she focused on the heat of a life-and-death battle. He was shaken, oceans away from the standard protocols that lent him steady confidence and his ready sense of command. It was her job to support and respond.

Battling on, Emma jammed her personal feelings into a steel vault. That vault allowed for functionality while she prayed for this nightmare to end.

"Scalpel."

"Scalpel." Emma delivered the instrument with a smooth snap.

A line of sweat darkened the bottom hemline of his scrub cap. Doctor Oliver Brandich never perspired. He never faltered. Cool poise was his hard-earned calling card. Now, cracks appeared in that granite façade ready to give way as he attempted the near impossible — a crash Cesarean section in a curtained-off cubicle of the ER.

The procedure was fast, and saved lives, but it was brutal, and so many missteps had already occurred. They needed every precious minute to accomplish a miracle.

"Commencing a Pfannenstiehl incision . . ."

Heat crawled beneath Emma's loose-fitting scrubs and her skin went moist with perspiration. For as long as she lived, she'd never forget the whirlwind of activity that swept through the cubicle, the bright lights, the astringent aroma, the blood, the tears. She had noticed the signs and failed to act on them because of emotion. Because of entanglements toward Oliver that haunted her still and left behind a gauzy trail of wretched consequences.

The on-call OB/GYN stepped in following a 'stat' call and from there, the horrific episode faded to gray . . . then black. A black shrouded by the consult with the father, with gathered family, that final surrender of a young woman's life. They'd lost Gabby, but were able to save the baby girl.

Rousing from sleep, her heart pumping erratically, Emma came alert. Doused in clammy moisture, she threw back stifling blankets and checked her alarm clock. Two-forty-five in the wretched, blasted Monday morning.

Work. Aaron. Memories. Loss and guilt, layered by a haunting degree of pain that existed on multiple levels.

Surrendering the quest for additional rest, Emma groaned and pushed hair from her eyes. The best remedy for sleeplessness was cleaning. She made her way to the kitchen and opened the cabinet beneath the sink. Spray-on bleach, surface cleaners, and a fresh sponge would do.

Emma, rest. Stop cleaning what's already been restored. Rest.

Tranquility and peace moved toward her in soft, mind-easing swirls. Ignoring the Spirit summons, she went to work scrubbing the bathroom tub, then the toilet and its surrounding tiles. Labor was therapeutic. Lulling. An anesthesia of sorts . . .

When Aaron's face materialized, she blinked free of his allure and redoubled her scouring efforts. Hard work expended the last of her energy and by three-thirty in the morning, Emma was exhausted.

She toppled into bed, spent. Teardrops tracked from her eyes as sleep, at long last, overwhelmed.

7

Despite oxygen tubes running a line across his face and into his nose, despite being latched to a pack of IV saline solution, Jonathan Fisher was still a formidable figure. His strong, large frame was swathed by warming blankets. He bid his family farewell then indulged in a final, lingering kiss with Anna. Seconds later, he was wheeled away to surgery.

Emma turned to his family. The three Fisher sons and the diminutive, but thoroughly charming Hailey Beth Thomas huddled next to Anna and followed her to the waiting room. Once settled, Hailey Beth dropped her purse and tugged out a deck of cards.

HB cast a glance toward Ben, and then summoned the group at large. "Canasta, anyone?"

Immediately, a game launched. The hours were marked by coffee breaks, a snack of muffins and fruit, and quiet conversations centered on speculation regarding Jonathan's surgery and recovery.

"Soon enough it'll be done." Anna took a deep breath. "Soon enough, we'll have some answers, and a battle plan. We'll be on our way to healing, I pray."

Phillip, Aaron, and Ben closed ranks on their mother, clasped hands with Emma and HB, and bowed their heads in a moment of beseeching — but restorative — prayer.

Emma felt honored to join them in storming heaven's gate.

"He'll be fine, Anna," Emma whispered after the family prayer was finished.

"I'm comforted by the fact that you're with us, Emma. Thank you for everything you've done."

"I didn't do —"

Anna shushed Emma's protest with an arched brow. "You sent Dr. Rhodan my questions. Then, you even translated his answers for me as we prepped for the procedure so I'd understand all the medical verbiage. After that, you assured me it'd be OK when Jonathan moves slow for a couple of days after this, that he'll recover, and he'll be OK."

"It's what I do. That's all."

"You even sent me information from the

cardiac rehab team so I'd know what to expect as he recovers and rebuilds his heart muscle."

"Honestly, there's not much to worry about on the diet and exercise front. You feed him well, and healthy."

"I've tried, but as the blockages took over, moving became harder and harder, with shorter spurts of good, sustained physical activity."

"He's under a lot less stress now, with more time to focus on staying healthy, so that's all good news."

Aaron stepped up from behind, resting a hand on Emma's shoulder. "Thank God for that. Phillip's return has really helped the family turn a corner. From business activities being kept under careful watch right down to maintenance work being completed on the house and equipment, life is looking up."

Dr. Rhodan entered the waiting room. His expression was relaxed. "The surgery was a success and I'm very pleased with Jonathan's overall stability."

A wave of relief swept through the small space.

Anna's tears welled as she pressed trembling fingertips to her lips. "What can we expect, doctor?"

"Today's procedure of inserting two stents will provide some immediate benefits. He'll be in recovery for a while and we'll page you when he's ready for visitors. For now, a nurse will monitor him. Eventually a bruise will form, then a small knot, but that's normal, and shouldn't cause you any concern. The incision will also feel tender for about a week or so. Jonathan will be placed on blood thinners for a short time because we want to guard against clots. We'll also conduct some follow-up imaging — x-rays most specifically."

"For?" Aaron leaned forward.

Emma slid her hand over his and held on fast.

"All standard procedure, so no concern. We want to be certain the stents perform as expected. We'll want to check him every six weeks or so, then we'll taper off until it's simply a yearly check. From a physical standpoint, Jonathan should be back to normal activities within a week or so."

Dr. Rhodan paused before addressing Anna. "We want to remain diligent about diet and exercise. He works hard, and his diet is good, but heart issues like this don't often distinguish between those who live healthy and those who don't. I'm hopeful that we've contained the problems and he can move forward."

The entire gathering relaxed; an atmosphere of hope and renewed joy encircled their table. The warmth of this family's love for each other invaded Emma's soul.

"I'm glad to see his recovery is in such good hands. My hope is he'll be around for a lot of years to come."

Aaron's smile spread free and easy. "That's all we want, Dr. Rhodan — thank you for giving us, for giving him, that chance."

8

How had the simple, connective beauty of church socials become a thing of the past? No level of cyber-driven social media could ever replicate the vignette that unfolded as Emma entered the activity center.

High school students, sporting purple latex gloves, delivered food to waiting attendees. They wiped damp cloths across vacated tables, emptied trash with fast efficiency while joshing and cat-calling. Colorfully designed chalk boards touted a dinner menu that included fried chicken, fish, salads, an assortment of veggies and desserts. The fairy-light scheme that Aaron and Phillip had teased Ben about was tacked into subtle swags across the length of the ceiling and added warm, inviting illumination to the room.

Emma found Jonathan and Anna seated comfortably at a nearby table, surrounded by friends and family. She made her way toward them, weaving past an open kitchen area where volunteers manned their stations. Several scout troop members attended the social as well, dressed in full regalia, most likely earning service points while they took in money for food and handed out raffle tickets for an array of items spread out across several tables.

Aaron, meanwhile, browsed the dessert table.

She grinned and moved to his side. "Why am I not surprised to find you stalking the sweets?"

"What?" He answered in wide-eyed innocence, fast-chewing about half of the fresh-baked brownie he'd stuffed into his mouth.

"Busted."

He delivered a grin that melted her at the knees. "Sue me."

"No way. I want to join you."

"Done." Aaron secured a second brownie which Emma laughingly rejected.

"But I just got here! I haven't even eaten yet!"

"No law against eating dessert first."

"Try selling that notion to Mom. She never bought it when we were kids. Hey, Em." Phillip sauntered up, hand-in-hand with a lovely, petite brunette. "Em, have you met Mila Thomas yet? Mila, this is Emma Briggs, extraordinary RN. Emma, this is my equally extraordinary fiancée, Mila Thomas."

The nickname tickled Emma's heart, delivering a heady shot of inclusiveness. Mila's lively brown eyes and kind smile were all it took to kindle an instant wish for friendship.

"Emma, I'm so happy to finally meet you." They shared a tight, solid handshake. "Sorry we didn't have a chance to hang out and chat when you've come to church the past couple weeks. It's been crazy at the soda shop and grocery — and planning this social has been nuts. Aaron's told me so many good things about you."

"Has he, now?" She smiled. "And, no apologies necessary. You've been busy, I know, and you've done great work with this event. Congratulations."

Mila looked around, visibly satisfied. "Well, I sure didn't do it alone, but that's so nice of you. Thanks. Let's get you settled and fed."

They joined Jonathan and Anna amidst a chorus of wide-open welcome.

Aaron left their table to and purchase raffle tickets for the prizes being offered to raise money for the church's classroom remodel. "Got the winners right here," he declared upon his return, waving the slender band of perforated paper.

The display table laden with merchandise was off to one side. Name plates identified each offering along with the name of the person or company who donated. There were homemade goods of all kinds, like sealed pouches of ravioli made by Antonio's Restaurant, apple pies from Carolyn Findlay. There was a colorful four-set of Anna Fisher's knitted pot holders and a quilt from church member Janice Mayberry. An assortment of gift certificates and goodies were provided by local merchants.

All around her, people came together, shared news and laughed. Kids scurried through the crowd sometimes waylaid by family and friends who were eager for a chat or a lightning round of catch up.

This, Emma decided on a breath of contentment, was life at its best.

Nabbing his sister-in-law-to-be, Aaron strolled with her outside where they could catch a breath of fresh air and chat in peace. "So, what was with that whole 'Aaron's had so many nice things to say about you' remark you made to Emma earlier?"

Mila snickered. "Oh. You noticed that?"

Aaron glowered.

"I'm trying to be welcoming. Or maybe I'm just prompting things along. Isn't that the phrase you used a while back when we were talking about the way you've been trying to help Ben and HB make a connection?"

Mila's sweet-as-you-please smile left Aaron equal parts irked and admiring. She was a formidable force. "You didn't used to be so mean."

"Actually, I was even worse. You just didn't recognize the trait." She grinned and gave him a light shove. "Don't let grass grow. Go get her. She's a gem. Music's starting. Dancing awaits. With a lovely lady. *Go.*"

Aaron listened to Mila's advice, but opted to divert a bit and resettle before approaching Emma. He'd approach her as friend, as a grateful recipient of her professional expertise. He paused at the table occupied by his family and gave Mom's shoulder a tender squeeze. "Dance with me?"

Her smile burst like a firework; her eyes danced like stars. "I'd be delighted."

Aaron accepted her hand and led her into a smooth glide that matched the beat of the music.

Mom gave his hand a squeeze. "You know,

when you're finished dancing with me, you should go and be as welcoming to Emma. I see the way you look at her, and it's got to be hard assimilating to a small town where everyone already knows each other and —"

Aaron cast a beseeching glance toward the heavens. What was *with* the women in his life these days? "Mom, are you, by any chance, matchmaking?"

"No, not exactly. Try friend-making. That's a much better analogy."

"Sure it is." Aaron squelched a skeptical chuckle and leaned back with a knowing grin. "You're a fibber. You want to get rid of me."

"Never."

They moved to the tempo of the music for a few beats.

"Women are tricky."

"Guilty as charged." No woman raised three sons without possessing a strong personality of her own, and Anna Fisher could write a textbook on the topic.

"Do you want to know why I'm so picky?"

"Sure. Fill me in."

"Because you've set the bar very, very high." Aaron kissed her cheek.

"Oh, my darling." Tears welled in her eyes, but she blinked them back and tossed her head. "Aren't you sweet?"

"I have my moments."

"More than a few." She kissed his cheek and the softest scent of gardenia drifted.

Once the song ended, Aaron led her back to the table, there Dad waited, a contented expression easing the time-lines of his eyes and mouth. He looked great, from his posture to the renewed, ruddy hue of his cheeks. Mom gave his arm a concluding squeeze.

"OK, son, it's my turn now." Dad claimed Mom's hand. After kissing the back of her fingertips, he led her to the dance floor.

"Go, Aaron," Mom encouraged as they walked away. "Talk to her."

That last bit of coaching left him with no other choice . . . not that he really wanted one.

9

"Hey . . . Emma?"

Aaron's quiet summons drew Emma towards him.

"Hi there." She would have bet her smile spoke volumes. So much for being subtle.

"I was wondering if you'd like to dance."

Emma nodded, magnetized by the idea of being held in Aaron's strong arms, his large, work-roughened hand sliding against hers and holding snug while they moved together.

He tucked an arm around her waist and drew her against the solid contours of his chest. He laced his fingers through hers and they moved in a slow, steady rhythm across aged planks of wood that creaked and sang, offering a testimony to the couples and loves that had crossed its surface through the passing years and decades.

"You're a good dancer." Emma's compliment was sincere, just this side of flirtatious.

A curious lack of forethought and hesitation in speaking was a highly unusual development for her. Best to think about that later.

"Thank you, but don't sound so surprised." A teasing glint lit his eyes. "Mom insisted on her boys becoming well-turned gentlemen."

"Then I'll be sure to tell her she succeeded."

"I'd appreciate that. Sometimes she needs reminding since we've definitely put her through her paces over the years."

"I have no doubt."

Smiles bloomed between them, a tender exchange as a beat of silence went by.

Emma leaned into his embrace and allowed herself the luxury of pure enjoyment.

"Would you allow me an observation of my own? About you?"

Emma's sense of ease vanished beneath the swell of a big, silent 'Uh-oh.' "Not at all. What is it?"

He no longer swept her into the motions of a dance. Rather, he held her close, and they continued to sway, but he focused on her eyes. She focused on his full, long lips, her imaginings going wild.

"Every time I look at you, I sense something."

Double uh-oh — and his voice? Softest velvet. "Yes?"

"Like you're searching. Seeking something. When I'm around you, I pick up on a longing for peace, for rest. Am I anywhere close to the mark?"

Emma nearly stumbled. *Only with a bullseye, buddy.* "Ah . . . I mean . . . I guess we're all looking for . . ."

"No, Emma." He stroked her cheek. His tone was so loving — so rich and smooth. He didn't want to push, but rather seemed to want to know her.

Her lashes fluttered; she sighed, captured by his lingering touch against her skin, the steadiness and warmth of him. Which scared away any sense of logic.

Unaware of her turmoil, Aaron continued. "I don't want some ready-made answer you'd deliver to an acquaintance or a patient you're dealing with. Please. Talk to me."

Once again, his gentle patience took her by storm. Aaron's refinement touched her, because she knew he didn't come by the trait with ease. Rather, he moved forward carefully, and questioned her out of genuine affection, not aggressiveness. The recognition left her unable to reply right away; she needed to catch her breath.

"So, you'd like to talk?"

Aaron nodded.

Emma teased him with a smirk. "How long have you got?"

"I've got a long time. How about you?"

Emma's heart stuttered. So, he didn't buy her show of humor. He didn't flinch or hesitate. Maybe it was time. Maybe Aaron's support, his perspective, was what she needed.

Emma cast a sidelong glance across the dance floor. Why did she feel as though every set of eyes rested upon them? Upon *her* — the mysterious town outsider? And she had the feeling Aaron understood what remained unspoken as he followed her gaze around the room.

"If you come with me, we could take a walk outside." His comment cut through a heavy silence. "The moon is full, and a bit of fresh air sounds good to me. How about you?"

"I'd love it."

Outside the hall, the air was sweet and cool. Emma drew in slow, refreshing breaths, nourishing herself for what lay ahead. This, it seemed, was the time to chase nightmares into submission, if only for a short time. All around her, field grass whispered, swayed by a breeze that caused wispy tips to ripple, to shimmer and sing

238

beneath the milky-white light of the moon. Insect song added a delicate rhythm and cadence to the night as they ambled along the gravel path that surrounded the hall.

"You're so lucky to have this, Aaron. This town, this moment, is timeless. I keep circling back to that fact tonight."

"Despite Antioch's watchful eyes?" He caught her hand in an easy, natural grip as they walked.

"Oh. Sorry. Didn't mean to be obvious about a bit of discomfort." Her skin tingled when his thumb glossed a caress against her wrist.

"Nothing to apologize for. You weren't obvious; I just think, maybe, I'm beginning to learn your mannerisms or something."

They shared an eloquent look that chased off any semblance of chill in the air.

"When you live here long enough scrutiny becomes second nature. Kind of hard to ignore, eh?"

"True."

"Does that bother you?"

Emma fought her way to the most honest answer she could find. "Yes and no. I don't mind kind, harmless inquisition, and that's what church was about. That's what tonight is about. I know that, but" — She sighed, focused on the crunch of their footsteps pressing against tiny, loose stones — "at the same time, it's tough to be the unknown quantity."

"Then make yourself known. That'll end speculation real quick."

"Easier said than done, especially for someone who isn't born and bred. Someone who's reserved, and private to begin with, who has a past others might not understand."

"With that, I think we're inching closer to the 'but' you've been dodging lately."

Emma couldn't elaborate right away.

Aaron stepped into her path, swallowed at once by shadow and the bloom of a crisp autumn evening. "Emma, I don't think I've ever come across someone so in need of peace."

She fought so hard to deny the truth, wishing she could remain unaffected by the observation. But in that instant, she looked up, lost in the depths of calm, dark eyes that flashed in the night. Without preamble, her resolve burst against a pressure-filled, over-burdened dam of emotion. A flood of anxiety, sorrow, and fear released into Aaron's safekeeping. That sense of peace he alluded to was precisely what she craved. Emma's history, the guilt and shame of her exit from Detroit, all poured free.

Aaron simply continued his walk with her, listening attentively, his arm snug at her waist, his body warm and solid against her side.

"An emergency C-section saved the baby," she concluded, "but the mother hemorrhaged uncontrollably. There was nothing more we could do."

Emma's world faded on the breeze that slid against her skin. She forced herself to breathe in slow — three count — then out slow — three count. The action was therapeutic and stilling. "A lawsuit was filed a couple weeks later. After the botched ER episode, Oliver shut himself off from everyone — from everything. The only way I can describe it is this: he left me; he pushed everyone away and closed down. I tried to empathize. Then, I tried to bully him. Finally, I drifted into a weird kind of isolation where I was faced with two choices: move on, or end up like him, an unhappy shell."

"Moving on as you did was the smart choice. Not easy, but smart."

Emma shrugged. "In so many ways, I'm still fighting to find my way, and not become isolated."

"Keep. Fighting."

Emma stopped walking. Aaron's intensity,

the magnetism of him, yanked her straight out of hiding — but comforted and soothed her as well. "After being raked over investigative coals that were both legal and internal at the hospital, what I craved beyond anything else was anonymity. A do-over with a clean slate in a place where no one knew me, or my history, or my troubles. No one could question, or press, or worse yet, try to sympathize. I needed a new start."

"Are you finding that do-over here in Antioch?"

Emma nodded, eyes downcast.

"What happens once you recover? What happens once you come to terms?"

"That's where I'm at right now. That's what I'm trying hard to figure out."

"Whether to stay permanently or use this time — this season, I suppose you might say — as a bit of a mending station, like at an ER." His attempt at humor was lackluster, a probe with meaning that he didn't seem any more eager to explore in depth yet than she was.

"I hope I'm not being quite that clinical. I want to find a path to the future, Aaron, obviously, but what I didn't plan on was facing a double-edged sword."

"Meaning?"

"Meaning small-town life, with its anonymity, with its peace and slow-pace, and even its connections to others" — she allowed a meaningful pause to slip by, hoping he'd understand his importance, his impact — "would put me at the center of speculation. A well-meaning quest on behalf of new acquaintances to find out more about a mystery lady. A mystery lady with growing ties to a family that's part of Antioch's history."

"And those well-meaning folks would discover . . . what exactly?"

"Lawsuits, scandal, failure. All of it is just an internet search away."

"If a person were interested enough to dive that deep, anyone with a brain cell would realize none of that was on you, Emma. None of it."

"Oh, yes, it was." Her head lifted; her mood went instantly sharp and intent. "Aaron, I'm ashamed of myself. Ashamed of what I let happen." Tears welled. For the millionth time since life slipped out of control, Emma blinked them away and swallowed hard, reasserting control. "I was on the team, and I was trusted. Instead of making things right, I became part of the mess because of self-doubt and my feelings for Oliver. That family counted on me to be part of a solution. I failed, and I can't disavow that fact, and I certainly can't disavow the way I ran from Detroit."

"Those observations are fair enough, but don't let them keep you from absorbing the fuller harvest of what you went through. The leaving you talk about might have been just what you needed at the time." Aaron paused to let the words sink in. "Maybe, in the here and now, you can stop running. I don't know much, but struggles of my own have taught me a fundamental truth."

"Which is?"

"Which is, when God wants you to move, he makes you uncomfortable where you're at. And that's no cliché. That's no piece of psych-speak. I learned that truth from experience."

"I see your point, Aaron. Truly I do, but you've led an idyllic life here in Antioch." With a broad, sweeping gesture, Emma spread her arms, indicating lush farm land cloaked by darkness and shafts of moonlight. "I don't mean that in a spiteful or resentful way — it's beautiful. With the family you have, I'd find it hard to believe you've ever had to confront being heartwrecked by those you love and trust as I did with Oliver."

"You might be surprised, Emma." A beat of tension passed between them. "Do you want to hear my history?"

Something about the way he posed that question — the underlying note of challenge, perhaps — triggered her pulse and an eagerness to hear what he had to say. Curious, emboldened by the progress they had made, she simply nodded.

"Pretty much as expected, you can look me up in the Antioch High School yearbook and discover I was the guy voted most likely to stay local, marry the homecoming queen, and continue the Fisher family legacy. What that brief snippet doesn't tell you, is that I wanted choices. I wanted to make my own way. Instead, it was Phillip who broke free. So, not only did he fulfill something I secretly yearned to do, from my point of view he turned his back on me, and our family, in the pursuit of self-satisfaction and success. You want to hear about the raging fury I swallowed back day after day when he graduated college and immediately hit the road to pursue a life of riches and financial safety in the business world?"

Emma had to catch her breath in the face of the intensity, the rapid-fire push and heat of Aaron's words. He clenched his jaw once again, seeming lost to a world, to a series of memories, and battles, that he alone could see. A beat later he schooled himself against what she could only assume were swelling emotions.

"I lost my big brother. For years. Beyond that, I had to carry on when he turned his back on the farm, a way of life, that had been in place for generations. The weight fell on my shoulders and I couldn't let my family down. And then Dad got sick and he's still trying to get back to where he was regarding his health."

His voice was low, but, Emma knew him well enough to recognize the way his anger simmered, the way his temper bubbled. That smooth mask of his covered a tempest. "Phillip chased a dream. A dream of financial success, stability, and a life made on book smarts rather than the caprice of weather patterns, good seeds, and physical toil. Everything for him and his choices looked great on paper, but reality is life's great equalizer. Not long after he left, he returned to Antioch, burned by the very world he thought would save him. He was laid off, broke, but became the errant prodigal who was greeted like a victor. That added fuel to my emotional fire."

"Because you were the 'good son.' The one who'd fulfilled promises but felt as though he was languishing with forced expectations." A bittersweet ache built through Emma's chest. None of this was Aaron's fault, but none of the blame belonged to Phillip, either. As Aaron had correctly observed, life was the great equalizer between them.

"Loyalty and bitterness were like cold and hot running through my veins until it all exploded when he showed up at our doorstep a year ago. So, when it comes to locking away pain, I could write an owner's manual. Emma, you're not alone in facing demons. I was so resentful and angry toward Phillip I couldn't stand to be in the same room with him. But after I socked him in the jaw for turning his back on me — on all of us — I was forced to grow up. To examine my perceptions and move forward. The past had to be put behind us. Your past doesn't fully explain or define you. What you've left behind is a chapter in a book. Don't allow it to become the whole story."

"I hear what you're saying. Phillip returned. He faced what he had done. Right?"

"No argument here."

"That's where I get stalled, almost into a rut. I feel as if I'm in a muddy mess. I can't seem to spin my wheels hard enough to leave what happened behind me. How do I face what I've done? How do I atone?"

Night air skimmed by.

Aaron paused, taking in her words. "Same as you, life didn't work out the way Phillip planned, or the way I planned, but it's better than we ever dreamed, know what I mean? He met up with Mila Thomas and the arrow struck home. His aggressive businessman persona vanished and his roots resettled in Antioch, and I'm finding a place of my own working the farm that I love and can see myself continuing that in the future."

"So, settling isn't always a bad thing." Crickets chirped and another of those intoxicating, softer-than-velvet breezes kissed her skin and left strands of her hair to ripple.

"Nope, it isn't." Aaron fingered back the dancing strands and moved close. "The same kind of hope, the same kind of promise, can hold true for you, too."

For some reason, a moment in time came to life for Emma, one of her last memories of leaving Detroit. A colleague of hers questioned the wisdom of leaving the 'Big City' for the tedious checkerboard landscape of Indiana. Now, saturated by its unique beauty, Emma couldn't imagine anything more beautiful. How could anyone deem the crop-ripened flatlands of Indiana boring or tedious?

"Finding home the way you have, the way Phillip has, is something a lot of people dream of. You've been given that gift, Aaron. Protect it, OK? Treasure it. See it for what it is. Grace from God. I thought I had that kind of life locked up and waiting."

"I'm working on that as we speak. I just ask one thing in return."

"Which is?"

"Find the same for yourself. And, while you're at it, promise me you won't write off your dreams just yet."

"Tough to dream when reality crashes into me and sends me in the opposite direction of where I thought I belonged. Where I was most comfortable and secure." A push of contrition caused tears to spring to life, blurring her vision as she blinked them back and swallowed hard. "Why didn't God step in for that mother? Why did God leave that brand-new father stranded? Most of all, why didn't I ignore my feelings for Oliver? Why wasn't I more forceful when he labeled pre-eclampsia as a bladder infection? She was in solid health just twenty-four hours earlier. There's fragility, unpredictability to every aspect of what we do in the medical field. I know that, and I accept that, but —"

Aaron shook his head and silenced further elaboration by touching a fingertip to her lips. "Emma, I refuse to let you put a qualifier at the end of that sentence. You can't qualify a truth that's absolute. There's no 'but' when it comes to this. Life isn't in our control. Life is delicate. We're fragile, just as you say. You say you've accepted the inability to control the outcomes you face, but those are just words. Your actions, and reactions, tell me otherwise. I don't think you do. Not here." He tapped a spot just above her heart. "Not where it matters the most, and affects you the most. Think about that. You're too precious to be allowed to waste away."

Precious.

The word seeped into Emma's blood with a dizzying rush of power.

Aaron dipped his head.

Emma barely had time to absorb his affirming words before he captured her mouth and sighed — or maybe she was the one who sighed — and she fell headlong into a dream the likes of which she had never allowed herself to imagine, let alone embrace as reality. This, she knew at once, was love. Deep, abiding, true love.

She weakened, a delicious sense of surrender washing through her in a current that carried her straight to the depths of a world-shattering kiss. Her knees melted.

Aaron's hold on her waist increased by a quick, possessive degree that left her feeling not only secure and protected, but treasured as well.

Mini-sparks danced along her senses; she feasted on musky flavors and soft dew while his lips moved and teased, while his fingers slid into her hair, performing a tender dance. Emma was assailed by hunger, by a need to taste, to explore his textures, to saturate herself with the beauty of their precious first kiss. His mouth glided in perfect time to hers; the give-and-take left her spirit to spin.

Aaron's raspy exclamation punctuated a night filled by the melody of whispering grass, chattering tree branches . . .

Emma clung to his shoulders, her fingertips digging slightly, holding tight, refusing to let him go. She dissolved into the moment, her world tunneling to nothing more than Aaron, her thundering pulse, an escalating sense of connection — of need.

At long last they tempered flames to steamy, crackling embers.

Aaron drew her in tight for a hug that soothed her soul. "We'd better get back inside before we're missed."

Emma made an agreeing sound but

couldn't help noticing the gruff, affected tone of his voice.

10

What on earth had she allowed to happen?

Emma lifted from bed the next morning, groggy yet strangely rested, as though she had slept sound for the first time in ages and her body longed for more of the same.

But with sunrise came a flood of uncertainty that pushed the serenity of sleep into the farthest corner of her mind. Why would Aaron, why would a kiss, why would a blooming rush of feelings, leave her so thoroughly off-center? No matter what the circumstance, she was generally more controlled than this.

But not this time.

What was she doing? Where was her fail-safe composure? With sincerity, she had talked a great game when lauding the anonymity and fresh start of her life in Antioch. Then, she had allowed Aaron to kiss her senseless. Utterly, beautifully, world-rockingly senseless. In addition — and she still blushed at the thought — she had responded in kind, swirling into a moment of communion that, even a full day later, stirred her pulse to a heated scamper.

What kind of fireball was she toying with?

No, she amended. Toying wasn't the right word. Almost prepped for work, Emma frowned at her reflection in the mirror. She had finished applying a dash of makeup and began to run a finalizing brush through her hair. She wasn't toying with Aaron, and he wasn't toying with her either. Clipping her ID badge into place at the V-point neckline of her scrub top, Emma groaned. This level of convoluted emotion was far from playful, or casual.

And that was just the trouble.

How could she explain herself? How could she justify allowing such strong roots to extend, wrap, and secure themselves around her heart when all she wanted to do was cocoon herself into a solitary, life-sheltering safe zone?

Emma spent the front half of her day buried in work, happily moving from patient to patient at Briar. Thus far, the day's agenda provided for a light and fairly routine caseload. There were a few Autumn into winter allergy issues, some stitches required for eight-year-old Eric Wyler who had split a lip while playing a heated game of kick-ball with his older brother. Eric endured the procedure with admirable strength and just a few teary moments. Following that came a standard pregnancy check that spotlighted a perfectly developing baby and glowing mother. Moments like that still snagged her heart, but happiness, and the prenatal enthusiasm exhibited by today's couple, smoothed away any ripples of unease.

During her lunch break she heated up a sweet-and-sour chicken dish then settled at a small, chrome table to review personal e-mail and check her phone for any incoming calls or messages.

Usually that daily exercise took only a few seconds. Today she stopped short twice — first by an e-mail from Parkview Hospital and second by a voicemail left by Anna Fisher. Brows puckered, she replayed Anna's message.

Emma, hi. It's Anna Fisher. I hope you don't mind me reaching out. Everything is fine, so, please don't worry about Jonathan. I enjoyed our time together at the social this past weekend, though, and wondered if you might like to get together for tea or coffee sometime soon here at the farm. Let me know. I look forward to hearing from you, and I hope you can make it.

From there, Anna relayed her phone number. Emma reached into the chest pocket of her scrubs, quickly extracting the notepad and pen that accompanied her everywhere as part of the job. After recording the digits, she tapped the surface of the notepad with a restless fingertip and pursed her lips. She wanted to return Anna's call straight away, but the e-mail from Parkview Hospital piqued her interest. She clicked on the message and gaped as she read . . . and absorbed . . . a note from Dr. Maxwell Rhodan.

Emma ~

I hope this note finds you well. I wondered if you would be interested in talking about a position coming open on my staff next month for a critical care nurse. You'd be stationed in the Cardiac Unit under my group, and I'm eager to discuss the opportunity. You impressed me when we discussed the Fisher case, and our post-op meeting with the family left me wondering if you might be underplaying a superb skillset in your present position. If you're happily engaged, I wish you well and understand completely, but if the opportunity I present is of interest, feel free to call me and set up a convenient time to have a discussion.

He signed off with his contact information. Chewing on her lower lip, Emma stared at the screen. She posed her fingers. Prepared to type. Froze.

Tried again and failed.

The offer Dr. Rhodan presented was flattering, but still, Emma was stunned.

Blowing out a puff of air, she checked the time on her phone. She had about a half-hour left before her next patient arrived. She accepted Anna Fisher's unexpected but delightful offer of tea and conversation. They agreed to meet in a few days at the Fisher farm.

The next step was Dr. Rhodan.

Emma ignored her food. She began to tap a reply and stopped. She ate for a few minutes, but her pulse rocketed. She flipped the protective cover over her device and finished lunch, determined to wait on answering Dr. Rhodan's e-mail until tonight. She needed to still herself, to think and pray before delivering any kind of reply to his offer.

It wouldn't hurt to hear what he had to say, right? A conversation didn't equal an offer. And, if an offer were made, she wasn't required to accept it, right? She thought of Aaron immediately. Fort Wayne wasn't *that* far from Antioch . . . but still . . . it was further away, and a total life shift. Again. What would his reaction be?

Emma strolled to the nearby sink. She cleaned her dishes, hoping that spot of manual labor might help to focus her thoughts. She released a turbulent sigh then did what she knew was best. She bowed her head for a few precious moments to pray.

Aaron stood a yard or so away from Phillip, working a rake as they piled dead leaves and small brush into a mound on a large metal sheet. Positioned nearby were two large buckets of water — this would be a small, final burn before winter set in.

Phillip continued the thread of a conversation that centered on — what else — the impact of Emma Briggs. Aaron couldn't seem to escape her, but in truth, he didn't really want to.

"So, what you're telling me is that you figure she's looking for peace. But what I'm telling you in turn is to be careful, 'Cause from where I sit, she's hanging out with the Fisher brother most likely to burst into a whipcord of intensity and gut-triggered reaction."

Well, wasn't that nice? Aaron stopped tugging leaves into place and scowled at his sib. "Aww, don't get all mushy on me, now,

Phillip. You jerk."

Phillip shook his head, laughing. "And the award for proving my point goes to . . ."

Aaron rounded on him once more, torn between laughing and snarling. "Do you want another bash to the jaw? I've got some extra time to indulge if you're interested."

Phillip made an exaggerated show of flexing his jaw, wordlessly causing Aaron to recollect the greeting he had extended the day Phillip returned to Antioch those long months ago. Lots of change since then — some of it turbulent, some of it spectacular.

"Nah. I'm good. Thanks for the offer, though."

They swapped grins, teasing glares. Lord, but they had come a long way. Thankfully.

Aaron kept raking, digging up the old, dead bramble to make room for winter's freeze and the promise of spring. "Look, I know what I am, and I know what I'm not. Thing is, I'm . . . *different* when I'm with her." He paused to lean on the wooden handle. "In fact, I just might be different *because* of her."

"And the changes are evident. Really. All kidding aside."

He appreciated that Phillip noticed. With a broad shrug, he returned to the task. "I know how to be careful, how to be gentle when warranted." *And I know how good it feels to hold her safe in my arms, to feel her go all soft and trusting when I touch her skin, or sink into those warm brown eyes.* The unspoken addenda filled his heart like an explosion.

"So, you're saying she's warranted?"

"Warranted and then some." Aaron slanted his brother a deliberately telling look that Phillip absorbed with the acceptance of a nod and an arched brow.

Before long the fire was lit and they stood guard over gathering ash, surrounded by the crisp, earthy spice of burning leaves, the warmth of flames dancing and sputtering.

Suddenly, Phillip cracked a smile. "Emma drives a burgundy colored car, right?"

The sound of wheels on gravel, the hum of an engine, signaled the approach of a vehicle. Phillip faced the driveway and Aaron watched him, puzzled. "Yeah, why?"

"It seems the folks are having company."

Huh? Emma wouldn't drop by his parents' place unannounced. Plus, wouldn't she let him know if there was a meeting of some sort? Wouldn't she text or something, or . . . ?

Aaron yanked his cell phone from the pocket of his jeans. No notifications, no missed calls. He spun toward the driveway.

She climbed out of the vehicle and turned her face toward the sky, a smile curving her lips. She seemed to be enjoying the aroma of the fire . . . a fire which Aaron and Phillip couldn't — and wouldn't — leave unattended.

Emma opened the passenger door of her car and pulled something out from the back seat — a package of some sort — but Aaron couldn't tell what it was. His brows pulled, curiosity eating at him.

What was going on?

What a beautiful aroma. Emma breathed deep, absorbing nature's incense of sweetness and spice stirred by the burning of wood, leaves and brush. Nothing spoke as eloquently of Autumn's advent, and exit, as a leaf fire.

Aaron and Phillip stood a few hundred yards away, next to a mini-tower of refuse that turned slowly to ground cover. She would have loved to say hello but didn't want to leave Anna waiting. Besides, unexpectedly coming upon Aaron sent a giddy, uncertain rush through her veins. She was melting into an ocean of emotion for which she considered herself thoroughly unprepared. Life kept right on taking her by surprise.

To accompany tea, Emma had offered to bring pumpkin spice cupcakes topped by cream cheese frosting. Steadying the package of treats she held, she ignored the siren call of Aaron's presence and trooped up the front porch steps. She knocked firmly on the front door and was greeted promptly by Anna's warm smile.

"Come on in — I'm so glad you could make it!" She wiped her fingertips on a hand towel and led the way to the kitchen. "I've got finger sandwiches set — cucumber and mini-BLT's."

"Sounds great."

"I made some egg salad sandwiches as well — they're a family standard, but not in such dainty and refined servings."

Anna's laughter had Emma laughing as well. "You went through a lot of effort. I'm flattered."

"Oh, Emma, as the mother of three boys, and as a woman who loves all things domestic, please believe me when I say I love having the chance to host a 'girl's luncheon.' This is special to me."

Warmth rolled and Emma smiled at Anna. "That's right. You're a home economics teacher."

"Closing in on retirement in a few years." Sadness touched the older woman's eyes.

"I'm part of a dying breed, I'm afraid."

"Our world seems to be straying from the importance of building a home and the art of caring for a family, isn't it?"

"I wish I could argue the point."

Somehow, it comforted Emma to know women like Anna Fisher continued to stand strong, and fight a good fight. Respect swelled. "There's such dignity and grace to be found in teaching young people how to create and tend to a home."

"Right down to paying the bills and managing a checking and savings account," Anna replied. "As such, today is a small means by which I can let you know how grateful I am that you're helping my family. You're doing so much to give me more good years with the man I love. Jonathan means everything to me, so I want you to consider our tea time celebration my heartfelt thank you."

"Anna, no thanks are necessary."

Emma continued to absorb the sweet, calming atmosphere cultivated by Anna's home, and her gentle — but strong — presence. Her eyes rounded when she caught sight of a three-tiered china serving stand laden by all the delicious food Anna had described. Delicate lace doilies even rested beneath each serving.

"Anna, this is incredible. Here . . . let me help you." Carrying the food and a carafe of tea, Emma followed her to the dining room.

Even here, Anna had left no detail untended. More fine china had been commissioned for use. Creamy white plates and saucers were bordered by a tiny wreath of lilac blooms. Silver utensils shimmered atop crisp, folded napkins.

The vision stopped Emma in her tracks. "Oh, my. This is way too pretty to spoil."

Appearing a tad sheepish, Anna smiled and settled the platter of cupcakes into place. She gestured for Emma to sit. "I went a bit over the top, didn't I?"

"Not at all. This makes me feel special."

"Good. That's the whole point."

Emma sat and unfolded her napkin, spreading it across her lap. "Your generosity is fantastic, and very much appreciated, but I mean it when I say you don't owe me a thing. Just a healthy life for Jonathan."

Anna shrugged lightly and lifted a teapot from its trivet, filling their cups. "I like to spoil the ones I care for. Emma, you're a fantastic nurse who has taken excellent care of my husband. You've gone above and beyond to accompany us on visits to specialists. But, most of all, I appreciate this time together because it seems you're walking through the front door of Aaron's heart."

Straightforward kindness and honesty. Emma hoisted her cup for a sip that both calmed her nerves and stalled for time. *Go for broke. You're in safe hands.* "He's walking through the front door of mine as well."

Anna sipped and smiled over her cup. "I thought as much. He's my complicated, deep son. The way I see it, the world his dad and I tried to show him was like the hand-me-downs he received from Phillip while he was growing up. Most of them were a size or so too big. He had to grow into them. Just as he's had to grow into the life he's inherited — like it or not. And he's got a stubborn streak. He's tough and a little volatile . . . but his heart is so big, and so good. When it comes to Aaron, I've always trusted. I've always had faith that he'd come to terms. I know he'll grow into the hopes and dreams we've always had for him, and the life God called him to lead. He's stubborn and volatile because his feelings run strong and intense."

Emma pondered those revelations for a moment, and agreed with Anna wholeheartedly. "Sometimes I wonder if I might be his final fight of rebellion. You know — the town stronghold defying those expectations as he mixes it up with the outsider who's left behind a somewhat murky past."

"A murky past? I'm intrigued, and as a woman who entered Antioch from the outside back in the day, with some murky patches of her own, I think I might be able to relate to the way you feel." Anna delivered a look rife with affection, and firm resolve. "So, if I may, I'd appreciate it if you didn't try to walk such a demeaning road. You're worth far too much to ever be pigeonholed. Your heart and integrity are beyond reproach."

Emma's breath caught, held. "I hope you'll still think so once you hear my story."

"Oh, Emma . . . I was hoping you'd share." Anna relaxed against the back of her chair and sipped from her tea, patient, serene, yet interested. All over again, her grin spread slow and easy — full of promise, and full of knowing, too.

From there, Emma's words poured free — the history, the mistakes, the powerlessness and fears . . . "I should have been more forceful."

"He was the doctor. Not you. On a smaller scale, I've done battle with principals, with superintendents, when I felt the situation and curriculum warranted it — but in the end, I had to bow to their authority. They're in the leadership position, whether they honor that truth or not."

"That might be true, but it doesn't take away my sense of responsibility."

"Or the guilt, it seems."

"What if I —"

"Don't ask 'what if,' Emma." Anna held up a hand to quell further argument. "Ask yourself this instead: Did you do the best you could with the information and facts you were given?"

Emma nodded.

"Did you do everything in your power for a successful outcome?"

Again, she nodded, but Emma's eyes narrowed. Skepticism came alive like a vibration and she was about to speak, but Anna concluded.

"What more could you have done? You're not God. Neither was the doctor."

Emma stared, captured by a truth expressed by Aaron as well. An instant later, she broke down and wept. Uncontrollably. In a simple series of words, Anna had hit upon the crux of the matter. She, and Oliver, had attempted to equal themselves with God. Not out of arrogance, or self-importance, but out of determination to succeed and claim life from death . . . beauty from ashes.

"Oh, my dear. What have I done?" Anna's words resonated with alarm and the gravelly residue of helpless sorrow.

Never would this woman deliberately hurt anyone; Emma knew so on instinct, with no form of history, so she focused on setting the record straight. "Nothing. Anna, you've done nothing except offer unconditional acceptance and care. I'm grateful. Truly." Not wanting to ruin lovely linens with the black splotch of wet mascara, Emma nabbed a paper napkin from the wooden holder that rested atop the table. She swiped her eyes then promptly crumpled the piece into her tightly clenched fist. "You've said just what I needed to hear. It's me. I'm coming to realize I'm not much more than a hot mess right now, but somehow, you're managing to see past it all and you're determined to find something good in me, something redemptive in the havoc of my past. Aaron is, too. That's what captivates me. That what amazes me. It's overwhelming."

"Affirmation overwhelms you?" She nodded. "Emma, that breaks my heart. Never, ever, should you doubt what God has given you in the way of healing gifts and a heart full of compassion." Anna reached across the table top, rested her hand atop Emma's, gave her fingers a lingering squeeze. "Find a way to overcome what happened. If you don't, it'll keep eating at you. Your life is too beautiful a thing, with too much to offer, for that to happen. Don't you think?"

"I used to. I used to have such faith. Now, I question everything, right down to instinctive decisions in the ER that used to come to me on automatic. I trusted my judgment. My gifts as a nurse."

"And then?"

Emma expelled a deep breath, closed her eyes for a moment so she could focus. "And then everything changed. Nothing has been the same since that episode. The day that led me to Antioch, to this whole new life, was a bad day that just kept getting worse. A day when every good effort led to a spiraling downfall. When every honest motion forward came against its opposite and ended in a young mother's death. The father lived. The baby lived, but the mother died, and I have no one to blame but myself because to this very second, I still believe I could have stopped it. The obstetrics attending was unavailable. Oliver had no choice but to attempt delivery in the ER. It happens. Sometimes a situation snowballs out of all proportion and control, especially in the ER. We're trained to handle these . . . events . . ." She blanched at the clinical term, so void of feeling and depth of impact, but the terms created a necessary emotional buffer. "The thing is, I still can't make sense of what happened. Everything Oliver did was per protocol. Sure, I tried to step in and advise based on what I knew, but I'm only an RN. He was the physician. I followed his lead and tried to help, but instead of progress, we kept spiraling backward."

"As I said, he was the lead."

"And we were also involved."

"You . . ."

"Oliver. And me. We were involved. We were dating at the time. I refused to question him, or his abilities. I was falling in love with him." Or had thought she was . . . until now . . . until Aaron. Anna probably sensed that unspoken truth; as such, Emma decided to clarify. "More to the point, I *thought* I was falling in love with him. It wasn't love, and I know that now."

"What happened afterward? With Oliver?"

"He pulled back hard and fast — with finality — after the hospital launched an investigation into what happened that day." Emma sank back against her chair, toyed restlessly with the handle of her cup. "Love doesn't operate that way. I was ready to support him. I didn't even question him, because my personal feelings wrapped around a nightmarish situation over which neither one of us truly had control."

"Then you learned from what happened. He lost, not you. Instead, you moved on, and you learned. You grew. And, Emma, never doubt it. You're a beautiful person. Worthy."

Anna's words acted like a storm burst through her body, releasing pain, releasing guilt, releasing sorrow for what might have been in favor of all that might come to be. If only she could believe, and reach out. "Thank you, Anna." The choked reply was all Emma could manage.

But Anna wasn't finished. "Over the past year, I've struggled with watching my husband's health falter dramatically. I struggled with watching my oldest son lose himself to a promise of high ambition and a life of material security. I've struggled with watching Aaron maintain a farm I know he loves and cares for but never dreamed of taking on as his own. The Book of Wisdom teaches us to realize the brevity of life so that we can grow in wisdom — in appreciation of the precious gift we're given with every moment we're given. In each of those instances, I was powerless, just as you were in the hospital on that awful day. But God saw it through — and he's seeing you through to

271

redemption. To better days. To peace."

Peace. The exact word Aaron had used.

"It's hard for me to picture you as the outsider you mentioned earlier." Emma made the comment as she resumed their meal. "You fit into the fabric of Antioch as though you were born and raised."

"Nearly. I had family here, but I moved here after graduating college because I was offered a teaching position at a time when I needed it most."

"And you've never looked back."

"Never wanted to. This is home."

After tea concluded, they hugged and bid one another an affectionate farewell with promises of a return engagement. That's when Emma knew for sure. She didn't want to look back any longer either. She wanted home.

And she wanted home to include Aaron.

11

Emma spent almost every evening after work with Aaron. They grabbed dinner at his house, or at the deli in town. They caught the latest romance/adventure movie at Grady's Olde Towne Theatre and even braved a walk through Remington Park as barren tree branches clacked and creaked against a cold, invigorating wind. While winter gusted in with its first early-November dusting of snow, the level of farm work decreased. Aaron's time turned to relaxation, taking on an air of quiet restfulness that matched the onrushing change in seasons.

Following Sunday dinner at the farm, Aaron drove her home. Emma's stomach churned, because of the upcoming interview . . . professional conversation, she amended firmly . . . with Dr. Rhodan in Fort Wayne. She hadn't mentioned it to Aaron, excusing her reticence with the argument that, technically, the upcoming meeting was nothing more than two like-minded colleagues discussing their profession, and its opportunities. Since Monday was her typical day off from Briar, she had scheduled the meeting for ten o'clock tomorrow morning.

The next morning, Emma made the drive to Fort Wayne, paying particular attention to the commute. At just after rush hour, the journey took about forty minutes. She could handle a fifty-minute to one-hour commute if they somehow found a way to build a future . . . to commit to one another.

Emma freed her mind of the distraction known as Aaron Fisher. Instead she focused on bullet points she wanted to bring up during the interview . . . *meeting* . . . to come with Dr. Rhodan.

She announced herself at the reception desk, glossing shaky fingertips against the lines of her rust colored skirt. A white, lightweight sweater finished the outfit. Once she settled in a chair of the waiting room, she toyed nervously with the edges of a long, patterned scarf looped loosely around her neck. What on earth was she getting so worked up about? This was nothing. Really. Just . . . nothing . . . simply an exploratory session.

"Emma!"

Dr. Rhodan's cheerful summons disrupted the quagmire of her thoughts, and she couldn't have been more grateful. Emma extended her hand in a gesture he accepted with smooth ease and professionalism.

"It's good to see you again, doctor."

"You, too. Come on back, and let me show you around."

Following a tour of Dr. Rhodan's clinic, they landed in plush leather chairs opposite one another across a conference table in a small room appointed with warm, homey features.

Dr. Rhodan wasted no time. "Emma, as I said in my e-mail, I'm interested in seeing if we might have a fit, a partnership, worth exploring when it comes to the work I'm doing."

"Which is why I appreciate your interest, and the confidence it shows."

"Your personality and your knowledge base impress me. First, when we met with the Fisher family on a consultancy basis. Next, when we provided the family with a debrief following Jonathan's stent procedure." He glanced at his folded hands. "You strike me as being tenacious about providing exceptional patient care, and that's a key objective of my practice — not to mention exactly what's required of a critical care nurse. That's also something I take very much to heart as a physician."

"Then we're very similar, Dr. Rhodan."

From there, they launched into a rundown of Emma's history as a nurse. Since she felt every issue needed to be placed in clear view, she didn't shirk her past in Detroit. Evasion would be wrong and hiding would be senseless. Her background was nothing more than a phone call or computer click away. Sharing her experiences with Aaron and Anna left Emma determined. She refused to hide, or surrender to shame any longer.

So, after explaining the history of her exit from ER care, Emma concluded. "I've always taken pride in paying careful attention to the details of my work. I'm more aware of its importance now than ever before, because, to coin the cliché, a rug can be pulled out from under you in a millisecond. In ways you might not have ever seen coming. A crushing loss can happen no matter how talented you are, and no matter how diligent your efforts. That's my takeaway from the whole nightmare I fell into. I suppose that makes me overly cautious and tentative, but, so be it. Operating with caution and care are the only ways I've found to survive." Speaking the words became transformative, a stunning and unexpected form of liberation that left Emma temporarily speechless.

Fortunately, Dr. Rhodan stepped into the breach. "Emma, your commitment is admirable. So is your determination. Never — ever — are we protected from outside circumstances that can build into a disaster. I've always believed if you practice medicine long enough you eventually find yourself on the losing side of a battle. Especially in the field of emergency health care. Your attitude affirms the belief I held from the start that you'd be an invaluable part of my team. I'd love to have you join our ranks, if you're interested."

A short time later, their meeting concluded. Emma tooled around Fort Wayne for the remainder of the day, lost in a daze, encapsulated by a surreal sensation of floating, of finally . . . *finally* . . . finding a path toward the bright, engaging future of which she had always dreamed. She ate lunch at a local restaurant, grateful for solitude as she lost herself in thought. While sipping soda and savoring a turkey club and coleslaw, she went through an internal review of the finer points of her conversation with Dr. Rhodan.

Success. She could dub it nothing but a success.

Later that afternoon, she returned to Antioch, knowing just one thing to be true. Now, she had to explain this offer to Aaron. She needed his input, but most of all, she needed to know whether the feelings they had found would transcend a move forward that would take her away from a home base she had grown to love — on numerous levels.

12

A rolling bell chime signaled an incoming call to Aaron's cell phone from Emma. He paused from clearing the last bits of brush and dead leaves from the flower beds in front of his home. He yanked his mobile device from the pocket of his coat, fighting a shiver with the warm anticipation of talking to Emma. Already, he smiled.

"Super Nurse."

Her chuckle traveled to him through cyber space. "Hey there, Farmer Man."

It was Aaron's turn to laugh. "Nice. How are you doing?"

"Good. You busy? Have a few minutes to —"

"Never too busy for you." He cut in fast. "Come on by. I'll treat you to dinner after you help me bag some landscaping refuse."

"I can do that."

"On second thought, maybe I won't even put you through manual labor. I can't wait to see you."

Her laughter tickled his ear, and his senses. "Right back at you, charmer."

Prickles of expectation left Aaron cheery. He whistled through his teeth, grinned like a fool. Yep, he was a goner. With all the certainty in his heart, he knew he had found the woman he longed to hold and cherish . . . forever. Never had he messed around with emotions. He wasn't the type. On instinct alone he had always been wired as an 'all in' or 'all out' kind of guy. Never did he doubt the direction of his heart. Sometimes that was a blessing, sometimes a curse, but Aaron could live with the consequences either way, provided he owned up to the truths of his heart.

After he cleaned up and changed from work clothes to more presentable attire, Aaron stood before the tall oak bureau stationed near the entrance of his bedroom. He pulled open the top drawer and drew a restorative breath when his fingers wrapped around a black velvet ring box. He pulled the case free, turning it around and around. They were inching closer and closer. It was time. He slipped the box into the front pocket of his slacks and squeezed it tight a few minutes later when he watched her car turn into his driveway. She parked and he met her on the porch.

Aaron pulled her in tight, claiming her lips, feasting, allowing their precious connection to warm his body, and his very soul.

"Mmm." Her happy murmur vibrated between them.

That's when Aaron realized — one of those gauzy, floaty skirts she favored peeked from the bottom hem of her hip-length wool coat. She wore makeup. Some snazzy jewelry. Emma was polished, as though coming home from work, but today was her day off — and besides which, her attire was definitely not a standard set of Briar-sanctioned scrubs.

"You're dressed for success today. What's up?"

His words seemed to flip a switch. Easy affection transformed to a blush, a seemingly guilty hesitance . . . Aaron reached for her hands to assure and received another shock. Absent of gloves, her skin was ice cold. "You OK, Emma?"

"Of course. I just wanted to . . . you know . . . talk. I just wanted to see you."

Aaron's stomach tightened when he sensed she shared only half the truth. "You don't need to sell me on that idea. Come on inside. Does tea sound good?"

She relaxed and smiled. "Perfect, yes.

Thank you."

After hanging Emma's coat in the entry closet, Aaron grabbed a pair of mugs from the cabinet, claimed the handle of a nearby teapot then double checked the variety of blends he kept available in a chrome tea caddy — thanks be to Mom. He placed the box in front of Emma, who settled on a padded stool at the breakfast counter. The counter provided a welcome sense of openness while dividing his eat-in kitchen from the great room, and the sight of her there, in his space, warmed Aaron through.

When she remained silent, he decided to push. "So, tell me about your day."

"Actually, I spent the day in Fort Wayne."

Though taken by surprise, Aaron kept quiet. He made note of her hesitance, though, and the nervous way she laced and unlaced her fingers.

Tentatively she continued. "I had a meeting with Dr. Rhodan."

"Wow. Tell me about it." He poured hot water into a teapot and set it to boil before joining her at the breakfast nook. She didn't offer much right away. The kettle sang and he poured, watching Emma steep her selection of orange jasmine. At last, he reached out, tucking his fingertips beneath her hand and giving a gentle squeeze designed to draw her away from her stall tactics. "C'mon, Emma. You can talk to me. What's going on."

She blew out a puff of air then turned toward him, eyes earnest, beseeching. "He's offering me a position on his critical care team. A really good one. It appeals to me. But, it also terrifies me. Additionally, if I accepted, I might have to move from Antioch."

"For Fort Wayne?" When she nodded, he took the initiative. "Fort Wayne's not far, though."

She shrugged. "Am I that easy to send packing?" Full lips tipped upward, but the playful, teasing gesture didn't ring true.

Aaron delivered a mock glower. "I won't even dignify that question with an answer."

"I'm just not sure." Her shoulders sagged beneath a weight it seemed she alone could see . . . and bear. "The job would be a pressure cooker. It'd put me back in the hospital setting, combining my work on his surgical team with his private practice, and it would take me away from a town, and people, that are such a blessing to me. All the same —"

"All the same, what?" He posed the query gently, but his nerves stung, and he hung on every beat of silence that passed.

"This job opportunity brings back a lot of

283

memories. A lot of bad memories. Gut-twisting anxiety. A potential for heart break . . . again . . . if I have to say goodbye to someone, someplace, that I care for so much."

Hope sang a song through Aaron's spirit, and he clung tight to the uplift. "Those are understandable feelings, all things being equal." He slid his hand into the pocket of his slacks, and squeezed the ring box as he reigned in every instinct to push and press. Instead, he prepared to jump off a precipice with no safety net to catch him if he made a mistake. Instead, he pressed on. "Maybe now, considering the offer, you can finally stand up for yourself, and your gifts, and look God — and life — in the eyes all over again. Seems to me like this opportunity is divine provision."

Emma nibbled on her lower lip, and Aaron stared, captivated by the vision, hoping and wishing and praying as he moved inexorably closer to his heart's point of no return. "Fort Wayne is just a stone's throw. Now that things are stabilizing at the farm, maybe I could find work in the city. Farming organizations are always in need of field officers who are knowledgeable in the ag industry. There's more I could do than just harvest work at the farm."

"You're not serious."

"Try me."

Emma blinked; her chest rose and fell. "You mean to say you'd do that? You'd leave all of this to . . ." Emma took a deep breath, and she trembled as she looked outside the great room window, at the now dormant rolls of brown land sliding into the deep sleep of winter.

"I would, for you," he affirmed quietly. "We could live somewhere in between."

Now, she trembled outright. "We."

"We. You know. In the future."

For an instant, her eyes went soft, and wide with love. "Aaron, you have to think this through."

"I already have." Soft, giving fibers of velvet skimmed against his fingertips when he tucked his right hand into his pocket once more.

"What would happen during the summer? What would happen during the harvest? Those are the times when you're most needed at the farm. You can't split yourself in two right when everything has evened out and come to fruition for your family. You need them, and you need the farm, and you need proximity."

"Emma, we're talking about the potential of living maybe twenty minutes away from

Antioch. That's hardly a deal breaker. Makes me wonder. What's really the issue here? Residual fear, maybe?"

Emma's jaw dropped; she stared, but regrouped fast. "Fear? Hardly! You should have seen and heard me today, Aaron. I presented myself for what I am — a survivor. A re-emerging force to be reckoned with. I was confident."

"Just as I'd expect. It seems to me Dr. Rhodan is right to offer you an exceptional opportunity. He sees what we've all seen in you. You're a woman of skill and character. But, that's your job. What about the rest of your life? What about your heart? Will you hold back? Will you keep looking for reasons to step away from life's risks?"

"That's not fair." Color bloomed in her cheeks. "If I wanted to step back, I never would have met with him in the first place, and . . . well . . . with regard to you . . . and me . . . I . . . I'm looking at the future as well."

"Are you sure about that?" She paused just long enough that he nodded. "Take the chance. Leap, Emma. Then, fly. Don't lock yourself up so tight that you take to the sidelines instead of the battle at midfield. To coin another cliché, no man is an island. You've got skills, and you've got a lot of good people in your corner. Let them in. Let *me* in. Trust, and have faith."

She looked at him for a long while, her lips trembling. "I'm learning. At least, I'm trying to."

"Me, too." Aaron turned. With his free arm, he pulled her close until she settled snug and perfect against his side. "And, maybe this will help."

At last, he tugged the ring box from its hiding place and flipped open the lid. Emma gasped, reaching up to touch the round-cut solitaire. Even in the recessed lighting from above, the diamond he offered sparkled with a captivating shower of vibrancy and life.

"Oh, my goodness. Aaron . . . this is stunning."

He melted, because he could tell she didn't just mean the diamond ring.

He was traditional, and he was only doing this once in his life. Since he was about to lay claim to his soul mate, Aaron knelt before her, keeping her left hand secure in both of his. "Emma, I don't come by the softer side of life, and emotions, with ease, but you bring that out in me. You bring out the best in me, and I love you. I want us to build a life. A life full of love and laughter and arguments and pain and joy that we share. *Together.* Stick with me. I know how much you crave that clean slate, but you need to realize something. You're already there. Through guts, tenacity, and love you've made it. You've gained traction and you've found your way to what you want the most. Trust that path. Trust God's direction. And after that, I hope you'll know one thing more to be true. I'm with you. All the way."

Tears spilled over the lush curves of her lashes. She stroked his cheeks and all over again, he melted, softened, going easy and giving in ways he had never dreamed imaginable.

"You're this certain?"

"Emma, I've been sure of you since the moment we met. I've never felt this kind of love before. I know enough to realize it's sacred. You're sacred. Being with you is what God wants from me next." He smiled into her eyes. "That is, if you're willing to take me on."

In an official manner, she straightened and extended her left hand, her eyes sparkling so beautifully the precious gem he offered was put to utter shame. "My answer is yes . . . yes, yes, yes."

He pulled the ring from its case and tucked it into place, kissing her knuckles before he stood and swooped her into his arms with a spin and a much richer, headier kiss. "So, you're ready? You're ready to take this on and follow God's lead?"

"I am. For always, and with all that I am, as long as I'm with you."

■ ■ ■ ■

THE JOURNEY

■ ■ ■ ■

In loving memory of Homer Evans.
Your 'Journey' through this life created
an incredible legacy. You championed a
large and boisterous family, yet always
had a way of making each and every
one of us feel special, and prized.
What a gift — and I treasure it still.

1

He said to them, "Come, follow me. I will make you fishers of men."
~ Matthew 4:19

An early-spring daybreak spread across the flat farmlands of rural Indiana. This was the time of day Ben Fisher liked best. Peace and the kind of contemplative solitude his spirit always seemed to crave held sway at sunrise. Settling against the thick cushions of the front porch swing, releasing a chest-deep sigh of contentment, he set the seat into motion, pushing a booted heel gently against creaky floor boards. The porch's wrap-around awning needed fresh shingles, but that was an issue he'd contend with later.

He considered the moniker held for gener-ations now. *The Fisher Farm.* His lips curved automatically. This spot formed a legacy purchased through generations of sweat and toil. This place provided not just nourishment of the land, but of the community. His family had taken that fact to heart for close to two centuries as some of the first inhabitants of Antioch.

It's not a coincidence our town is called Antioch, Dad had said time and again, pride swelling through his broad chest, lifting his wide shoulders as he walked the soybean fields. *The founders — my great-great grandfather among them — were very deliberate. They looked to the Bible for a name and chose Antioch. Antioch is where the first-ever Christians gathered as a formalized community. I guess our ancestors figured we'd be keeping good company.*

Nowadays, so many people would consider such sentimentality corny, or outdated. Ben's take was different. He understood the vibrations of Antioch. It was home, and he valued the atmosphere of the small, tight-knit community where he had been born and raised.

Except . . .

An increasingly familiar itch, a yearning he hadn't even recognized before, slipped beneath his skin as he stared out across dew-kissed fields of soybeans that rolled for hundreds of acres. Fog lifted slowly, like eerie wafts of steam. The itch had followed him ever since last week's sermon at Antioch Christian church, when Reverend Maxwell Taylor had launched a spirited proclamation on missionary opportunities. Ben stretched his legs. Relaxed rather than anxious, he continued to mull things over.

A cardinal swept across the yard, drawing him back to the view. The vivid red bird flitted and chirped. Ben cradled a bistro mug of coffee between his hands. Warm, earthy fragrance tantalized his nose and he absorbed the subtle increase of bird song as he sipped. Against the eastern edge of the sky, translucent hues of pearlescent gray melded into pink. Hints of orange, buttery yellow swirled through wispy white clouds. Light shimmered, iridescent as the sun peeked and then rose. Low-lying crops shimmered and swayed against the soft caress of a breeze. That gentle ripple of air stirred freshness, a floral infused welcome to spring. Ben was surrounded by his father's soybean crop and the scent of moist soil.

We're entering the spring season, a time of regeneration. In life and in mission. Embrace the idea of taking on a challenge. Answer a call to help our brothers and sisters at our twin parish in Pine Bluff, Arkansas. If this call to service speaks to your heart, please don't shy away or question God's prompt. Explore the pathway and determine if there's a fit. Because there certainly is a need, my friends. Reverend Taylor's words to the church community played out for, oh, probably the hundredth time.

This time, disquiet wouldn't be quelled, or ignored. Ben hummed a low, frustrated exclamation, his eyes narrowing until he refocused. What was going on? He wasn't unhappy or dissatisfied with his life at the farm, so why did he ache all of a sudden? Why did he find himself Google-searching missions, and Arkansas these days?

Subtle pots-and-pans clamor sounded from the kitchen, through an open window just behind the spot where he sat. Mom was up, likely fixing breakfast for herself and Pop. Oatmeal spiced by cinnamon, a touch of brown sugar, along with a heap of fresh fruit made the menu most days. Toast, too, because heart condition or not, Pop insisted on the crunch and sweet of toast covered by a slather of homemade jam.

Reclaiming his typical sense of calm, Ben smiled. The jam came courtesy of the Thomas family. His brother Phillip's fiancée, Mila, had dropped off a fresh jar when she came over for dinner the other night. They'd be getting married at the end of July, and Ben couldn't wait to stand up for his oldest brother and celebrate a most unexpected love affair come to perfect fruition.

Thoughts of Mila Thomas led quite naturally to the image of Mila's younger sister, Hailey Beth. A natural connection due to family ties . . . and nothing more. Sure, Hailey Beth was a person he'd known since he was old enough to walk. Sure, she was a petite, big-eyed dynamo who could go from butter soft to steel strong in the time it took to blink — a fascinating combination — but beyond that, she was simply a good friend. A familiar and appealing part of his life. Affection for her came as naturally as . . .

Ben's gaze tracked to the ancient, massive barn that crowned a swell of land on their property. Studiously maintained, its hay-covered floors had been the spot he had shared his first kiss. At seven-years-old. With HB.

That coy and sweet little fireball.

His smile curved wide at the image he held of her perfectly shaped figure, the long waves of chocolate brown hair that tumbled around her shoulders, those full lips. Oh, man, did he need a distraction. Polishing off the last of his coffee, Ben stood, intending to join his mom. Maybe he could score a helping of food if he chipped in with preps.

Just as he turned toward the door, a rumble, steady and increasing, drifted across the now gold-burnished fields of the farm. In seconds, a train whistle echoed across the dips and flats, coming closer, with chattering wheels and a rhythmic pulse he could have sworn he felt vibrating through the wooden floorboards, the soles of his work boots.

The train wasn't that close, though. The stirring of the air and his body was purely phantom. Psychological. A call to move. A call to action.

A call — mysterious and scary — urged him away from the only home he'd ever known.

Hailey Beth Thomas swallowed a bite of cereal — a favorite breakfast-for-lunch option — taking a break from her regularly scheduled duties at Thomas's Grocery Store. She sat a large, time-worn wooden desk in the office she now occupied. Dad had opted for full retirement from daily operations at the mercantile almost six months ago, giving Hailey Beth free rein to run the business that had been in their family for over a hundred years.

While she ate, pairing cereal with a freshly toasted English muffin topped by a smidge of butter and a layer of her mom's home-made strawberry jam, HB reviewed supply orders and processed some invoice payments. Multi-tasking at its best.

Crunching into the muffin, she savored the creamy sweetness that melted over her tongue and tapped out an e-mail to one of the distributors she worked with, finalizing delivery of a couple cases of canned goods in need of stocking.

She paused for a spoonful of cereal and her cell phone came to life with a rippling wave of music. Incoming text. Benjamin Fisher. Hailey Beth's heart performed a literal skip-flop.

Mom's making toast with jam for dad. And for me. Makes me think of you and your fam. Prob be by l8r with a grocery list to be filled.

Sharing breakfast, with Ben. All matters work related fled on a cloud of delight. Hailey Beth didn't sigh out loud, but her smile spread fast and large as she picked up her phone and rapid-fired a reply.

Ha! Well, enjoy the irony. I'm just finishing an English muffin with jam. Great minds and all. Stop by. I'm here all day.

A laughing emoji followed shortly thereafter, as well as: *C U then HB.*

"Well aren't you just beaming as bright as a sunbeam?"

Hailey Beth jostled to proper focus, a hot blush warming her neck and cheeks as her older sister Mila sassed off and breezed into the office with a knowing grin curving her lips. Hailey Beth stashed her phone and cleared her throat — guilty convictions both — while Mila plopped down in the chair in front of the desk. Mila said nothing more. Hailey Beth attempted to return to those inventory orders and invoice payments. She had to retype her e-mail twice all the while trying to ignore her sister's presence and pushy silence.

Mila stretched her legs, released a contented sigh. "You know, I've got all day."

"No, you don't. You have a shop to run, same as me. What's on your mind besides being a needle?"

"I'm a needle? Really? I certainly don't mean to be. All I did was compliment your . . . you know . . . glow."

Oh, Lord help her. Hailey Beth knew a sweetly-laced bout of goading when she heard it. "I'm glowing?" She scowled, turning slowly to face her sibling, hoping her killer gaze would scare her sister into submission.

"Well, no. Not anymore." Mila relented, leaning forward. "Seriously, though, you seemed pretty happy before I walked in and tweaked you."

No sense hiding from Mila. She knew Hailey Beth better than anyone on the planet. "I just got a real nice text."

"From?"

Oh, who do you *think would send me into an all-over glow?* "Ben." She offered nothing else, and spoke casually, too. Naturally, that only returned Mila to a prodding, irritating silence. Unable to tolerate the empty void, Hailey Beth groaned. "He's enjoying Mom's strawberry jam. And it just so happened that I am, too." With a flourish, Hailey Beth waved a hand toward the remains of her muffin. "I got a kick out of the similarities."

Now it was Mila who glowed. "HB, that's so cool! He reached out just to share a tidbit? That's so . . . tantalizing . . . so *not* like our reticent Ben Fisher!"

Hailey Beth heaved a gigantic sigh. "Oh, please. Calm down and come back to earth, my sister of romance. You're letting wedding butterflies and rainbows color your entire world. Speaking of, what's the latest on the nuptial front?"

"I'm so excited! Rochelle is coming into town from Chicago this weekend and she's staying at my place for a couple weeks so we can start alterations, plan details, and just hang out together, like we used to before she moved away."

The diversionary tactic worked like a charm. It was one thing for Mila to know Hailey Beth had a crush . . . since forever . . . on the youngest Fisher man, but to dwell on such a hopeless topic wasn't worthwhile. Hailey Beth was a BFF to Ben, and vice-versa. Things had been that way since their childhood, and there was nothing on the horizon set to change that fact.

Unlike Hailey Beth, Ben didn't want anything more.

Mila continued with wedding details and Hailey Beth tuned back in. Rochelle was Mila's best friend growing up; renewing ties would be great fun. "We'll finally have all four bridesmaids assembled in one place, at one time, for an epic shopping adventure."

"That we are. It's becoming very real for me, and for Phillip, bless his heart. He's been a rock."

"And so have you. Not a bridezilla to be found." Hailey Beth shared a smile. "Are you still leaning toward the teal lace cocktail dresses?"

"Definitely. I love the flounce of the skirt once you get all that tulle action going on beneath it. Those dresses have such a cool, vintage vibe."

"I agree. The cap sleeves and sweetheart neckline are very classy and Audrey Hepburn chic." Hailey Beth propped her elbows on the desktop, fully captured by the idea of love, and celebration, and marriage . . . and the dresses *were* divine.

"You like that choice?"

"Love it. I'm all in."

"I think a white pashmina shawl would polish it to perfection. You never know what the spring weather might hold, and the reception will be at Phillip's farm, beneath a silk tent, twinkle lights galore."

"I'm sold, I'm sold."

"You better be, oh, maid of honor." They exchanged grins. "You know, while we're out this weekend, you could pick up a second little cocktail number for the Founder's Day Celebration in a couple weeks."

"I could. If I had a date. And if I had any interest in actually attending the dance."

"Stop being antisocial."

"I'm very sociable, but I'm certainly not going to the dance solo."

"The dance is only a small part of an entire weekend of festivities, which you know. There's the carnival, the silent auction. You have to take part. It'll be fun."

Hailey Beth ignored the logic. "But the dance is the big event. I don't see a lineup of men pounding on the door asking me to join them."

"That's only because every available guy within a ten-mile radius knows you're off the market."

Hailey Beth reared back. "As if! I'm not off the market! I'm not involved with any—"

"Strawberry jam, anyone?" Mila cut in with decisiveness, and an arched brow.

Hailey Beth gaped.

"Think about it, HB. With that, I'm off. Sundae Afternoon calls."

Before any type of a sputtering reply could be delivered, Mila was gone, vacating the back offices of the mercantile as swiftly as she had arrived, leaving Hailey Beth prickly and alert. Edgy.

Wistful.

In deliberate retaliation, she growled, muttering beneath her breath. "And so it goes in the life of HB Thomas. Sheesh." Irritated and piqued, she buried herself in the tasks at hand: running the family grocery store and packing away her feelings for one Benjamin Fisher.

2

Sunday morning, Ben left the farm an hour before his folks woke up and got ready for church. Kind of like a guilty thief skulking away from the scene of a crime.

But he *wasn't.*

He was twenty-four. He continued to live beneath his parents' roof for several reasons that had nothing to do with dependence or a lack of ambition. His father's health was a factor, as was an on-going need for physical assistance at the farm. Phillip ran the business side. Ben and Aaron contended with crop production, machine maintenance, home maintenance.

And, like Phillip, Aaron was set to be married before too long. Romance was blooming in Antioch, Indiana.

Hailey Beth's face drifted to the fore.

It was time to lay roots, or break free, and if he didn't break free, he'd have nothing to show for his life except for what he had been given by his family's name. There was nothing wrong with that, but he wanted something of his own. Something he created from his own calling. He rebuked HB's image with calm finality. She was one of his dearest and most trusted friends. Never, ever would he take a sledgehammer to such an important relationship by entertaining the idea of romance.

Ben enjoyed hands-on engagement with the earth, with the home into which he had been born and raised. The farm was large — five bedrooms, an office, a huge dining room and living room. There was room to breathe. He enjoyed woodworking as well as mechanical tinkering — such things kept him sharp and focused. Centered, too.

Except for that blasted sermon from a few weeks ago.

Except for Hailey Beth. Why the sudden itch where she was concerned? An eminent separation, perhaps? The idea of not having her close by any longer?

Turning off that bout of internal static, Ben cranked the engine of his truck, easing down the gravel drive, heading toward the outskirts of town. Soon, he could see the gleaming brass spire of Antioch Christian Church, piercing a dark blue sky unfettered by clouds and kissed by a breeze that slid through the open window of his vehicle.

He strode into the communal space like thousands of times before. From there, the scariest walk of Ben's life took place along the length of a long, nondescript hallway dotted by doorways that led to classrooms, meeting spaces and offices. He knew every square inch of this place, but never had he approached its walls with such anxiety and uncertainty.

Lord, please help me, Ben beseeched. *I want to serve and honor you. Always.*

With all the work and effort required at the farm, should he even entertain this meeting and idealistic mission program? Should he throw his life into the ring of a service project about which he knew nothing?

He was ready for this scheduled meeting with Reverend Taylor. He wasn't signing up yet. Besides, the very decision over which he agonized could easily be a polite but firm, 'No, thank you.' There might even be ways to support the church's outreach to Arkansas by donating tools, or money. This was a fact-finding mission. Nothing more.

A closed door marked by a plaque bore the Reverend's name. Shoring his resolve, Ben squelched his anxiety and knocked.

"Come on in."

Ben twisted the knob, stepping inside.

Ben sat through the services that followed, head spinning, unfocused and unabsorbing of the sermon that took place.

Reverend Taylor walked to the front of the church, ambled the aisles, friendly and warm.

Ben didn't hear a word. His attention centered on the pew before him. There, the Thomas family lined up as they had for generations. Ben couldn't take his eyes off Hailey Beth. As soon as services were over, he intended to pull her aside and talk. Like, seriously, at-length, from-the-heart talk. She was a terrific listener, a confidante he relied on, and from the first memories he possessed of HB, he counted her as one of his sweetest, dearest friends. He needed to lean on that relationship and his HB Sounding Board in a major way.

An ache settled hard against the depths of his chest. Thick waves of long brown hair tumbled against the lip of the dark wood pew, tempting his fingers into a twitch. Hailey Beth was angled away from him, but she looked straight ahead, attentive to the sermon. He required no direct access to envision large, rich brown eyes, or the subtle curve of soft lips.

Ben called a halt to idealistic thought patterns, frowning as his gaze skimmed across her slender shoulders, along the lines of a diminutive figure clothed by a simple white button-down blouse, a black skirt. Crossed knees drew his attention to slim legs, leather heels, and an escalating need that pulsed just beneath his skin as unexpectedly . . . and powerfully . . . as the idea of being part of a missionary assignment far from home.

Ben forced his way through the conclusion of church, trying hard to engage, but failing. He prayed with sincerity for mercy and understanding, knowing he received it. All the same, he didn't like the idea of not being mentally present for worship.

When services finished, Ben ignored decorum. By and large, he bypassed socialization and homed in on HB, greeting friends only as necessary. Singularity of purpose led him to her side, guiding him to the moment when he stepped up to her from behind and slid a familiar hand against her arm, up to her shoulder.

"Hey, HB."

Did he imagine the rise of goose flesh along her skin? The way she trembled just slightly?

"Ben. Hey."

"Got a minute?" He murmured the words

quietly, into the curve of her ear, trying to be unobtrusive as she concluded conversations with the Havershill family. She smelled like gardenias and jasmine. His nerve endings danced in response.

"For you? Always." Polite and kind, she concluded her mingling session.

Ben added his own greetings before leading Hailey Beth away with a directing touch at her elbow. It always felt so good to have her at his side. In his corner. "Sorry to interrupt." He apologized as he led her toward his truck in the parking lot. "Can you break away for breakfast?"

Her brows furrowed. "Right now? What about breakfast with the families?"

"There's always supper, right?"

Hailey Beth nodded, her surprise continuing.

Suddenly, he realized how desperate he sounded for her company. How could he explain himself in a brief conversation? "I've got something on my mind."

"So it would seem." Her eye sparkled playfully.

"I'd like to run something past you, if that's OK." Ben could have sworn he saw something in her eyes, felt something in the way she reached out, rested a hand on his forearm, that triggered a heated pulse. A pull.

"Just give me a second. Let me tell Mom and Dad I can't make breakfast."

Ben took hold of her free hand, delivered a squeeze. "I'll do the same with mine. Thanks, HB."

She stepped away, but turned back, looking over her shoulder, her concern visible. "Hey . . . you OK?"

Ben smiled his assurance, pulled in by her tenderness. "I will be now. Thanks for shuffling things. I appreciate it."

Her shoulders relaxed. "Not a problem."

Lesterfeld's was one of a handful of classic mom-and-pop restaurants that dotted the landscape of Antioch's town center. Ben guided Hailey Beth inside, again with that warm hand at the back which stirred a pleasant tingle against her skin. She admired him anew, wondering how something as conservative as a simple gray dress suit could cause her pulse to pound. A royal blue tie, white button down, and spotless dress shoes spoke clearly of a man respectful of traditions and Sunday worship. He was clean shaven, his chestnut hair styled into thick, smooth waves. Bearing a strong-muscled frame, Ben had always struck

Hailey Beth as a noble knight, a romantic guardian. She sighed inwardly, knowing she needed to either get over this infatuation thing, or be doomed to live in solitude for the rest of her life.

"There's an open table toward the back."

Distracted by her thoughts, Hailey Beth simply followed his lead and directing touch, settling across from him at a bistro table covered by red linen, cutlery, condiments, and menus.

Already knowing she'd opt for blueberry pancakes and sausage, Hailey Beth opened the laminated menu but paid only a cursory glance to the selections. Ben, she noticed, did much the same. She'd bet the family store on him ordering a western omelet.

Attention focused, Ben leaned forward, forearms propped against the tabletop. "So, I had a meeting with Reverend Taylor before church today."

"You did? About what?"

Their waitress delivered a pair of coffees, poured them each some iced water. Hailey Beth nabbed her mug and sipped. *Ah, bliss . . .*

"Mission work. Participating in the service program he talked about a few weeks ago. In Arkansas."

Shock struck home like a well-placed arrow. Next came a tight squeeze to her heart. A sting to her nerves. Hailey Beth swallowed fast so she wouldn't sputter liquid. "What?"

Ben nodded, eyes alight. "Yeah. The mission program he talked about with Christ Our Savior Church in Pine Bluff."

Their waitress approached and inquired about orders.

"Western omelet, please. Large orange juice, too."

Hailey ached while she murmured a request for breakfast. So much about him was familiar to her. Precious. And he was excited about leaving. Energized by the idea. Had he been so uninspired, so unhappy in Antioch?

The heart squeeze turned into a hard, fast plummet. Hailey Beth openly stared, powerless to quell the reaction. Seriously. Ben Fisher, the most grounded, rooted member of the Fisher clan — the tight-knit Fisher clan — would soon be on his way to new horizons far from the farmlands of Indiana.

Unreal.

In the face of her silence, the spark in Ben's eyes dimmed considerably. "You're shocked."

No way to deny it. "Yes . . . yes, I am . . . but . . . I mean, if it's what you want to do, then I think it's great." Such a lie, but what was she supposed to do? Deny him happiness because of unrequited, misbegotten emotions? No way. Her eyes stung with tears, so she bit her lower lip. Now, Ben's light faded from view.

"You think it's a mistake. Nuts."

He sighed, pulling at the corners of a paper napkin, focused on the fidgets rather than Hailey Beth. She needed to move fast.

"Oh, Ben . . . no such thing. Truly." She rested her hand on top of his to ease his nervousness and sooth her own uncertainty by touching him, forming a connection. "Tell me more."

She imbued the request with as much enthusiasm as possible, but her world hazed and slowed to a halt. He must have sensed the uptick in her attitude, false as it was, because Ben launched into an animated description of everything Reverend Taylor had detailed during their meeting.

"The goal of this project is to lend assistance to people who can't afford general home maintenance and upkeep. It's an agricultural region of the state, which is why our church twinned with them to begin with. There's mutual understanding of the positives and negatives of living off the land."

Hailey Beth kept quiet but nodded. What

was going on here? What had happened to him, to the appealing draw of hometown life? What had happened to routine and security and expectation? When, and how, had Ben's life shifted so dramatically without her even noticing?

He continued. "The Ozark Mission Project is endorsed by the Reframe Association, which is kind of a big deal."

"Yeah? Because?"

"Well, Reframe is a non-profit that only backs programs that maintain the highest level of home repair and remodeling. Reverend Taylor has picked a great group to work with, and I have skills that can be put to good use. HB, I can help these people, simply by supplying knowledge and a little elbow grease."

And heart. Miles and miles of heart. She could tell Ben was on spiritual fire for the challenges and joys to come. Nevertheless, a piece of her spirit shattered. She could almost see the piercing shards glittering as they sliced away her self-control, her hopes, a cherished dream . . .

"God gave me gifts. I want to use them. I want to serve." Ben hunched forward and shrugged broad, wide shoulders. "I'll be back. I mean, this isn't forever, but it's weird. I feel as if this is something I should

317

do. More than that, this is something I *want* to do."

Hailey Beth tried to speak; the lump in her throat made doing so a tough proposition. "Then you have to give it a try. If you're not where you're at, you're no place."

Ben's turbulent gaze lifted, tagging hers. Gratitude rolled off him in waves. "That's it exactly, HB. *Exactly.* I'm not here anymore. Not completely. Not from the heart."

With that statement, a door slammed closed on the deepest chamber of her heart, the one that belonged to Ben alone. He had made himself perfectly clear. She had no choice but to open her tightened fists and let him go.

Because he had never belonged to her in the first place.

Thankfully their waitress arrived with heaping platters of food and they began to enjoy their breakfast. Hailey Beth pasted on a smile, prepared to support him as the friend she was rather than the besotted fool who had carried a torch for him for way too long.

"I'm behind you all the way. I'll miss you like crazy, of course, but I think mission work is a wonderful path to explore. You need to see what it's all about. Home will always be here. Your family will always be here."

I'll be here.

The words nearly danced from her mind to her lips. She stemmed them just in time to maintain silence. Distance. Control. Still, the lump in her throat grew tighter, tough to contain and even tougher to ignore.

"I love my family, all my friends," his pointed gaze lingered on hers. "I love the farm. Those facts will never change no matter where I am. Thing is . . . I feel a pull. A pull that I can't even explain, and certainly never expected."

"When would you leave?"

"In a few months. After the harvest. I won't leave my family until after the fall. They need all hands on deck, and, I'd sign on for a year with the chance to re-up when the year is finished."

"I'm excited for you." Another lie. They kept piling up.

"You sure about that?" He pressed gently, as calm as ever, a teasing quirk to his lips. In his eyes, though, was concern. A search for her genuine response. "I really want your opinion about this."

"I'm surprised."

"Can't blame you for that."

Hailey Beth's pancakes and sausage tasted

like sawdust, no fault of the cook, and landed in her stomach like dead weight. Still, she smiled when all she wanted to do was cry.

"My folks will be stunned, too, I'm sure. Phillip and Aaron as well. You're the one I wanted to turn to first. I trust you, and care about your feelings. Am I nuts? Is it wrong to want to break away? To try something new? Something of my own? Is it selfish?"

Her gaze lifted to his. From the heart, she shook her head and answered. "Not at all. You're one of the least selfish people I know, Ben."

His shoulders relaxed and Ben breathed deep, his chest rising and falling while a smile — a real smile — crested. "Thanks, HB. That means a lot to me. You mean a lot to me."

Maybe. She didn't doubt his sincerity. *But I don't mean enough for you to stay in Antioch, and remain part of a world I can never leave.*

3

Ben stood at the entryway of the farm office, shoulder propped against the doorframe, his arms folded across his chest. "I have to do *what*, exactly?" His eyes narrowed, the only clear indicator of his irritation.

Phillip sat behind the desk, swiveling back and forth in the black leather chair that was older than the two of them. And Ben's eldest brother had the gall to smile. *Smile*, confound it all.

"You have to get fitted for the tux, Ben. We can't guess about these things."

"I have to stand in front of a mirror and go through the whole measuring tape thing? Seriously?"

"Part and parcel of the whole groomsmen's gig. Sorry. Not."

"No, this whole tux thing is the tough gig. Being . . . fitted . . . for it is humiliating."

"Was that a sneer I heard in your voice?"

Phillip rocked back in the chair, eyes sparkling with mischief. Phillip was an older version of Ben from a physical perspective. They both favored their father in build and coloring.

Aaron's features were somewhat more angular, his eyes clear and intense, with an amber hue that copied their mother, Anna. They were a good compilation, though Phillip and Aaron had withstood some nasty battles when Phillip returned home from Indianapolis once his cushy career failed to provide the success and security he craved.

Speaking of Aaron . . . "So, how's the best man holding up to all this nip and tuck and measure stuff?"

Phillip hooted. "Oh, about like you'd expect. Aaron's groaning, grumbling a bunch of trash-talk about being a male fashionista, rolling his eyes repeatedly. But, he's coming through, as always. Just like you. I appreciate it. Mila does, too."

Ben froze. He could talk about the mission opportunity. The perfect segue had just opened. He looked long and hard at his big brother and came to the decision at once. This, like Hailey Beth had correctly observed, was home. This was his safe zone. He could confide in Phillip. In fact, he wanted to.

Phillip read him with a glance and his eyes went sharp. "OK, what's on your mind?"

"What do you mean?"

"You went still. When you go all still and quiet, it's a sure sign you're rumbling on the inside. Classic Ben Fisher."

After a few more seconds of that classic Ben Fisher stillness, he moved forward and sat in the chair across from Phillip's desk. "Well . . . your attitude about my 'coming through' for folks just might change in a minute. Got some time to talk?"

"Always."

Not wasting time, Ben filled him in, not just on the mission project, but on his meeting with Hailey Beth a few days ago.

"Wow." Phillip tapped his fingers against the stack of papers sprawled across the wood desk.

"You're not the first to have that reaction."

"It's unexpected, too."

"I've heard that one, too."

Phillip rubbed at his lower lip, studying Ben. "But . . . it calls you."

"Yeah."

"Wordy, as always."

Ben shrugged and grinned at his brother, a sense of melancholy adding texture to the moment.

Sadness touched Phillip's eyes. "I think

it's a great opportunity. Have you broken the news to Mom and Dad yet?"

"I will once I'm sure matters are covered here at the farm. Otherwise, I'm not leaving. I don't want to leave anybody hanging, least of all Mom and Dad. All of us have been through a lot during the past year."

"And we emerged on top, thank God. I can't say you won't be missed. That'd be a flat out lie. We'll always be able to use your hand and care, but you're also talking to someone who knows how important it is to build a life to call your own. Things here are stable, Ben. Pop's in good shape. The surgery helped him turn a corner. He's found his leadership feet again. Aaron's rededicated to his role as manager and ag-specialist and I'm happy running the business end of things."

Sensing there was more to be said, Ben waited in quiet patience. Sure enough, instinct didn't prove him wrong.

"I have to admit, though —"

"Yeah?"

"I always thought that life of yours would include Antioch, and marriage, and a family."

Ben's pulse escalated. Visions of Hailey Beth danced straight though him, bright and alluring. What was going *on* with him lately?

"With that comment, I believe wedding fever has officially struck down the Fisher family like a virus." Ben's joke fell on somber ears. "Phillip, a volunteer stint for a year or two doesn't eliminate the prospect of marriage and a family in the future, or am I missing something?"

"I hope you don't." The declarative rested on air, pulsing with meaning, and entendre. "How'd HB take the news?"

Defensiveness rose to the top of Ben's normally placid surface. "Why's that important, versus the fact that I'm building a path out of town?"

Phillip watched him in a silence that built and lingered.

Ben could taste his sibling's exasperation.

"Know what? If you don't get it by now, Ben, I'm not gonna hand you a flashlight. Some things you need to learn on your own."

"What's that supposed to mean?" Ben barked the words.

"Just what it seems. Answer the question. How'd she react?"

"Surprised. That's about it."

"Really. That's all?"

Sure, there had been flashes of sadness,

maybe even a level of hurt, but they were lifelong friends. She'd miss him, and he'd surely miss her in return.

If you're not where you're at, you're no place.

Her words came back to him, amplified by a sense of truth, by the way she supported him, even though he sensed her disquiet. She was a true friend. She'd remain a part of his life in Antioch forever.

Until she got married and found her own path away from his. What then? Suddenly, Phillip's inquiry made perfect, albeit shattering, sense.

The idea of HB moving forward, apart from him, left Ben stunned to silence. He puzzled over the instant, painful tear that split through his spirit.

His big brother let him stew for a few minutes before returning to a layout of spreadsheets and numbers detailing farm production, revenue and expenses. Phillip chuckled beneath his breath and shook his head. "Just be ready for that ol' nip and tuck on Saturday morning."

Still troubled, Ben sighed stood. "Only for you, Phillip. Only for you."

"Don't speak too fast, bro. I'm sure Aaron'll be calling on your groomsmen services before too long. Then, someday, it'll be your turn at the plate."

Ben closed the office door with a bit more force than was strictly necessary to drown out the sound of his brother's relishing laughter.

Henderson's Formals and Tailoring was the only shop in town specializing in social occasion attire and fittings. The boutique's selection wasn't vast, but featured classic tuxedos for rent along with a number of lavish wedding, bridesmaid and prom dresses.

Hailey Beth hiked her purse higher, excited about the selection finalization and sizing session to come. Mila could have gone to Fort Wayne to purchase her gown and the dresses for her bridal party. Instead, she was keeping things local, feeding Antioch. That made Hailey Beth proud.

She followed four eager, bubbling women into the quaint, charming shop. Wood floors were covered by area rugs. Mirrors abounded, as well as a trio of matching crystal chandeliers that lent glittering illumination to three raised platforms where generations of brides, along with their families and attendants, had viewed and posed their selections. Glass cases featured jewelry, tiaras and satin gloves. Lining the far wall were a selection of shoes that were classic, and gorgeous. An archway divided the store in two. Behind that arch were lines and lines of suits, shirts, tuxedos, shoes, and display cases laden with every necessary accessory for the guys — cufflinks, cummerbunds, bowties, dress socks, and shoes.

Led by Mila, their party was greeted by owner Marilyn Henderson who already displayed the teal satin and lace covered sheath on a mannequin.

Rochelle Simmons, the only one who hadn't seen the dress yet, fell in love with the garment on sight. "Mila, this is stunning. I love the color and the style is fantastic!"

"I can't wait to wear it!" Emma Briggs, Aaron's fiancée, fingered the ample flounce of the skirt, brushing her fingers against fluffy layers of tulle. Emma had won Hailey Beth's friendship quickly. The blonde-haired, chocolate-eyed beauty was an increasingly important part of the fabric of town as a skilled and compassionate RN who divided her time between Fort Wayne and Antioch. "I love it as much today as I did when we found it last month."

"Same here. It's perfection." Hailey Beth chimed her approval, tucking an arm around her sister's slim waist. This wedding would be epic, and she couldn't be happier for Mila and Phillip.

"Are you sure?" Mila eyed her attendants nervously. "I don't want you to hate what you wear. That's always the worst when it comes to being in a wedding, isn't it?"

An enthusiastic chorus of support erased all doubt and excitement built.

Marilyn poured flutes of champagne, brought out a silver tray of cheese and crackers, then began the process of hunting down sizes and putting her seamstress to work. Meanwhile, the wedding party toasted the upcoming ceremony, reclined upon comfy couches, chatted, and gushed.

For Hailey Beth, the moment was perfect.

And, as maid of honor, Hailey Beth was the first one on the sizing block. Following a quick wardrobe change from jeans and a t-shirt into formalwear, she stood on a dais in front of a triple mirror while head seamstress Tara Ogilvee went about transforming her freshly-donned dress into personally tailored perfection. Behind her, a bell-chime sounded above the door, signaling the arrival of a customer.

Make that customers.

Phillip and his squad of groomsmen entered the store, and Phillip's attention homed in on Hailey Beth immediately since she was presently the only attendant being fitted. "Well, doesn't the maid of honor look stunning?"

Scandalized, Mila charged for her fiancée. "Get out of here! It's bad luck or something for you to see anything having to do with the wedding, and —"

Phillip's chuckle rumbled. "I'm not allowed to see your dress, love. The rest is fair game. Especially in a town the size of Antioch. Not much hope in all of us avoiding each other, but no worries. I arranged things with Marilyn so I'd be sure not to be near when you were modeling your chosen gown."

"You're a rat!" Mila chastised, but a rose-hued blush painted her cheeks and she melted into Phillip's arms when he drew her close and dotted her nose, then both cheeks, with tender kisses.

"I promised I wouldn't even peek," he declared with solemnity, still gazing into Mila's eyes. "Guys, are you looking at the dresses?"

Aaron snorted, and grinned, sweeping his future sister-in-law into a hug and a spin. "I've got better things to do."

Like his father, Aaron was larger than life, intense and passionate. Especially when he released Mila, and his attention homed in on his fiancée, Emma Briggs.

Hailey Beth could have sworn she saw

sparks, and stars, and an abiding vibration of love.

"Hey, Em, you keeping good notes? Our day is coming this fall, you know."

Emma, tall and graceful and bursting with sweet spirit, taunted her beau with an arched brow. "Wouldn't you like to know? You'll just have to wait and see what I have planned for you."

"I'm counting the days." Aaron captured her left hand, and kissed it gently. A lovely diamond solitaire winked beneath the lights.

The words were whispered, but carried clear to the depths of Hailey Beth's heart. Oh, to find such commitment, such depth of feeling.

When her attention rested on Ben, she felt vulnerable. Exposed. He had stopped short. He watched after her, and typically, his expression revealed not a thing. Calm, unreadable, he paused just long enough to absorb her with a long look before returning his focus to the guys in his pack and moving toward the men's section beneath the dividing arch of the store.

Just before the guys left, though, Rochelle tagged Ben, resting a hand on his forearm.

"Ben? Oh, my goodness! It's been *way* too long. How are you?" Cheek kisses ensued.

"I'm good. It's great to see you again, Rochelle. How long are you in town?"

"For the rest of the week. Until next Sunday. I'm hanging with Mila at her place. Wouldn't miss the Founder's Day celebrations. There's still a parade and a carnival, right?"

"As always."

"I can't wait. Everyone's already buzzing about the dance."

Ben laughed. "The social event of the season in Antioch."

"Other than your brother's wedding, of course." She stepped close, coy and playful. "I have so many great memories of Founder's Day from when we were growing up. I'm sure by now you already have a date —"

"Gentlemen, if you'll follow me, we'll get started on the tuxedo orders."

Thank the good heavens above for Marilyn's intercession. Frozen like a statue, Hailey Beth ignored the rustle of fabric, the pins, the background clamor of her friends. Powerless, she followed the conversation between Rochelle and Ben with an intensity that left her holding her breath. Relief poured through her veins once Ben was led away.

He glanced over his shoulder a time or two when Phillip's group was directed toward menswear. He focused on Hailey Beth, but he had also focused on Rochelle. Tough not to realize he had been flattered by her attention and flirtation. A chill of embarrassment danced against Hailey Beth's skin. She felt transparent. Foolish to the maximum degree.

"Would the white smoke billowing from your ears mean you've elected yourself Pope?"

Mila's whispered tease snapped Hailey Beth to proper focus. She glared at her sister, but on the inside, felt nothing but gratitude for the quiet understanding she saw in Mila's eyes.

"Wouldn't that be historic?"

"Almost as historic as confronting yourself in the mirror," Mila rejoined sweetly, but again in quiet tones meant for the two of them alone.

"Ridiculous."

"Tell me about it."

Hailey Beth tossed a bag of wedding accessories across the room in a fit of temper. She *really* needed to get over this whole Ben Fisher inspired roller coaster of emotion she seemed to be riding of late. The plastic sack landed in a heap on top of her bed. She released a growl and scowled at the world in general.

There she had stood, framed in triplicate like a total idiot, being fitted into layers of tulle and lace. Meanwhile, Rochelle had moved in on Ben and captured his attention. Hailey Beth sneered. Capture was such a mild word. In truth, Rochelle had visibly captivated him. Meanwhile, as the seamstress pinned and positioned, Hailey Beth had felt trapped — literally and figuratively — powerless to do anything but watch after them, and endure a piercing without so much as a flinch. Such had been the course of her feelings for Ben from the beginning.

Once his little flirtation with Rochelle had concluded, Ben noticed Hailey Beth. Sure, he had raked her with a couple of thorough, sparkling-eyed looks, but then he had stalked away after not much more than a quietly murmured greeting. He'd probably been stunned out of his mind to see her in fancy attire, standing before him like a gaping, crushing teenager. Which she wasn't. By *any* means.

Or was she? Was Mila right? Was she afraid to confront herself, and her emotions? Right on cue, without apology or preamble, Mila stormed across the threshold of Hailey Beth's room at their parents' home. "Well, that was an interesting shopping expedition.

Care to fill me in on whatever it is you're dealing with when it comes to Ben Fisher?"

"Leave it be, Mila."

"Sorry. I can't. This is all part of the Big Sister Manual, right under the chapter entitled: Never Let Your Younger Sibling Wallow in Despair Without Nagging Her to Death. Now. Spill."

"Go away."

"Try again."

"Go away, please?" For show, Hailey Beth delivered a sickly-sweet smile and fluttered her lashes.

"Try again — part two." After a mocking flutter of her own lashes, Mila relented and collapsed onto the edge of Hailey Beth's quilt-covered bed.

Thin, supple white sheers billowed against an incoming breeze. The wood plank floors creaked pleasantly while Hailey Beth paced. A braided rug cushioned her footfalls. This was comfortable space, her safe zone. Yes, she still resided beneath her parents' roof, in the room she had occupied almost since birth. She'd always enjoyed the connection, the ready support of working at the family store and living where she had grown up.

Until now.

Suddenly, she felt constricted, a prisoner of her own creation.

"Come on, sweetie." Mila stretched comfortably against fluffy down and pillows. "In all seriousness, what's going on? Please talk to me about him, and what you're feeling. You've been acting like the clichéd deer caught in headlights lately, and that's not like the strong, sassy sister I know and love."

"Mila, it's nothing." And that was the truth. Sadly enough.

"Bull. You've adored him forever and you're both too pig-headed to look the issue straight on and deal with it."

"Especially since he's leaving Antioch in the fall!" Hailey Beth shouted the words, playing her trump card, her excuse for all forms of bad behavior since she was heartbroken.

Mila reared back, jaw dropping. She gasped. "He's not."

"He is. He's leaving for Arkansas, and a mission program sponsored by Antioch Christian Church as soon as the fall harvest is complete."

"The one Reverend Taylor talked about during services a while back?" Hailey Beth nodded.

Mila lunged from the mattress and wrapped her in a tight, wordless hug.

The show of affection and understanding further undermined Hailey Beth's tenuous grip on self-control. Tear beads trickled over her lashes, running warm down her cheeks. "Mila, I'm finished with all this. I can't keep doing this to myself. You're right. I care about him. Very much. *Too* much."

"There's nothing wrong with that." Mila maintained her hold, rubbing her back.

"I'm a known quantity to him. Have been since we were both babies. There's no intrigue. There's no mystery. I'm boring to him. He looks right past me."

"I don't think it's that he looks past you, it's that he's comfortable with you. You've always been great friends. Tight."

"Yeah. What a thrill."

"My point exactly. Everything with you is as expected. You're a constant. A ready presence. Again, there's nothing wrong with that. In fact, it's great —"

"See also, *boring.*" Hailey Beth cut in. "I'm not compelling to him, or attractive. Look how he took to Rochelle today."

"Wrong. All you need to do is shake things up. Take him by surprise with a little something unexpected." Mila waggled her brows in a blatant display of sass.

"Oh. I see. I get it. Be artificial. That'll be perfect. Hang on a sec. Let me write that down in my journal somewhere before I forget."

"Oh, go ahead and snark if you want to, but my advice stands, and you know exactly what I'm getting at. Shake up the status quo. Surprise him."

4

Hailey Beth decided. She was going to the ball. Well, not a ball, exactly, but the closest thing there was to it in Antioch. She had made up her mind to attend the Founder's Day dance, and once she made a decision, she saw it through. No matter what doubts or second thoughts entered the equation.

She stood before the mirror of her vanity. Mila's advice formed a resonating echo through her brain, refusing to be put to rest. She opened the creaky, brass-hinged lid of her hand-carved, oak jewelry box — the one she had inherited from her great-grandmother.

An endeavor such as this required planning.

Reaching into the velvet-lined keepsake holder, she fingered the delicate silver chain of her favorite necklace, the one she had been given at her sweet sixteen birthday party. A heart-shaped locket dangled from the end, adorned by a small, centered diamond. She seldom wore the piece, but loved its shimmery, smooth look and texture. She drew out a pair of small diamond studs, held them up to her ears. A present from her parents when she'd turned twenty-one.

Jewelry, for her, wasn't meant to be frivolous or showy. It had to mean something. It had to hold a place in her heart before it would adorn a neckline, a wrist, a finger or an ear. She inched just a bit closer to the mirror, performing a critical evaluation on what she saw. A thick mane of sable hair needed some fine-tuning — a fresh set of layers and a clean-up at the ends. She released heavy waves from the utilitarian ponytail she had swept into place this morning. She stared at her reflection.

And sighed.

Plain, plain, plain. No wonder Ben looked right past her. No wonder a vivacious woman like Rochelle had scored his interest. Rochelle was fresh from the streets of Chicago, bursting with vitality, urban chic, and that elusive aura of mystery and freshness.

But Hailey Beth was anything but a quitter. She had some basics to play with. And, as Mila had observed, with a bit of make-up and the donning of that floral sun dress presently tucked at the rear of her closet she might look OK for the dance. Plus, right beneath that dress rested a smart pair of white, strappy sandals perfect for the occasion.

Determined and resolved, she pulled her cell phone from the front pocket of her jeans and dialed her stylist, Renette Steele at the Snip Snap Salon.

"Hey, Renette, it's HB. I know it's short notice, and I'm so sorry for that, but is there any chance you could squeeze me in for a cut before the dance on Saturday? Maybe a mani-pedi, too?" Renette's affirmative reply caused a smile to erupt across Hailey Beth's features, and she laughed deep. "Yeah, I know, I know. I'm going all out."

"Pretty rude the way you gaped at HB, then stepped lively with Rochelle." Phillip's censure drew Ben's attention away from the job at hand, an ambling survey of the freshly-sprouted soybean fields ripening across the Fisher farm.

"I didn't step lively. I barely had a conversation with her. How's it rude to welcome an old friend back to town? Furthermore, she came to me, not the other way around. Lay off!"

"Wow. Where'd that explosion come from, Mr. Calm, Cool and Collected?" Aaron froze, garnering the attention of both his brothers while he stared at Ben. "What exactly's under your skin?"

"Nothing!"

Aaron's gaze sharped, transforming from startled to knowing in a heartbeat.

Phillip snorted. "He's so clueless."

"I said lay off!" Ben nearly stalked straight back to the house. Mom had baked apple pie for the Founder's Day cook out tomorrow night, and the smell had been a delicious form of torture. Swiping a slice from the extra pie she had created would sure as get-out beat standing here, in the middle of a damp, earthy field, being egged on by his siblings.

"Hey, stop being the hot-headed reactionary. That's my gig. If you take that away from me, what do I bring to the table?"

Phillip smirked. "How about a big ol' bag of shut up?"

Aaron resumed walking, checking irrigation, squatting soon after to check on growth and any evidence of worm and bug infestation. "Oh, and I'm intimidated by that come-back. Not."

Ben cracked a grin at their antics, so familiar, so much a part of his life tapestry.

"Know what this reminds me of?"

"Couldn't begin to know." Phillip shot him a glance.

"That time in the emergency room."

Aaron snorted, using a swift, well-practiced touch to separate leaves, press fingers to soil, survey moisture levels. "Which time? We've graced the curtained cubicles of Weatherby-Thomas Hospital's ER more times than I care to consider."

"Let me refresh your memory. You and Phillip were practicing karate moves in your bedroom. You were polishing your skills for, what was it, the purple belt or something? You did that spin and kick move that went out of control and landed on me instead of Phillip."

Phillip laughed. "I remember. Poor Ben here toppled to his knees and then he lurched forward and split his head open on the metal corner of the bed frame."

Ben rolled his eyes but couldn't withhold a deep laugh. "Don't ask to see the scar. Besides, Aaron screamed louder than I did."

"I did at that. Out of fear of Mom and Dad's wrath more than your injury."

"Yeah. You're awesome like that."

Phillip ambled forward, but looked at his brothers. "Aaron also cried like a baby in the waiting room of the ER. And that had nothing to do with Mom and Dad. He was worried about his brother. The reaction was about looking out for each other. Remember those days?"

Aaron gave Phillip and Ben a long, meaningful look. "Seems they're coming around again."

"I'm grateful for that." Phillip's gaze took to the distance, toward the entry of the barn where sunlight and fields rolled for acres. "Especially now. We're headed to new places. All three of us. It's weird. It's good, but it's weird." Phillip keyed in on Ben once more. "Aaron made a point, though. Nothing gets to you. You're unflappable. What's up with you lately? Is it the prospect of leaving?"

Ben shrugged, honestly not knowing how to answer that question.

"Somebody really needs to teach you to stop monopolizing conversations, Ben." Aaron's muttered critique earned scowls from both of his brothers.

"Leave him be," Phillip advised, returning his focus to the land. "So, for next year, I'm thinking about double-cropping."

Ben arched a brow, rounding on Phillip as they walked the fields. "Really. That's an ambitious push forward."

"It is, but there's a lot of benefit to be

found. I figure we could plant winter wheat in the fall. The wheat goes dormant over the winter, and it's the first thing to mature in the spring. Once the wheat is cut, we'll plant soybeans in the same field and harvest two crops out of the same field in the same year."

"That'd be double the productivity, though, and we'll be down a man." Aaron's observation aligned seamlessly to Ben's gut reaction.

Phillip halted, hands on hips, surveying the freshly-budding field of rippling green leaves. "We can hire. We'll probably need to anyway."

Ben felt an unpleasant prickle dance against his arms. Just like that, life went on. Changes came and went, adaptation occurred. He was replaceable.

Aaron continued. "So, we'd leave the wheat stubble in the field for weed control."

"And a decrease in erosion." Ben chimed in, refusing to be displaced. "That'll help the soybeans we plant later take root a lot quicker, and stronger. As the residue decomposes, it becomes a fertilizer. Added bonus."

Aaron nodded. "Could be good all around." He eyed Phillip. "You're confident about this?"

"Depends on a lot of things." Phillip bent,

fingering the leaf buds. The stems and the undersides of the soybean leaves were fuzzy. Those fine, protective hairs acted as a natural form of pesticide, keeping any number of hungry bugs from indulging a feast. "Weather, insects, workload. We'll see. It's a thought to consider when we finish with the fall harvest."

Ben's senses prickled and stung all over again. He'd be gone by then. And all the certainty he had felt after meeting with Reverend Taylor began to sift through the cracks and crevices of doubt — and an unexpectedly potent pull of emotion.

5

It served Ben right for trying to be a gentleman.

But had he truly been a gentleman? An hour before the doors of the community center would be flung open to the citizenry of Antioch for the Founder's Day dance, he had just completed installation of the final strands of white fairy lights, the setting up of coffee urns, tables, chairs. He climbed down from the ladder to survey the overall effect.

Swags of lights, twined within garlands of evergreen, were adorned by a rainbow of flowers draped from the ceiling. A saffron glow painted the massive, open space with romantic, creamy light. Why in the world would that fact leave him thinking of Hailey Beth, and how stunning she had looked, pinned into the folds of that attention-grabbing, gorgeous dress, her eyes all wide and soft, her lips framed in a pout of surprise, full and supple and such a tempting beacon . . .

Dry at the throat, he had been powerless to speak but for a perfunctory greeting.

A gentleman wouldn't be to-the-bones enthralled by one woman and then . . . what was it Phillip had said . . . step lively with another. Ben had never meant to give Rochelle mixed signals, or lead her on, but no way could he be this tied into knots by feelings for a person he'd known and cared for as a friend practically since birth. Rochelle had stepped forward like a life saver. She had provided a much-needed diversion when heat climbed through his body.

Where did this tide of emotion for HB come from? Was the idea of leaving her . . . of leaving Antioch . . . wreaking this much havoc on his normally cool control and faultless perceptions?

Ben folded the stepladder and hefted it onto his shoulder, preparing to leave the hall. A frown puckered his brow. After stashing the ladder, he returned inside and gathered the rest of his supplies. He squinted against sunlight when he exited the building. A row of dusty, well-used pickup trucks lined the gravel parking lot that stretched wide across the length of the American Legion Hall. He angled toward his vehicle, still lost in thought . . . and tribulation. He needed to confront himself with honesty. In the contest of Hailey Beth Thomas versus Antioch, Indiana, Antioch came out on the losing end. Which is precisely why HB had his emotions in a tangle.

Humidity climbed, causing his skin to go damp. It would be one of the first hot days of the season. Heavy, earthy air carried with it the promise of long days to come. His favorite time of the year. Ben secured the remainder of his gear and climbed into the cab of his vehicle.

He knew his strengths and weaknesses. He was steadfast. Still waters ran deep, but he was always the calm in the storm. He didn't lose control. Suddenly, though, being near Hailey Beth pulled at him, to a fierce and increasingly unavoidable degree. His uncharacteristic behavior had even garnered the attention of his brothers. If Phillip and Aaron sensed a difference in his demeanor, then his feelings were riding entirely too close to the surface.

He cranked the engine and headed for the farm, knowing one thing to be true. Change needed to happen. Confrontation. And how in the name of all that was awkward could he conduct a conversation like this with HB? A lack of word-power and overt expressiveness landed hard on the list of his personality shortcomings. Besides, she was his friend. One of the dearest people in his life. Ever.

But if he didn't resolve this, one way or another, he'd land in a world of regret. A world patterned by a fateful, two-word question: What if?

"Well, would you get a load of Hailey Beth? Wow. She is lookin' good."

Ben cast a scowl at Aaron, who passed the comment then executed a slow, low, whistle. "She always looks good. Why are you so shocked by —" Ben's gaze slid to the arrival of the Thomas family — one and all, much like the Fisher clan had entered the hall just a short time ago. There was always strength in family. Especially farm families. When his search came to rest on Hailey Beth, his world ground to a screeching halt.

She stood framed in the wide, open entryway, backlit by a sky full of stars, by the darkened silhouettes of towering trees and milky moonlight, by colorful flowers tumbling from urns and the motion of people coming and going. A sweet breeze drifted, skimmed, curved, and his senses hummed.

He couldn't look away. He didn't *want* to look away. Ever.

Her normally utilitarian ponytail had been surrendered to shortened layers that skimmed her cheeks and face, tumbling softly to a spot just below her shoulders . . . shoulders that led to slim, creamy arms left bare by a simply styled dress painted by flowers in delicate hues of pink, green, blue and yellow. Yep. Tip to toe, she was a feast for the eyes. He couldn't help wondering. When had such fundamentals as vintage class and elegance been displaced by the raucous world they lived in? HB — the quintessence of being a lady — put every super model he could think of to complete shame.

And so, he stared. And so, he longed. And so, his soul swelled in the throes of an emotion that wasn't quite pride, wasn't quite primitive, but was most definitely built on protection, and possession.

Hmm — maybe that kind of reaction *was* a bit primitive . . .

Phillip whacked Ben on the back, jarring him unpleasantly from a delicious view. "Ah . . . bro? You might want to blink."

Ben shot his sib an intense glare. Fat lot of good that did him. Phillip and Aaron just sidled off toward the beverage table, snickering merrily.

It was far past time to grab a cold soda

and do some mixing and mingling. The self-assigned bout with socialization didn't help much, though. HB crowded him now, a beautiful invader never far from his sight.

Hailey Beth and her family occupied one side of a long cafeteria-style table. The Fisher family occupied the other. Life, she figured, was a strange thing to decipher. Her family, the merchants of Antioch, positioned straight across from the Fisher family, one of the town's longest-standing, most influential farm families. A tenuous line of friendship had always existed between the two clans. Growing up, Hailey Beth had heard tales of Jonathan Fisher and her father, Byron, having struggles with issues of friendship versus business. Crop harvests affected her family's store and its offerings, and Hailey Beth's dad acted as a local broker, negotiating prices for crop distribution throughout Indiana. Those same crop harvests provided food and shelter and a livelihood to the Fishers and others.

The salt of the earth often did battle against issues of sustainability via revenue and profit. At times, those battles turned intense.

"I'm so glad gatherings like this still draw a big crowd." Hailey Beth's mom, Corinne, shared the comment with her seatmate, Anna Fisher. The two of them surveyed the room with satisfied expressions.

"I agree. Know what else? The older I get, the more sentimental I become." Anna dug into her slice of blueberry pie topped by a rounded scoop of vanilla ice cream. She sighed with pleasure. "Juanita Norem makes the best blueberry pies. Seriously, I could never compete with this."

Corinne nodded, following suit with a crème drizzled bite of her own. "Perhaps, but then again, who'd want to?"

"Amen. The first pickings of the season and they're outstanding."

Like playful school girls, the women clanked their plastic forks together. Sharing a wink, they polished off the treat.

Jonathan Fisher sipped from a freshly cracked bottle of water then tucked an arm around the shoulders of his wife. "Why so sentimental?" Unlike everyone else at their table, he had foresworn dessert in deference to a health regimen that had turned an episode of near heart failure into a new lease on life. He nibbled from a serving of fruit and cheeses that rested before him on a paper plate.

Anna rested against him, and sighed. "Times like this, I get to thinking about how fast time goes by. How nice it is that some things remain constant. Wasn't it just yesterday that we were in our twenties, with the world and our whole lives just waiting?" Anna inched closer to her spouse, love in her gaze.

Laughter rounded the table before Hailey Beth's dad chimed in. "Feels that way sometimes, doesn't it? Now, it's our kids who are paving the way to marriages and mission work, and taking the helm of family businesses. New lives. New challenges. Circle of life, I suppose."

Hailey Beth leaned on her elbows, looking around. These were familiar faces, one and all. Beautiful, country-fresh décor warmed her, soothed her anxieties and welcomed her soul. Sure, the fixings were simple — wildflowers tucked into dime-store vases, dollar store twinkle lights strung above by the hand of Ben Fisher.

Rochelle Simmons worked her way through the crowd, renewing acquaintances and at no loss for friends and welcoming attention.

But Ben paid her no particular attention.

Hailey Beth couldn't help it — on instinct she had tracked his interaction with the sweet and lovely urbanite. He had been kind and gracious to Rochelle, but opted to stick close to his family. And hers. He stayed close to Hailey Beth, and that caused her heart to fill, and then promptly overflow.

She was blessed, and she knew it. As years passed, she became keenly aware of hometown beauty, the importance of sharing timeless traditions. Calm, beautiful simplicity could speak volumes in this world when tidewaters turned and times changed. Just like that, in rode melancholy. Ben's days as a constant in her life were short numbered.

"Remember the barn dances we used to have?" Jonathan leaned forward against the table, smile wide while Byron chuckled and nodded. "Dance space was broomed free of debris, tables and chairs were set up on beds of fresh-pitched hay so folks could sit and visit. We haven't had one of those in a long, long time. We should put one together this autumn. After the harvest. A celebration of the season. Like the old days."

"Those weren't the old days, that was just yesterday." Anna shared a commiserating glance with the table at large, and then nudged her husband in the arm. "And since when have you been a fan of dancing?"

An instant of dead silence fell between the two couples.

The unexpected interruption drew Hailey Beth fully into the conversation. She took note of the intent, yet unreadable look exchanged by Jonathan Fisher and her father.

Following an elongated pause, Dad cleared his throat and smiled. His focus homed in on Jonathan alone. "I believe you became a fan of barn dances on October thirteenth . . . exactly thirty-five years ago."

Jonathan acknowledged that comment with a nod, along with a smile of affection . . . and respect.

There was something in this exchange that piqued Hailey Beth's heart and curiosity.

"I do believe you've nailed it right down to the date, Byron." Jonathan's response returned the atmosphere to normalcy, but Anna's glance moved slowly, and again with a meaning Hailey Beth couldn't quite discern, between Byron and Jonathan.

Hailey Beth was about to lose her ever-loving mind.

Ben possessed all kinds of sexy, alpha mannerisms, rich with subtlety, potent to distraction, yet nearly invisible in the ways they could reach into her psyche and deliver a sensual tweak. Like right now. He sat next to her, and all he did was touch her. His arms were folded and he leaned forward slightly, engaged in the conversation.

But a pair of long, tan fingertips rested lightly against her forearm, brushing back and forth in a feathery touch of skin to skin. There was nothing overt in the caress; an outsider might miss it altogether. For Hailey Beth, the gesture proved infinitely seductive, and left her acutely aware of him.

Meanwhile, he chatted on, looking elsewhere, thoroughly a part of the conversation at hand.

"And then . . . do you remember the time Mom was raking leaves into the fire pit that Pop had built, and the hem of her apron caught fire? She tore that thing off so fast!"

"Oh, for heaven's sake, Benjamin — hush your mouth!" Anna condemned, but laughed harder than anyone else.

"Uh-oh." Phillip lifted his hands in surrender. "Benjamin. Next thing you know, it'll be Benjamin Alexander. Bro, you're in it deep."

Ben hooted, and shrugged off the threat. "As I recall, Phillip, you were running through the field, screaming and crying, instead of lending aid to our mother."

That piece of comedy was met with a mild spell of brotherly trash talk.

The evocative caress continued; Hailey Beth tingled, ached.

The table space formerly shared by the

two families became fluid as people came and went, as greetings and updates were shared. Their present assemblage reminisced and laughed, enjoying everything that was best about living in small-town Indiana — connectedness, history, tradition.

Ben moved away — just far enough away to lift a plastic tumbler filled with lemonade and down a swig. Just far enough away to break their connection. A sense of loss, of need, promptly followed. Soon enough, though, the connection returned, and his arm rested alongside hers on the table top. He brushed his fingertips against her arm once more, an arm that now danced with a spray of goose flesh. That's when she realized.

His actions were deliberate. Innocent, yes, but deeply and utterly intentional.

Time passed swiftly as she absorbed the undercurrents of the evening and continued to ponder the surprising circuit of electricity that had rippled through the earlier exchange between Ben's parents and her own. What was up with *that* whole vignette?

"Hey, HB? Feel like a walk?"

Hailey Beth surrendered introspection to find Ben looking at her, waiting, and watching. Closely. With an intensity that beckoned her far from the boundaries of a simple, long-adhered to friendship. She wanted to act on the prompt of her heart, reveal herself to him, before he was gone, and all chances were lost.

"That'd be nice. Sure."

But could she — *should* she — take that large a gamble?

6

Ben guided her from the hall, across the threshold of the large, wood-frame building. The instant they walked outside, cool air brushed against her skin, rippled through her hair. Hailey Beth indulged in a happy sigh. This brief bout of revival was just what she needed.

Until Ben's hand dropped from the small of her back and he captured her hand, lacing his fingers slowly through hers. Instantly her senses returned to high alert

"Before now, I kind of thought I was too young for walks down memory lane."

"Yeah?"

He nodded. "I guess the idea of leaving hits home at times. Tonight being one of them."

So, stay. The response bubbled and burst through her spirit, but she kept it herself. "You're not second guessing, are you?"

"Nope. I know change like this is a huge

shake up. I pretty much expected the bitter-sweet. I've got a meeting with Reverend Taylor this week. There's a group of about ten who have signed on for the first work session. Some are retirees. Some are college students commissioned to semester-long service for credit. Some are simply handyworkers, like me, who want to donate some time and elbow-grease."

Her heart dropped in time to every incremental rise of enthusiasm in Ben's tone and she promptly decided a topic shift was in order. "I agree about the walks down memory lane. Did you get the weird vibe of the conversation between your folks and mine?"

"Yeah. History. I'm sure over the span of their decades of knowing one another, there's been some tales to tell."

"Makes me wonder. Something hit home between them. Seemed intense. Emotional."

"And in the past."

The finality and apparent ease with which he closed off the past left her frowning, and puzzling.

Then he started to chuckle. "Speaking of memory lane, I still remember that pretty little kid from kindergarten who came to school one Monday morning with her formerly long hair all mangled up into a chop-chop-suey."

HB released a bubble of laughter at the way he described how she had self-styled her hair with a pair of barber sheers under the misguided notion that she could create her own short, feathery hairdo. "Benjamin Alexander Fisher! I was just sampling a bold and glamorous styling technique —"

"Technique, one. HB, zero."

"Now, that's just mean."

Ben laughed. "You gave yourself a set of bangs that looked like the jagged-edge teeth of my Pop's hacksaw, and you added in that asymmetrical cut in back that you tried to make stylish long before asymmetrical cuts were a thing."

"Oh, hush. What do you even know about asymmetrical cuts anyway?" HB linked her arm through his as easy as could be.

He sent her a long, probing look. "I like the cut you've got going on tonight. You look really good."

A complete turnabout took place between them.

Humor morphed into something warm, heavy with feeling. Hailey Beth's heart pounded. "We've had some adventures, haven't we?"

"Lots of history." He covered her hand with his.

HB hid a sigh of utter joy and contentment. This felt so right. So natural and good.

They continued their walk.

She opted to gamble a little. "You seem to be in a sentimental place tonight. Feeling nostalgic?"

"The table conversation got me to thinking. Guess I'm taking stock. Especially of the people I care about. What they bring to my life."

The admission caused her lips to tremble, so she pressed them tight and blinked against the sting of tears. Ben wasn't one to wax emotional. He possessed rich feelings, but didn't often use words to express them. He was, and always had been, action oriented. "You'll be missed."

"Will I?" With that, he turned, and the intensity that flashed in his eyes stole her breath. "HB, out with it."

"Out with what?" She rasped the words against the sudden abrasion of a too-dry throat.

"Everything we're not saying. Everything that needs to be confronted."

She trembled. Dark mysteries swirled, an intoxicating rush of . . . *feeling* . . . swept through her senses, her heart. Those mysteries, she knew, wouldn't remain hidden any longer. Her heart thumped hard in time to that truth. Ben stepped close, warm, musky, and vital, an intoxicant to senses already thrumming into overdrive.

He cupped her face between his hands, traced her cheeks with the gentle glide of his thumbs. "You're trembling."

"Yes, I am."

"Why?" He tilted his forehead until it met hers, until their eyes met, held, and, for Hailey Beth, made the entire universe vanish to nothing more than meaningless haze. "Because your presence is that powerful to me." She lifted her chin, hoping the gesture reflected a confidence she certainly didn't feel on the inside. Ever since Ben's bombshell announcement about leaving Antioch, she had become the queen of false bravado. "How's that for saying what we're not saying?"

"Good enough for me." He hummed the words.

A lasso of intensity returned, snaring her — pulling her toward him. Before Hailey Beth could steady wobbly legs, or draw a sharp, replenishing breath, Ben wrapped an arm around her waist, drew her tight against him. His head dipped. A heady ache consumed her. Hailey Beth sighed in surrender to the moment, senses alive and sparkling with expectation. His breath skimmed against her waiting lips . . .

"Ben, the audio's gone haywire and the DJ is wondering if you can troubleshoot —"

It didn't surprise her that they groaned in unison. Such was their history. Such was their connection. Phillip's interruption acted like a heavy dousing of iced water. Ben yanked free of their embrace and Hailey Beth cleared her throat, moving a few steps away from the call of his warm, solid perfection.

"Oh . . . I, ah . . . I'm . . ." Phillip winced and turned back toward the hall.

Before further embarrassment could be inflicted on the moment, Ben stalked toward the building.

From within, music, laughter, indistinct conversations and light poured into the deep, dark quiet of the night. Where had all *that* noisy residue come from? Had she been that far removed from the world?

Ben bumped shoulders with his brother. A brief but intent glance was shared between the brothers just before Ben growled in warning, "Leave it be, Phillip. I'm telling you right now. *Leave it be.*"

7

Arriving home after the dance, Hailey Beth still ached for Ben; she still longed for culmination, for what she knew would have been the most amazing, satiny glide of a kiss . . .

Blast Phillip well and true for the most epic-fail interruption of all time.

She sighed as she walked inside, but was heartened by the sight of a light on in Dad's ground-level study. The door was left mostly ajar, and Hailey Beth smiled, picking up on Dad's time-honored signals. No matter how old they were, no matter what the circumstance, if Byron Thomas expected his daughters to be coming home, he waited for them until they arrived. There was something precious in that truth that made Hailey Beth feel prized and protected. The gesture, she knew, didn't stem from a lack of trust, it stemmed from a father's love.

"Hey, Dad."

"Hey, Hailey-girl."

Dad had called her Hailey-girl forever.

"Did you have fun tonight?" His words came to her muffled a bit by distance, and the insulation of his office walls, but she recognized the invitation to pause for a moment, and share, if she'd like. Hailey Beth bypassed the wide stairwell leading to her bedroom on the second level to join him.

"I did. It was a great event."

She found him seated on the old, black leather love seat, shoes off, stocking feet crossed and propped atop the nearby coffee table. He set aside his book and gave her a smile of welcome.

"I'm glad to hear that. There for a while, it seemed to me as though you weren't too keen on the idea of going."

No sense hiding, or creating false spin for her mixed up behavior these days. "Yeah, I wasn't too sure about going solo." That was true enough.

"Ben seemed to step up and answer the call." Not surprisingly, Dad saw straight through her. "Care to join me for a bit before I hit the hay?"

"Sure."

She tucked next to him, resting her head on his shoulder. Dad was tall, lean, his features angular and almost aristocratic.

He'd always put her in mind of a nobleman with his thick silver hair and lively gray eyes.

"You spent some time outside talking there at the end. How's he doing with all the changes to come?"

She was glad the dim lighting hid her blush. "He's as well as can be expected, I guess. He's excited."

"Can't blame him there. New patterns of life are always exciting."

"And bittersweet."

"That, too."

"I'll miss him, Dad. A lot."

"I can tell. More than usual, your feelings for him are rising to the surface. Impending loss acts that way sometimes."

"Am I that easy to read?" It troubled her to think she was so transparent when she couldn't get a firm handle on just how much Ben felt for her in return. Sure, he was more verbose and affectionate than usual, but, he was leaving his entire life behind, for heaven's sake. Naturally he was holding on fast to his friends and seeking support. So, how much of what they shared tonight had to do with love as with the idea of letting go of one life in favor of another?

"You know? It's strange to think that both of my girls have fallen in love with Fisher men."

Hailey Beth lifted her head from his shoulder and uncurled her legs so she could face him fully. She breathed deep, unwilling to diminish herself by hiding, or lying. She nipped at her lower lip, studied him for a few beats of the old grandfather clock in the far corner. "I guess it's quite the coincidence, huh?"

"Not really, Hailey-girl." Dad looked into the distance, and he smiled, as though meeting with memories that were beautiful, but . . . as he had said moments ago . . . bittersweet, too.

"It's not a coincidence?"

"Well, suffice it to say, the history between our two families stretches back a long, long way. God brought us to where we're meant to be, and where we'll be happiest, but sometimes He does it while we're kicking and screaming."

"I'm not quite sure what you mean by that, but, I'll assume you mean I shouldn't fight against Ben and what he wants."

"That's exactly what I mean. He needs to make his way. Just like you. Just like everyone."

Her shoulders slumped. "So, it's the whole, 'if he returns to me, he's mine, but if he doesn't, he wasn't mine to begin with' thing."

"I'm afraid so." Dad drew her close once more and dotted her forehead with a kiss. "I learned that lesson the hard way when I was in my younger years. A beautiful, intelligent, sweet young woman came to live in Antioch when I was in my late teens. She stole every bit of my focus."

Hailey Beth listened, captivated. "Really?"

"She cared for me, too. A great deal. But, she *loved* someone else."

"That's awful. She led you on?"

He soothed a bit of her agitation with a head shake, and a tender look, full of deep reaching contentment. "No such thing. No such thing at all."

"Well . . ." Hailey Beth raged at anyone dumb enough to reject the love of her father. He was awesome. "Aren't the late teens pretty young for the big 'L' word?"

Dad chuckled. "Oh, I don't think I need to tell you that when you know, you know. After all, how long have you known Ben? How long have you loved him?"

His gentle admonishment put her still bubbling temper to rest.

Dad continued. "Things were simple. Straightforward. She was, and is, a very good friend to me, but I had to let her go. She didn't return. It broke me for a while, but because of her, I changed. Forever. And for the better. I found my way to your mom, and the life I was meant to live. I know, to my core, that this is the happier, more fulfilling path for me."

But what a painful thing to experience — loving, and releasing, and being left with a void. Sure, the pain was temporary — life constantly evolved and changed after all — yet with all that she was, Hailey Beth didn't want loss to be the end-song between her and Ben.

Nevertheless, Dad's counsel was spot-on, and she knew it. "You said she's still friends with you. She still lives in Antioch?"

"Yes, she does. She's a school teacher." He directed a long, pointed look her way, and waited for the realization to dawn. Anna Fisher. The table episode at the dance tonight now made perfect sense. Anna had been a teacher at Antioch High School for ages now, part of the home economics department.

"Oh." Hailey Beth sat up straight again, covering her mouth with fingertips that trembled. "Oh. My. Word. You're talking about Ben's mom."

"Ironic, isn't it?"

Indeed. As if something within the DNA of their families was destined to combine. Look at Mila and Phillip; look at the way she and Ben were struggling to figure out their hearts and emotions.

Still, Hailey Beth didn't know what to make of this new puzzle piece. "Mila and Phillip's story is playing out, but I get a sense your history is repeating itself with me and Ben."

"Mila and Phillip belong together and they've moved forward as such. As for you and Ben, you're right. God's still sculpting the story. It's up to the choices you make. It's up to the two of you to create what's next in your lives, but never, ever, without the hand of God leading the way. Despite the loss, I gained. So did Anna." He shrugged. "Loss and gain. It's part of the journey."

Her dad. Anna Fisher. Jonathan Fisher. Now, Hailey Beth knew, there were many layers and textures to the relationships between their families. "What about Mom? Did she know? *Does* she know?"

"Corrine knows me better than I know myself." The smile he wore was infinitely loving. "I never have, and never will, hide from her. And don't get fixated on the fact that there was once a love triangle in Antioch. That's not why I'm sharing our story with you right now." He cautioned her further by delivering a gentle squeeze to her shoulders. "I want you to focus on what led us to where we are now. Focus on smart choices. Focus on from-the-gut choices. Choices that you'll need to make in order to find your own way. And, Hailey-girl, no matter what that ending is, or with whom, you need to trust and have faith that you'll end up where you belong. That's the lesson I learned long ago, and hold fast to every single day. I hope you will, too, sweetheart."

She understood, yet remained fascinated by the history. Things would have been so different had another choice been made, another corner turned.

For all of them.

8

The interlude with Hailey Beth over the weekend changed everything for Ben. The near-kiss had knocked him way off center. The near-kiss had turned into a pulse of need, of promise. The near-kiss had him tempted to chuck all his grandiose plans and stay right where he was, sweep her off her feet, and seal their future together forever.

And he was supposed to handle that truth how, exactly?

Ravaged, he tried to pay attention during the biweekly mission planning and orientation meeting at Antioch Christian Church. Nothing doing. Instead, his mind drifted to Hailey Beth rather than the details of serving the destitute in rural Arkansas, details of a missionary exercise he had shifted his entire life plan to join.

He forced himself to engage as Reverend Taylor read a passage from Chapter One in the Book of Ezra. "Let everyone who has survived, in whatever place he may have dwelt, be assisted by the people of that place, with silver, gold, goods and cattle together with freewill offerings for the house of God in Jerusalem. Then, the family heads of Judah and Benjamin and the priests and Levites — everyone, that is, whom God had inspired to do so — prepared to go up to build the house of the Lord in Jerusalem. All their neighbors gave them help in every way, with silver, gold, goods and cattle, and with many precious gifts."

A hammer-strike of purpose brought him fully around. All it took was the revelation of Scripture to bring about renewed determination. God was speaking to him directly, right down to King Cyrus's call to lend aide and the call of Benjamin's name.

Reverend Taylor continued. "Eyes on the prize as we keep pushing for donations and community-wide, parish-wide support. That prize is sustainability. We're teaching men to fish. Hands-on training will empower a disenfranchised town to survive. We have a brain trust assembled around this table that can show them the means to utilize the gifts of the earth."

One of the half-dozen volunteers spoke up — Tim Abraham — a retiree who owned a storage and rental truck company. "I've got my former company on standby to store, and ship, so we should be good with transporting supplies."

Ben added those bullet points to his meeting notes and gave a satisfied nod. Things were coming together. He had already secured material and financial support from several local businesses. For starters, Pepperfield Farm Supply had donated fertilizer, soil, and a variety of flower and crop seeds. At the Founder's Day dance, Byron Thomas had said he'd chip in supplies as well as a monetary donation.

"That's perfect, Tim. Thanks." Reverend Taylor continued. "We're on our way. In a couple months, we'll be taking what we do on our farms, what we've learned through the course of our lives, and bringing that knowledge to a community in need. A community that's hungry for help and eager to produce. It's the truest essence of being a disciple. You're leaving home for new, fertile grounds, to spread a form of nourishment that's both physical and spiritual."

Ben's thoughts strayed all over again and he cursed himself as a fool for loosening the reins on his heart. The pattern of tonight's meeting cut to the essence of his struggle. His commitment remained solid, but the idea of leaving stirred a vibration through his soul, a push and pull that led him into conflict. This opportunity was incredible, but as the clock continued its relentless tick toward leaving, he felt scrambled. Nowadays he was torn, and left wondering. Could he do any of this without Hailey Beth? Only in those moments, when the image of her swirled to focus in his heart, did doubts creep in.

Once the meeting ended, he left as soon as decorum allowed. He needed time by himself. Uninterrupted prayer and introspection would soothe some of the rough edges. He'd get to work on some equipment maintenance at the farm, or maybe he'd start a project. He loved the long days of summer, when the sun didn't even set until after nine o'clock. He'd dive into creation, focus his energy, and pray. Through it all, God would speak.

A pair of Founder's Day banners still draped the span of Main Street. The hand-painted sign closest to him snapped in the wind. HB had been so beautiful that night, a soft, feminine silhouette bathed by milky-white moonlight and the mysteries of a flower-kissed summer night. Those last few celebratory markers would be removed before long. Life would move on through the weeks and months of summer. Ben crossed the church parking lot and climbed into his vehicle. Before cranking the engine, he paused, leaned against the steering wheel and looked up at a bright blue sky uninterrupted by clouds and a sun just beginning its descent.

Life would move on.

OK, he'd find a way to cope with that fact. Meanwhile, he wanted to make the most of the time he had left in Antioch. With Hailey Beth. A trip to one of the nearby lakes for a long bike ride and a swim, a kayak adventure, or a picnic maybe. Something special for the two of them alone. Or, maybe he could do something for her. Something tangible to leave behind, and remind her of her importance to him. As one of the program coordinators in charge of the mission, he'd be gone for a year, taking up residence with a local family, but a year wasn't forever.

Unless service projects like this one continued to pull at him and he continued the journey.

What then? If his time in Arkansas intensified the fire already building at his gut, the last thing he'd do was buck God's prompting. Instead, he'd need to trust. And risk the equally unexpected, and powerful, prompting of his heart.

Hailey Beth paused from lunch when she heard the doorbell chime and clang above the entrance to the grocery store. Mila bounded across the threshold, brown curls bouncing around her shoulders, smile wide and happy as she greeted friends, her arms laden by a bouquet of multi-colored tulips. Leaving her office behind, but bringing along the bowl of cereal — lunch should never go soggy, after all — Hailey Beth tagged up with her sister and admired the blooms.

"How pretty!"

"They're for you. I left my batch at Sundae Afternoon. Thought they'd brighten the check-out counter."

"I'm sure they will, and thank you!" She pecked Mila's cheek. "This is so sweet."

"Couldn't resist. Spotted them while I strolled through the farmer's market. I had a few minutes after lunch with Phillip, so I thought I'd try to get some flower arrangement ideas for the wedding. Is that old, curved vase still in the back storeroom?"

"Sure enough. Here, let me —"

"No prob. I've got it." In passing, Mila eyed the half-eaten bowl of crunchy, sugar-sweetened goodness. "Your food choices never cease to amaze me."

Hailey Beth pouted, donning a mask of affront. "What? I like breakfast, and I like cereal. Come sit with me for a minute. Your visit is perfectly timed."

"Oh?"

"Yeah. I was stalking online photos for wedding ideas and found the coolest table favors. I want to run my favorite past you and see if you want me to order it."

"What I need are flower ideas." Mila trekked to the rear of the store, securing the vase from a cabinet beneath the sink. She filled it with water and blew at the fringe of her bangs, shaking her head. "Actually, what I need most is to elope. I swear, I'm getting so nervous and jumpy these days. The shower is only a couple weeks away, and the wedding is coming up so fast after that."

"Don't be silly. You've always dreamed of your wedding day, and the big white gown, the church, and your friends. It'll be fine."

"That was then. This is now."

Hailey Beth laughed. "Leave it to your maids, Mila. We've got this. Your only objectives are to be gorgeous, to glow with love, and nab yourself the eldest Fisher man."

"But, what about the youngest Fisher man?"

Oh, why had she mentioned the Fishers?

Since a light, breezy quip had landed her in hot water, Hailey Beth tried to battle back. "I think Phillip would be a tad put out if you focused on the youngest Fisher man. Green with jealousy, in fact."

"That's not what I meant, and you know it."

Hailey Beth opted to ignore the comment. "Put the flowers out front, then sit down and give me your undivided attention. Let's talk table favors. And flowers. I have some ideas on both. Tell me what you think."

After fulfilling Hailey Beth's request, Mila pulled a chair into place and they teamed up behind the aged desk. Before them hummed Hailey Beth's open laptop, already displaying images she had culled during her luncheon/breakfast break.

Hailey Beth clicked on an image, making it large. "Look at these!"

"Oh, my goodness — HB, fans, made of sandalwood? That's brilliant!"

"Isn't it? Look at the carvings! They're so delicate looking, but they're made of wood, so they'll last. They're collapsible, and they even come boxed. They'll smell delicious."

"Plus, around here, you never know what kind of weather you'll get this time of year. Could be cool, or rainy, or it could be hot and humid."

Hailey Beth's enthusiasm mounted. "Exactly. But, no matter what the weather, they'll be a super nice keepsake. Plus, we can have them personalized with your names and the wedding date. Check out the white silk tassels, too, which are a nice touch. Do you like them?"

"Honey, I love them! Consider your fan idea a major score."

"Awesome. I'm placing the order tonight, with personalization. Next on the hit parade? Flowers." Mila heaved a sigh, her gaze all dreamy and happy — just as Hailey Beth wished.

"You're such a God-send. Truly."

"Aw, shucks, sis." Hailey Beth bumped shoulders with Mila, then scrolled through her own set of inspirational photos and floral motifs. She made ready to click on the image of a floral arrangement she thought would be perfect for the reception. Mila grabbed her hand and stilled her effort to execute a mouse-click.

"HB, what's that?"

"What's what?"

"Those Mason jars. The ones stuffed with flowers and greenery. They're gorgeous. What beautiful colors. I feel as if I could reach out and touch them. The twisting fairy lights are a perfect touch."

Confused, Hailey Beth zoomed in on the image. "Those aren't table arrangements. They're wall-mounted decorations. They're permanent. I added them to an on-line design page I created because I was thinking about doing something like that to give the walls of the store some pop and fresh color at some point."

"Imagine some green spikes, and some hyacinth, or lilac, or lily of the valley. That would look awesome, and smell like a slice of heaven. Plus, you could switch out the flowers and make the decorations seasonal. Some daisies or sunflowers for summer, some big fall mums."

Hailey Beth chuckled. "What about winter, when there isn't a fresh flower to be found in all of Indiana?"

"When did you become such a cynic? You could do evergreen, dusted by faux snow, capped by tiny, colored ornaments." Mila speared her with a look. "If you don't do it, I'm going to. Sundae Afternoon would —"

"Slow down, sis. This is a project, and you have enough on your plate. So do I. It's a great idea, and I'll take it under advisement. After life settles down. That's why I saved it. Kind of the purpose of these idea pages, know what I mean?"

Mila pursed her lips. "Suit yourself. It's

awesome, though."

Hailey Beth scrolled on, clicking on what she hoped would be a gorgeous addition to the reception festivities. "Look at this arrangement. Can't you just see those giant peonies, in all different colors, filling up a clear, glass holder? The vase would be square, just like in the picture, and low, so it won't interfere with table talk and socializing . . ."

9

"Hey, Ben, have you got a second?"

"Sure." Knowing Mila, the request had to do with wedding details. There must be thousands. If he could help knock something off her 'to-do' list, he was on board. After all, that's what a future brother-in-law was for.

He sat counter side at Sundae Afternoon, nursing a soda, making short work of a hot dog and fries. The meal was his indulgence in health-defying food, enjoyed far from the confines of Mom's kitchen. With good reason, and full support from the entire Fisher clan, Mom's kitchen was completely heart healthy, with no wiggle-room. Dad's turn-around from a severe battle with heart disease had made them all believers in the whole exercise/diet balance of life.

All the same, everyone needed an occasional splurge — even Dad — who could be found scrounging the occasional peanut butter snack cracker or maybe an every-once-in-a-while slice of homemade cheese cake.

Finished crafting and delivering a root beer float to a customer just a few stools away, Mila joined him and leaned against the counter. "So, I need a favor, if possible."

"Sure. What's up?"

"Can I show you rather than try to explain?"

"OK." Ben's brows furrowed as he polished off the last of his relish and onion topped dog and chased it with a final swig of cola. "Lead the way."

Just beyond the kitchen and storage area was a small, glassed in office barely big enough for the desk and computer that filled its space. Mila tapped the keys of her laptop, rousing it from sleep mode and clicked her way to a popular ideas website.

Ben groaned inwardly. Honestly, what was the allure of this cyber-venue? Ever since wedding plans had ratcheted to full-gear, even Phillip had been known to prowl the site. What was he setting himself up for?

"Here we go. Take a look, and tell me what you think."

Ben leaned in to study the image Mila had clicked to enlarge. Hmm. Nice. On display was a picture of big, fluffy flowers, their stems tucked into simple, every day Mason jars. The jars were hung upon planks of distressed wood, ready to be installed as wall décor.

"Mila, they're awesome, but what are they for? What's this about?"

"It's about Hailey Beth."

The bomb-blast declaration stopped him on a dime. Ben's senses ticked upward by a good fifty or sixty points. "Yeah?"

Thankfully, Mila didn't seem to notice his hitch. "Mmm-Hmm. It's like a gift to her, for all she's doing for the wedding and everything. I want to create maybe three or four of these, and hang them throughout the grocery store. Can't you just see them, all full of flowers, maybe with lights strung through? Maybe I'm off my rocker, but I think hangings like these would add a cool touch of charm and country-style to the place. Character." She shrugged and looked at him over her shoulder. "Besides. Something like this would mean a great deal to her, coming from you."

"Coming from me." He arched a brow, answering Mila's unspoken challenge, but he was more than a little afraid of where this conversation might lead.

"Yes. Umm. Yes. You're so good at this kind of thing, and you're special . . . you're part of the family now . . . and . . ."

Ben grinned, deciding to let her off the hook, and spare her the awkwardness of saying everything that couldn't be said. "You don't need to sell me, Mila. Consider it done. In fact, I know just how I want to set them up."

Her eyes sparkled; she gave him a tight, spontaneous hug. "Really? Honest? Oh, Ben, that's awesome! Thank you! I'll pay you, and I know how tight time must be getting for you now, but —"

He stilled her with a firm shake of his head. "I already have the supplies. If you don't mind, can it come from both of us?"

"Of course!"

This was perfect. In fact, this was a moment of answered prayer. Without even realizing it, Mila had given him the idea, the means by which to make HB something from the heart, something made by his hands, something to let her know she was special to him, and always would be.

No matter where the future took them.

"Can you do it? Are you sure? I don't mean to impose."

"Absolutely. I'm on board. E-mail me the link so I have the pictures to go by. I can take care of the rest." He shot her a meaningful look. "Right down to the flowers. OK?"

Mila's hard blink indicated surprise, but then, she issued a smooth nod, and her lips curved knowingly. "OK. Deal. The project is on you. Right down to the flowers."

In the days that followed, Ben went work. First, he set up a bike trip and picnic outing with Hailey Beth for this coming Saturday at Walloon Lake, an expansive oval of spring-fed blue that was cool, and deep, and located just a couple miles east of town. Second, he secured a trio of weathered, planks of gray pine wood which he had already sawed in half and edge-sanded to a smooth finish. He loved crafting things from wood. He loved the sweet aroma of fresh sawdust. He had distressed the wood further, using a combination of vinegar and steel wool. These would form the bases for a series of wall decorations soon to be installed at Thomas's Grocery Store.

On Friday morning, he woke up early, dressed fast, and grabbed a pair of banana nut muffins from a sealed plastic tub next to the fridge. After securing a few napkins, he filled a thermal cup with coffee then crossed through the flourishing soybean field burnished to a shimmering gold by the sunrise. On his way to the barn, he whistled a nonsensical tune, grinning as he imagined HB's surprise at the treat in store. Once stationed inside the space — which doubled as a work area for any number of his hand-made projects or equipment overhauls — Ben sat on a hay bale. After a stilling session of prayer and calm, he ate breakfast, then began the process of securing steel bands around the mouths of each jar. Next, he'd create a small loop in the fastener. From there, he'd screw each jar into place on the planks. He measured, placed, and decided three jars per plank would create a great display and catch the eye.

But what about lights? Mila's picture had featured a bunch of those tiny white lights strung along the wood and jars. Maybe he could nab a few of those battery-powered, remote controlled LED strands. Far less electrical hassle. Pulling his cell phone from the front pocket of his jeans, he tapped the device to alert, wanting to open e-mail and confirm that —

"Well, hey there, HB . . ." He rumbled the words when he discovered a text from Hailey Beth that stopped his pursuit of anything else. Heat and pleasure combined into a pleasant skim against his skin. His features folded into an expectant smile.

FYI . . . I'm making strawberry shortcake kabobs 4 2morro. Drizzled in white chocolate, btw. This means ur not allowed to cancel! LOL!

Ben hummed a happy sound, tickled that she seemed as eager for their outing as he was. He tapped a reply.

Cancel? Me? Not a chance.

Hailey Beth wanted to stop the clock, to wrestle the hour and minute hands until time stood still. Until there was no possibility Ben would leave. Until her heart, and his, reconciled to whatever the future might hold.

Just ahead of her on the bike path, he pedaled the circumference of Walloon Lake. Grass overgrew the edges of the road. Towering pines dotted the view of a crystalline body of water that sparkled like diamonds beneath the noon-time sun. Beneath her oversized t-shirt and pull-on shorts, Hailey Beth had donned a one-piece swimsuit. As the heat index climbed, so did her longing to chuck their bikes, their as-yet untouched picnic basket, and dive into the refreshing waters of the lake.

Truly, the universe could wait for anything else.

"Hey, Ben, let's pull off and go for a swim. Seriously. I'm dying."

"Wimp."

"And proud of it, babe."

His laughter carried to her through a spiced breeze laden by humid air and the ripening heat of a mid-summer afternoon.

Ben angled toward a nearby clearing and they dropped their bikes near the thick trunk of a weeping willow tree.

Hailey Beth peeled off her day-glow orange t-shirt and white shorts, b-lining for the water. Swim trunks set to go, Ben disposed of his t-shirt by tossing it across the handlebars of his bike. Hailey Beth barely crossed the shoreline when Ben caught up to her and swooped her into his arms. She squealed, catching on to his intent as he trounced ankle, thigh, and then waist deep into the lake . . . and then he tossed her as hard as he could.

Sputtering, laughing, gasping for breath, Hailey Beth rocketed back to the surface of the water and launched straight for him, fully intending some form of revenge. But then, a better plan emerged. Floating free about a hundred yards away or so was a flat, square diving platform. Revenge could wait. Hailey Beth caught his eye, nodded toward the wide raft. "Let's go!"

"Deal."

They spent the next half hour diving,

swimming, chasing and dunking each other. Plenty enough revenge to soothe her soul — though as they romped, Hailey Beth couldn't escape the sensation of being held in strong arms, water shimmered and beaded on his skin like diamond-dew. Her heart sang, filled by the pure simplicity of the moments they shared.

Returning to shore, laughing like mad, they laid out a pair of terrycloth beach blankets and promptly collapsed.

Hailey Beth closed her eyes and sighed with unfettered delight. Water droplets evaporated from her skin as the pleasant chill gradually transformed to languid warmth.

And her stomach growled, which caused them both to crack up all over again.

Ben turned his head. "I guess we should eat, huh?"

"I suppose."

Ben snorted at her lazy response. "I thought I was the one who was always short on words."

Although their blankets were separated by a bit of distance, he stretched his arm, capturing her hand and lacing his fingers through hers. Delicious, she decided in a lush, happy haze. Absolutely delicious. Hailey Beth kept her eyes closed. And savored. "You just want those desert kabobs I made."

"There's that, for sure." Now it was Ben who closed his eyes, breathed deep of the grass spice, pine, and floral sweetness.

"I suppose I should get up."

He turned his head toward her. One of those chocolatey brown eyes popped open. "Mm-hmm."

"And I guess we'd better eat."

"Mm-hmm."

Groaning, feigning exaggerated reluctance to relinquish the lazy moment, Hailey Beth lifted to an elbow, then sat, then groaned again and stood, grabbing a wicker basket from the metal carrier strapped to the front of her bike.

Ben laughed at her theatrics. "You gonna be OK, there, HB?"

"Oh, I'll survive."

"Here. Le'me help."

When he stood, sunlight framed him, bright and golden. The dips and planes of his chest, his shoulders, overpowered her senses, as well as her ability to remain strictly friends, strictly comfortable, strictly removed . . .

Ben stepped close, his body warmed by the day's sun and exertion.

Hailey Beth could breathe him in through

the humid atmosphere that surrounded them. Senses piqued, she caught her breath when his fingertips slid against hers. Ben drew the handle of the picnic basket from her suddenly too-loose grip and delivered a lingering look into her eyes.

Hailey Beth fought a swoon by helping him lay out an additional blanket, sturdy paper plates, plastic cutlery. Chicken salad, mixed with diced grapes, smoked almonds, and pasta was paired with an assortment of bite-sized veggies. Sitting cross-legged on the blanket next to Ben, Hailey Beth uncapped a small tub of ranch for dipping.

"This is outstanding."

"Pretty much healthy, except for the mayo mix in the salad."

Ben chewed and chuckled. "You're sounding like my mom. She's all over our diets like mad."

"I can see why. Your dad looks great, and he seems to have ten-times more energy than this time last year."

"No doubt. Which is why living by Anna Fisher's dietary rules is easy to embrace. We tease a lot and give her grief, but, what a blessing. Time. You can look at the ticking clock as a countdown, or a count forward. I'm all in for the 'count forward' approach."

Simple truths. Ben's life, his world, was

ruled by simple truths. So was hers, which was a large part of the reason they'd been inseparable since childhood. Hailey Beth drifted with the flow when their conversation slipped into a comfortable, contented silence.

"Are you ready for the shower next weekend?"

"Oh . . . yeah . . . you'd never understand the complexities, though."

"Like?"

"Like pining for the perfect lace sheath to wear, and pairing said dress with shoes that won't destroy your feet."

Ben frowned. "Bridal showers sound dangerous."

"You have no idea. That drama aside, the menu is all set, and I've got a bunch of cute decorations ready to be installed at the restaurant. Lots of help, too, so I think we're good."

"It ends at six, right?"

Hailey Beth puzzled, wondering why he was so interested in the timing. "Around there, yeah."

"Hmm. Phillip said he's been asked to show up afterward, to say a thank you to everyone and help Mila pack up."

Oh, so that was why. He was thinking of

his brother. "He's such a good groom-to-be."

He pegged her with a playful grin, then a wink. "The Fisher men were raised right."

I'll say. Hailey Beth agreed in silence, captivated by the view as Ben dipped and popped a pair of Roma tomatoes, enjoying the veggies with visible gusto.

10

Sunday evening, Hailey Beth entered Thomas's Grocery, intending to check on the day's activity before she saw to closing the shop. Post bridal shower festivities, her feet were killing her — as expected — and she was dying for the comfort of shorts, flip-flops and a loose, comfy t-shirt.

She had been on her feet, in heels no less, since ten o'clock in the morning. Now, at half-past six in the evening, she was delightfully exhausted. The celebration of Mila's upcoming marriage had been a resounding success.

Followed into the family mercantile by Mila, the creaky wooden door had barely clanked shut behind them when an unexpected site caused Hailey Beth's footsteps to stumble, and stop dead.

There was Ben Fisher, halfway to the top of a metal ladder, installing wall hangings just like the ones she had shown Mila weeks ago. There were even flowers. A big batch of pastel-hued daisies rested on the cashier's counter. There were green spikes and leaf sprays, too, everything ready and waiting to be cut and placed.

No way.

"Hey, HB. Hey, Mila. How was the shower?"

Her features graced by an all-too-smug grin, Mila brushed past Hailey Beth's statue-like form just as breezy as could be. The wench. "It was over-the-top awesome. Phillip and I are stocked for the next decade, I'm sure. What a great party, and it was so wonderful to see everyone."

At last, Hailey Beth found proper footing, as well as her voice. "Ah, Ben, we'll be right back, OK? I need to chat with Mila for just a quick second."

Ben remained focused on positioning those beautifully crafted flower holders against the wall, but his grin spoke volumes. Even though she didn't have a direct sight-line, she'd bet the bank his eyes sparkled with mischief. "Yeah, 'cause I'm sure there wasn't enough conversation to be had at a bridal shower."

Hailey Beth bit back a growl. "Excuse us, please."

His installation efforts never missed a

beat. "Take your time."

As soon as they were sequestered in the quasi-privacy of the store office, Hailey Beth rounded on her sister. "You did this!"

"Oh, no, no. This was *your* idea, and I've got the website to prove it. All I did was mention it to Ben. After that, voila!"

"You mentioned it. To Ben."

Mila nodded, eager and pleased.

Hailey Beth gaped at her sister's audacity. "I thought you were my friend!"

"Nope. I'm your sister. Big difference." Saucy to no end, Mila grabbed the single-serve box of cereal always stationed at the corner of Hailey Beth's desk. Mila shook a handful of the go-to comfort snack into the palm of her hand then tossed the sweetened, round-shaped cereal into her mouth.

Hailey Beth scowled, skewering her sister with a dark glare. "I think I hate you."

"Go ahead, if it helps. I promise to survive. But I wonder if you will."

In sharp emphasis, she grabbed Hailey Beth by the shoulders and turned her toward the office doorway. There, Ben was plain to see in all his worker-man, alpha-male glory. He stood atop the metal step ladder, hard at work with measuring tape, a leveler, his electric drill powered by brawn and muscle.

Ahem. She physically shook herself, convicted by her own behavior while heat performed a cascade from head to toe. The buzz of Ben's drill cut into a suddenly oppressive silence. Mila had a point. Hailey Beth was gawking at him like a love-struck teenager, but, really, this was a gesture of friendship. Nothing more. Shame on her. Ben deserved better. She steeled her spine, determined to be reasonable. Practical.

Realistic.

He was simply making her shop even more country-quaint and beautiful. The offering might have been inspired by Mila's prompting, but, from now on, his touch, his handprint, would linger upon her daily world like the sweet, inviting scent of flowers and earthy undertones of fresh-cut greenery. Despite every noble intention, Hailey Beth continued to focus on him — on those long legs, that trim waist, all done up in denim. Those broad shoulders worked a steady beat beneath his un-tucked, button-down work shirt with its sleeves rolled up against tan, sinewy forearms. She longed to just stand there — savor.

But in just over a month, he'd be gone.

Just like that, the spell broke. A lump squeezed against her throat. Seeming to sense Hailey Beth's building emotion, Mila gave her a firm shake at the shoulders, then a tight hug. "I love you, kiddo. And, I figured, what better maid of honor present could I give you?"

Days passed into a week. A week of routine for Hailey Beth. Except . . . one thing was most definitely not routine. Especially at the store.

Once again, for probably the millionth time, she caught herself looking at Ben's wall display. A dreamy, happy haze swept through her soul. The dawn of a smile, probably the millionth she'd shed this week, curved her lips. Then came recognition. An immediate frown.

Blast him.

Blast him good and true.

Benjamin Alexander Fisher had gone and done it. Every time she looked at those cheery flowers, tucked neat and sweet, cuddled by green leaves and a few tender green spikes in their clear glass jars framed by fairy lights, she thought of him. It was impossible not to. And it wasn't as though he needed help capturing her attention . . .

Blast him.

Maybe she could rebalance herself by doing something for him in return. At the very least, she should thank him. Separate schedules and increasing activity for the wedding precluded any extended time together the last several days. Hailey Beth rang up a customer, bagging flour, milk, sticks of butter, and a stash of onion soup mix for Melvina Oberman, who seemed to be stocking up to make bread sometime soon.

Bread.

Hailey Beth pursed her lips, inspiration dawning as she bid Melvina a good day. Ben loved homemade banana bread, and she could abscond with a few bananas from Mom's overly ripe stash. Maybe that would help re-level the playing field between. Yeah. That would work. Friendship for friendship.

Satisfied with the move-forward plan, Hailey Beth rededicated herself to life at Thomas's Grocery, chatting with customers, sorting stock, and tracking orders.

Late that day, while early evening cast long, supple shadows across the crop fields and flat lands of Antioch, Hailey Beth drove to the Fisher farm. She turned right, into the long driveway, where at the end, a white, wood-framed, two-story home stood sentinel. She braked to a stop in front of the detached garage. Nabbing a wrapped loaf of freshly baked banana bread, she climbed out of the car. Gravel crunched beneath her shoes until she trotted up a trio of wooden steps that led to the front door. Her knock was answered by Anna, who greeted Hailey Beth with a hug and welcoming smile.

"How are you, sweetheart?" Anna ushered her across the threshold and into the great room.

"I'm good, thank you. I was looking for Ben." Hailey Beth lifted the baked goods, rapidly excusing her presence since there wasn't much activity on the main floor of the house. Was Ben gone? Her heart sank at the idea. "I made him a little token of appreciation. Wanted to thank him for the beautiful wall hangings he created for the store."

"I saw them the other day when I ran into town to pick up a few things. I had no idea he was even making them."

"I didn't either."

Anna smiled at the sheepish admission, giving Hailey Beth's arm an affectionate pat. "They sure do look nice. He'll be so glad you've come by. He's in the barn seeing to Dollie and Marcus for the night. Go, say hello."

"Thanks. I will."

After a final hug for Ben's mom, Hailey Beth followed the slight curve of a different gravel pathway, this one angling from the side of the house. Narrow and flower lined, it was a spot of beauty. There was a pond just yards away where frog music and the chatter of insects could be heard. The perfume of hyacinth and summer roses filled the air. At the end loomed the massive expanse of the family's red and white barn. The doors were flung open. From within came the sounds of music and a rhythmic dig and heave that led her to believe Ben was pitching hay for their two horses.

Entering the barn transformed low-lying sunbeams into bands of pale gold. The pungent spice of hay and horse flesh filled the air. Translucent particles danced in the breeze, shimmering, glowing, filling the blocks that poured through the doors and the wide, high windows above. As her eyes adjusted to the shift in light, Ben came into sharp focus.

Bare chested, oblivious to her arrival and the world at large, he prepped the stalls, bobbing his head and moving in time to some classic rock. The music blasted from the speakers of the shelf-top radio. The vignette was perfect. Hailey Beth trembled on automatic. On instinct. A wave of longing magnetized her senses.

Ben kept to himself, by and large. He was quiet, reserved, but deep. Perception and empathy lent such richness to his character.

Such feeling . . . She stared, and ached, and wished, and prayed . . .

Some women might have absorbed his essence and shied away. Not so for Hailey Beth. That mysterious, undeniable pull went to work, driving her toward him via silent, stealth-like footsteps. The closer she came, the more acutely she realized: he smelled of hay spice, dewy earth, and the hot rays of a late-summer sun. Every nerve ending along her arms, neck, and chest sang with energy. Dizzying warmth swept through her once Ben registered her arrival.

He grabbed for his t-shirt and slid it on, moving toward her, eyes inquiring.

No one had ever struck a match to her senses like Ben. *Ever.*

Why exactly was she here again? She stumbled and bumbled, about to lose her grip on the simple loaf of banana bread she clutched. Meanwhile, Ben's solid frame blocked the sun, his features now backlit by gold, like a burst of rays.

"Hey. HB. What's up?"

A level of concern layered his eyes, tilted his lips downward a trace. She fought for air and gave herself an inner wake-up call. Ben took hold of her hand — so simple a thing — until his thumb stroked back and forth, slow and light against its back. At that point, her pulse stirred into a heavy pound. She noticed the way Ben tracked the motion of his caress, the way an expression of wonder lit his eyes.

Hailey Beth cleared her throat. "I . . . I wanted to . . . I wanted to . . ."

"What do you want, HB?"

He whispered the words, a seductive ripple of sound against her ears, her senses. His breath skimmed softly against her cheeks. What a loaded question . . . and when had he stepped so close?

She cleared her throat again, and tried once more. "I wanted to say thank you, and . . ."

His caress had continued. Drawn to the vision of their connected hands, Ben cut in quietly. "Your skin is so soft." His gaze lifted to hers after taking in her gift. "Is this for me?"

The song ended. Silence ripened the atmosphere.

Ben took custody of the bread, relieving her of its weight. He placed the loaf on a nearby work shelf.

Hailey melted, dissolving into an ache, a tingling rush of undiluted wistfulness. "It is. I appreciate what you did at the store, and I hope you like it, and I really appreciate what you did at the store, and —"

He touched a fingertip to her cheek, stilling her at once. "You already said that, HB. No problem, and no thanks necessary. It was my pleasure."

Again, with that husky whisper. He rested his forehead against hers, stared into her eyes.

Hailey Beth's control snapped. She wrapped her arms slowly around his neck, drew him down, nuzzling his mouth with her lips before laying claim to a long, slow kiss.

Ben answered that call with hunger. With surrender. His low hum of pleasure spurred her on, destroyed her hesitance at being so forward. "You taste like sunlight," she whispered, pulling just far enough away to meet his gaze. But she wanted his kiss, his touch, his presence. Forever.

"What does sunlight taste like?" Ben resumed a physical connection, nibbling her neck, glossing his lips against her skin. Her pulse danced harder; her heart beat accelerated. Snugged as they were, she wondered if he could feel its beat or see the vibration that jumped at her throat.

Ben returned to her mouth. He kissed her hard and deep, bold for the first time ever, lips dancing and moving in time to a private, shared measure of music only they could hear, and only they could ever create.

"Sunlight tastes warm. Sweet. Perfect." The kiss intensified, pouring through her in a free-flow Hailey Beth welcomed.

From beyond their private sanctuary in the barn came the squeak and rumble of an approaching vehicle. Phillip's old red pickup kicked stones free and sent a plume of dust into the air as he navigated the drive leading to the Fisher farm.

The timely interruption returned Hailey Beth to reality, to the truth of the road to come. A road leading to just one destination.

Heartbreak.

The realization brought tears to her eyes, tears that rapidly spilled over her lashes. Alarmed, Ben brushed the pads of his thumbs carefully against her moistened skin, stroking away the wetness, but not the pain.

"HB? What's wrong?"

"Nothing's wrong, Ben. Everything is right. Everything right here and right now is exactly the way I had always imagined. My sister is set to marry her soul mate in a few weeks, her life will be brimming with happiness. My family is well. I've got a great business to care for. I'm healthy and strong.

I have wonderful friends. I have everything but love. I have everything but you."

The final words seemed to strike home with Ben, causing his eyes to go wide, his touch to become even more tender, if such a thing was even possible. He cupped her face between his hands, looking at her urgently, pleading.

"HB, I —"

She shook her head, unable to bear the idea of him saying anything right now. *Absolutely anything.* Because there was something else she needed to add.

"Ben, don't. Just . . . don't. Please. This is the kiss I've dreamed of since I was a little girl. There's just one thing wrong."

He waited, keeping to himself, continuing to question her with a long, intent gaze.

"To me, this isn't a kiss of beginnings, or hope, or promise. It's a kiss goodbye." Her voice faltered, she spun from his embrace. "I have to go. I'll see you later."

Framed within the mahogany oval of a tall, standing mirror, Ben surveyed the overall reflection. In the center stood Phillip, tuxedo in place, fussing with his bow tie. To Phillip's left, Aaron finessed the alignment of his cummerbund. To Phillip's right, Ben stood stock-still, absorbing it all. Twisting on the inside.

This moment was huge, on many levels.

"Black-tie. At a country church wedding and farm reception. Seriously, Phillip, what were you thinking?" Aaron's light-hearted muttering was met with a mock-glare from their eldest sib, because how else was Phillip expected to treat his designated best man?

"Don't blame me, blame my bride-to-be. She's all about the romance."

"What's romantic about black-tie?" Satisfied with his attire, Aaron straightened his jacket.

"She said she melts a little when she

411

thinks of me in a black tux."

"She needs glasses."

"You need a life."

Ben burst out laughing, slapping Phillip on the back. The repartee was timeless, perfect, but most of all, bittersweet.

"I'm getting a life, my brother. Next year, when Ben's back from his mission trip, you guys are returning this favor for me and Emma when we take that fateful walk down the aisle."

Phillip made a final tweak to his boutonniere, a teal lily framed by baby's breath and a pair of small, green leaves.

"Can somebody help me with this flower thing?" Completing the ensemble, Dad stepped up from behind, trying to pin his boutonniere into place without much success. "Your mom always does this for me."

"No problem, Pop. I've got it."

Phillip's words came out quiet. Husky. Ben watched as he made short work of the task, then held Dad's arms, looking him in the eyes. "Thanks, Pop. For everything."

Following an understanding nod, Dad cleared his throat and waved away the gratitude. "Hey, I'm just standing here. You're the one who deserves the thanks. Boutonnieres. Whose nut-brained idea was that?"

Phillip hooted. Wrapping an arm around Dad's shoulder, Phillip caught on to the reflection thing. He pulled Dad into center-frame of the mirror, into the reflection of all that they were, and all that they would become . . . from this moment forward. The four Fisher men. Ben was captured by a sentimental yearning for the past, but excitement for the future rode just beneath the surface. For each of them.

With stealth and grace, one of the two commissioned photographers for the day moved into place and snapped pictures. Ben supposed their quartet made a nice image, all spiffed up for the wedding, dressed in identical tuxedos. But he knew, with absolute certainty, no photograph would ever compete with the image that burned itself promptly onto his heart.

"Hey, Phillip?" Phillip looked at Aaron, waiting. Aaron's lips curved into a slow-building, devilish smile. "Wait until you see what Ben and I did to decorate the getaway car. It's awesome! Totally classic!"

"Come on! Seriously?"

Phillip lunged for Aaron who backed off fast, his grin at mega-watt strength, his hands held high in surrender. As usual, Ben stepped between them, but belly-laughed hard. Just like that, sentimentality vanished into the sound of cat-calls, hoots, and their relishing, sparkling-eyed father playing referee over it all.

Tears sheened Hailey Beth's view for a moment as she looked down the main aisle of Antioch Christian Church, ready to join the rest of Mila's bridal party at the altar. Yesterday and tomorrow melded into an overwhelming moment of love and joy. She blinked to clear her view. Never would their lives be the same. That was OK, though. Happy horizons called Mila to the side of her forever love, and Hailey Beth knew that as sad as it was to let go of one season of life, one season of their shared time and experiences, the times to come would provide just as much happiness, just as much fulfillment. The relationship she shared with Mila would be additionally blessed by today's exchange of vows.

Her gaze fixed on Ben, who stood next to Aaron at the head of the church, and her heart lifted into a fluttery spiral. The music of Pachelbel's *Canon in D* accompanied her down the aisle. Once she stepped into place, the flourish of the pipe organ filled space and time. All at once, the church filled on a thrilling rise of melody as Beethoven's *Ode to Joy* began. Guests lifted solemnly to their feet.

And Mila made her entrance.

Grateful for the monogrammed handkerchief she held, Hailey Beth dabbed at her eyes as her sister moved forward. The delicate, snow-white square had been stitched by hand, given as a pre-wedding gift to the bride and each attendant by Anna Fisher. So many beautiful threads and connections crowned this moment, and Mila looked like a brunette Grace Kelly, her wide, lace dress moving in time to her walk toward the future.

Reverend Taylor opened the ceremony with a welcoming prayer, and Hailey Beth's heart overflowed.

"Our first reading," he continued, "is from the first book of Corinthians, Chapter Thirteen, Verses Four through Seven. Love is patient, love is kind. It does not boast, it is not proud. It does not dishonor others, it is not self-seeking, it is not easily angered, it keeps no record of wrongs. Love does not delight in evil but rejoices with the truth. It always protects, always trusts, always hopes, always perseveres. Love never fails."

Although stationed at the opposite side of the altar from Ben, Hailey Beth felt the touch of his gaze as sure as a caress.

Love never fails.

Statuary of angels caught her eye. Crafted of creamy white granite, their wings were spread in an eternal display of protection and comfort. Scripture was truth, of that there was no question in her mind. Yet, seldom was life as simple as that direct, three-word declaration.

At the end of the ceremony, Aaron took hold of her hand, as practiced at rehearsal, and tucked it gently against the crook of his arm. He escorted her down the aisle in a recessional parade given tempo by the exhilarating strains of Mendelssohn's *Wedding March*. The instant they stepped outside, a cascade of rose petals filled the air, thrown by wedding guests assembled just beyond the open church doors. Meanwhile, kids laughed and squealed, blowing soap bubbles that sailed high into the deep blue sky.

"I'll turn you over to Ben just as soon as decorum allows," Aaron teased, sotto voce.

Hailey Beth leveled him with a glower. "How gracious. Dumping me like a bad prom date so you can dance the night away with Emma."

Aaron feigned guilty conviction. "You're on to me." Just as quick, he turned big brother, treating her to a wink. "Still, save a dance for me, HB. You give as good as you get. Always have." He kissed her cheek, assuming their spot in the reception line. "You'll be rewarded for that, I have no doubt."

"Sure, sure." At that point, Reverend Taylor moved past. Before he could get away, Hailey Beth touched his arm to win his attention. "Reverend Taylor, you did such a great job. What a beautiful ceremony."

Small talk ensued. For the next hour, guests were greeted. Hugs, kisses, moments of reunion carried her away. After that, guests adjourned to the Fisher farm for the reception while the bridal party remained at the church for a brief session of formal portraits.

Hailey Beth noticed the way Ben tracked her, the way he'd catch her eye and linger in the moment for a few beats. During a break in the outdoor picture series, he chatted with Reverend Taylor as well. She supposed the topic was of the upcoming mission. Less than thirty days remained before departure, but she refused to let the future ruin what was left of the present. As a groomsman, Ben had been paired with Rochelle, but Hailey Beth felt no disquiet in that fact. She read him, his caring and connection, so vividly now.

Intimate sharing and soul-quenching kisses tended to assure her that way. Every time she thought of their interlude in the barn, she couldn't quell a smile.

By the time their chauffeured limousine left the church parking lot, a sunset evolved, painting the sky as their driver executed a scenic route through town. Celebratory horn honks, glasses of champagne, laughter and reminiscing took them to the Fisher farm. Squeezed happily next to Ben, Hailey Beth sank willingly into the joyful party.

Wispy clouds danced through a sky decorated by every hue of pastel imaginable. The sun transformed to an orb of rich, solid gold, sinking low as night slid its bluish gray fingers across the sky, the flatlands, of Antioch.

At the Fisher farm, a fairytale fantasy-world came to life.

Tent panels of whisper-thin silk rippled against a gentle evening breeze. Its long, wide expanse was illuminated from within by thousands of tiny, roof-top sparkle-lights and from without by lines of perfectly spaced ground stakes. Walking through the opening, and entering the reception of Mila and Phillip's wedding, was akin to stepping into a translucent, saffron-colored dream.

Hailey Beth clutched her bouquet. She

held fast to Aaron's arm at the back of the bridal party line, the maid of honor and best man awaiting their introductory cue from the DJ. Pair by pair, they marched inside to a loud chorus of cheers and applause.

After everyone assembled, a towering cake from Mascott's Bakery was wheeled carefully into place at the center of a makeshift dance floor. Phillip and Mila cut into the masterpiece, shared bites, and didn't smash one bit of the luscious confection into each other's faces.

After dinner, the DJ cranked up the sound and went to work entertaining the crowd.

Phillip and Mila shared their first dance as husband and wife to the romantic strains chosen for the event. Rather than pairing up groomsmen and bridesmaids for a traditional bridal party dance, Phillip and Mila urged everyone to form a circle. Shoulder to shoulder, arms around each other, they sang along to a contemporary Christian tune celebrating the bonds of friendship, swaying, laughing, shedding a few tears, and creating a memory that promptly stored itself in the vault of Hailey Beth's heart.

Afterward, she sank onto a seat next to Anna and kissed her cheek. "Thank you again for the beautiful handkerchief. I'm certainly giving it a workout today."

"Which is as it should be. Happy tears are my favorite tears."

"Mine, too."

Before their conversation could continue, Ben stepped up, offering an outstretched hand to Hailey Beth. "Mind if I steal you away for a bit?"

"Only if you're leading me to the dance floor. This song is one of my favorites."

"I could be coerced."

"Me, too."

They drifted to the floor, hand in hand, beginning to twirl as the artist sang with longing and love.

Hailey Beth rested her cheek against his, lost in the song. Ben, too, seemed content with the silence, with the simple joy of moving in time to a beautiful piece of music.

At last, as the finer details of the reception area captured her attention, Hailey Beth felt compelled to clear her tight throat and speak up. "I can see that making those decorations for the store was good practice for you."

"How's that?"

She leaned back to look into his eyes. When she came upon tranquil, deep brown, her spirit swooned. "I believe I detect the fine hand of Benjamin Fisher in the directional signs outside, as well as the 'Mila and

Phillip Fisher' sign standing front and center at the bridal table."

Ben dipped his head shyly. "Yeah. They seemed to like that one. I learned a lot about working a scroll saw, and wood branding when I made it. I'm pretty pleased with the results."

"You should be. They're beautiful." Hailey Beth was moved by the thoughtful gesture. "Did you make the smaller ones, the ones on easels at the gift table and guest book stand?"

Low-key and humble once again, he shrugged, and nodded, continuing to sweep her effortlessly across the floor. "Yeah. There's one at the photo booth, too."

"Which we need to visit before the night is through."

Ben gave her a bland look. "If you're into that kind of thing."

"Which I totally am." Hailey Beth giggled and slugged his arm. "Come on. You'll love it, and it'll make a great keepsake."

"Now, that's true enough." A seductive vibration coursed between them like an electrical charge. "Four poses per sitting, right?"

Tingles skated the length of her arms, up her shoulders, burning her cheeks. "I do believe."

Ben's smile dawned, pulling her like true north, drowning her in yearning. "Let's go."

The visit to the photo booth turned into corny poses and a riot of laughter. Ben squeezed into the tiny space and Hailey Beth had nowhere to go but his lap. She settled demurely, then Ben initiated the photo sequence.

The first two shots were pure comedy — Ben poking out his tongue, Hailey Beth pulling a funny face and going cross-eyed — Ben giving Hailey Beth rabbit ears, Hailey Beth pulling his ears out like an elephant as she made a crazy face.

Still stationed on his knee, Hailey Beth's heart lurched when she saw the last two on the reel. They were simple and beautiful, with both of them wearing big smiles, heads together, eyes sparkling. This was them. This was her Ben, captured forever in precious, split-seconds of time.

"I think we'll have to figure out a way to divvy these up."

Ben looked into her eyes. "Or arrange some form of joint custody."

"Ha. I have a pair of mini-scissors in my evening bag."

Ben's eyes went wide. "Because . . . yeah, of course you do."

Hailey Beth sighed in exaggerated frustration. "Part of a bridal survival kit. A MOH never travels without a stocked sewing kit on her person."

"MOH?"

"Maid of Honor."

"Well, no question you fit the title to perfection, HB."

Her senses danced. "Flatterer."

They shared the photos, but after that, Ben seemed reluctant to leave her company. "Want to get out of here for a few?"

Hailey Beth sensed he wanted to talk more than vacate the reception, but why? She nodded and allowed him to lead the way through a pair of open tent flaps. Grass shimmered with dew, tickling her ankles as they walked. They reached the boundary of the back yard and soybean fields. Ben's ambling came to a stop.

A full moon lit a clear sky glittering with stars. Even in the dim light, Hailey Beth sensed Ben's intensity, a tension that alerted her senses.

"This is for you. This is for me. This moment is for us, HB. I'm going to kiss you — and it most definitely won't be a kiss good-bye."

Ben didn't pause. He barely allowed the words to pass before he toppled her into a kiss that began as a silky, soft stroke of the lips, a dewy caress, and ended in depth and richness, bolstering an emotion that pushed its way into the depths of her soul. She tasted his warmth, his earthy spice. She breathed in the essence of cool, night air, intriguing flowers, sweetness, and life. His fingertips slid through her hair, loosening the clip at the base of her neck, causing waves to fall through his fingers, into the breeze that skimmed across her cheeks. Their mouths sealed; Hailey Beth closed her eyes while savoring sighs — his, hers — blended with the cricket-chatter and leaf whispers of the night. The kiss poured through her, fateful.

And more than a little foreboding.

12

A couple days later, Ben returned his tuxedo to Henderson's Formals, his gut well and truly in a stew.

It most definitely won't be a kiss goodbye.

Yeah, Fisher. Sure, it wasn't. Maybe not that night, and maybe not today, but he was deluding himself. Goodbye was coming fast as a freight train, with an equally devastating power of impact.

He pulled out his wallet to pay the tab and came upon the sepia-toned pictures of them from the wedding. One goofy. One beautiful. While he waited to be cashed out, Ben studied the frames, his fingertips glossing the image, his gaze snagged by the more serious image.

Looking at Hailey Beth sent him falling back into the kiss they had shared. Potent enough to leave him questioning everything, right down to a future he had planned and counted on for months now. His head had been there for weeks now, that circular battle between his love for her versus that undeniable pull to make use of his God-given talents and serve. He had meant it when he said their moment at the reception wasn't a goodbye kiss. He didn't want to say goodbye to her. Ever.

Transaction concluded, Ben accepted his receipt and folded his wallet, replacing it in the back pocket of his jeans. Thomas's Grocery was just a block away. He clicked on his phone to check the time, send Hailey Beth a text to see if they could somehow meet. Since it was close to noon, Ben decided to surprise her and find out if she was interested in a spontaneous lunch date.

When he entered the store, he came immediately upon Hailey Beth's winsome smile, sparkling eyes, and knew his unscheduled visit was a good call. She manned one of the three wooden cashier stands, finishing up with a customer.

"Hey there!" Her greeting came when she plucked off her overhead service light to close her station. "Picking up supplies?"

"Nope." He propped a hip, savoring the vision of her — dark blue apron on, emblazoned with the 'TG' logo and name. Her hair was pulled back, revealing that slim, creamy neck, emphasizing that heart-shaped face, those huge brown eyes. "I'm picking up the prettiest girl in town, if she's interested in getting a bite to eat. Can you take a break?"

"You bet. Care to come with me to the market?"

"Sure. You after anything in particular?"

"Actually, I need replacement blooms." She nodded toward the mason jar wall hangings. They were lit, and they looked great.

"The flowers don't seem bad."

"I fuss over them. Replace them every three days."

That tickled him. "That's the only bad thing about live flowers. They don't stay alive for long."

"But I wouldn't change a thing."

They shared smiles.

"Want me to drive?"

"Sure. That'd be great. Le'me grab my purse."

When she returned, the apron was gone revealing a simple, but lovely cotton dress in a mild shade of pink that looked great on her. She had also taken her hair down. She raked her fingers through freshly tumbled waves that tempted and stirred an itch along his fingertips. She moved toward him and Ben's senses performed a heated sizzle. He helped her step into the cab of his truck.

Hailey Beth closed the door and rolled down the window. When he kicked the vehicle into gear, she thrust her hand out the open window, fingertips sweeping up and down along wavering currents of wind.

"That's a sure sign of summer."

She gave Ben a glance, then closed her eyes as air blew across her cheeks. "What's that?"

"You, hand-surfing."

Hailey Beth pulled her hand inside the car and blushed. Ben was glad for light traffic through town because he was thoroughly distracted by that petal-soft rise of a pink against her cheeks.

"You're taunting me."

"I'm enjoying you."

At the next stoplight, she feathered his cheek with a tender caress. "Ditto."

The farmer's market was located at the southernmost edge of Antioch and consisted of not much more than a gravel parking lot and acres of grass dotted by tents that surrounded an ages-old but still sturdy metal structure. Styled like a glass and metal atrium, the market proper had sheltered shoppers and produce display tables for over half a century. Trucks of all sizes dotted the grounds and Ben navigated his pickup to a stop near the entrance of the building.

It didn't take Hailey Beth long to get lost in the mix of fresh-grown vegetables, flowers, and crafts. Ben enjoyed the way she lingered here and there, poking her nose into rose bouquets, or the way she trailed her fingertips over zucchini, squash, and lightly thumped a few musk melons.

He joined her as she chose her flowers — fluffy peonies — and the shades she mixed and matched were beautiful hues of pale blue, pink, purple, and snowy white.

Ben tucked in close, tracing the tips of the velvety petals. "Nice."

"They're my favorite."

"I can see why." He extracted his wallet, nodded toward her chosen array. "May I?"

Her eyes went soft, shy. "Oh, Ben . . . you don't have to do that, I —"

"I want to." Before she could object, he nodded to the seller and handed over payment.

Delivering a smile that struck home like a high-powered arrow, Hailey Beth thanked him, and then accepted the handles of the brown paper bag.

They continued their walk, hunting for luncheon food now, and Ben absorbed the way that plain old sack brimmed with bursts of color, with big-headed blooms dancing and bouncing against her thigh as she paused to take stock of some sandwich offerings, some chopped veggies and dip, some cookies.

Seeming to realize he lagged behind, Hailey Beth returned to Ben's side, inched in close, aligned to him in perfect synchrony as they wandered. Her shoulder pressed against his and she slipped her fingertips against his, holding on tight.

Man, did this feel good.

They selected fresh-made tuna salad sandwiches for lunch. Ben added a pair of mixed fruit bowls to their order while Hailey Beth shot him a sly glance and nabbed two caramel apples.

Ben agreed to that with a wink and a nod, directing the way to an empty picnic table shaded by the branches of a thick, tall maple tree.

Hailey Beth lifted her face to the sun, resting on a deep breath.

Ben followed suit, lulled by the peace of birds chirping, the white-noise of indistinct conversations taking place all around them.

"This is perfect."

It was.

Perfect.

Ben swallowed, braced, fought every instinct hot-wired into his DNA that, since he could talk, had geared him toward conservancy of opinion, of risk-taking, of high-level emotion. "Hailey, can I ask you something? Something weird, but . . . something . . . something I want you to think about?"

Brows pulled, frowning with concern, Hailey Beth nodded.

An inner quake started at the core of his stomach, branching out fast. The characteristically silent, observant one was about to bust out of that shell. "Why is this perfect?"

"Umm . . ." Her brows furrowed; she looked at him in confusion, and concern.

An idea caught fire, amplifying his intensity to push through. "It's us, HB. It's you and me. That's what makes this perfect."

Her bottom lip disappeared beneath the press of her teeth, the only revelation of her nerves. Her gaze remained steady.

Ben continued. "What if . . . what if I asked you to come with me? What if I asked you to join me on this mission trip? What would happen?"

Now she openly gaped. "Happen? What would happen? If I deep-sixed my entire life for a year of volunteer work? I'd be certified insane, that's what. Ben, what are you getting at?'

Something in her response, its readiness

and smooth analysis perhaps, cued Ben in on the fact that she had considered the issue. "What I'm getting at is, you could come with me. Obviously, you wouldn't leave as soon as I am, but you'd train up, you'd learn the ropes, and join me when you could, for whatever time you could spare. We could make choices . . . about the future . . . together."

"The future. Meaning us. Meaning lives beyond Arkansas and a year spent apart."

"Yes."

"Ben. No. You're not at all serious."

"HB. You know me as well as anyone else on earth. Do you think I'd put this out there lightly? I'm beyond serious, and, yeah, the logistics need work, but not the intent. Not the end result. The way things stand right now, the way I feel, I'm finding it difficult to even think about leaving anymore."

Now her lips trembled. So did her hands, which he clasped gently, then swept lightly with his thumbs.

"I can't be the reason you stay, Ben. I can't be what holds you back."

Ben felt something within him crumble. Suddenly the bright, bustling beauty of the farmer's market felt garish, overwhelming.

"Hailey Beth, come with me." He reiterated his request with deliberation, with the added impact of dropping her nickname. "I told you at the wedding I don't want to say goodbye. I mean it. I want you there. I want you at my side. I want to share this with you, day-by-day, as we always have. I know, now, how important it is. How important you are."

Her eyes went wide, glittery with moisture, her jaw slacked.

Ben pressed on, relentless. "I know it's asking a lot. I know this is completely off track from anything you had planned in your life. Joining the mission was a surprise to me as well. But, all that being understood, I knew it was a call I had to answer. Could you ever feel the same? Is there any way you could be convinced to give it a try?"

"Leave?"

He stared her down, and then gave a sharp firm nod. His words, by now, were spent. She pulled her hands from his and despite the hot, late-summer day, a sense of cold crept through Ben's body.

"I . . . I . . . couldn't. I can't leave Antioch. I've never even considered such a thing. Me? Mission work? My mission is here. My mission is the people I know and love who —"

"Maybe God, and your heart, could call you to a wider view."

Her breathing went ragged, her cheeks flamed. "No, Ben. You need to understand. This place is my home. It's my anchor."

So, that was it. She was scared. She was grounded by what she knew, the life she had lived since birth. He understood completely. "Anchors weigh you down, HB. Sometimes anchors need to be pulled up. If they're not, the boat will never sail, and meet its purpose. Think about that."

Her eyes went guarded and way too calm. The phrase 'Uh-oh' struck home real quick. Meanwhile, as he always tended to do of late, Ben's gaze dropped to her lips. Generally soft, lush and full, tempting beyond all get-out, they now pressed into a tight, telling line of banked temper.

"How can you say something like that to me? I'm not staid. I have a life, Ben. A life I worked hard to create and continue to work hard to maintain and grow. How dare you belittle that!"

Shocked straight back to the conversation at hand, Ben gaped at her. "What? I've done no such thing! I have too much respect for you to ever belittle your life, Hailey Beth, and you *know* that. You're running scared. I see it in your eyes. Your rejection isn't about life-change, it's about fear."

He seldom called her by her full name. In

less than five minutes he'd used it twice. He hoped she noticed the fact.

Still livid, she stabbed a long, slim finger — tipped by shiny pink polish — straight into his chest. He bit back a pained oath.

"Tread very carefully, Ben Fisher, and think about the things you've said to me just now. In retrospect, I think you'll come to know you've come blasting at me with no justification. If you ask me, I think maybe it's you who's scared right now, and afraid to leave home. Maybe that's my sudden allure for you. Maybe you don't care so much about me as the idea of what I represent. Home. Safety. Stability." She blinked hard, clearing those sparkling, tear-filled eyes of moisture. "For now, I need to get back to the store, so I'd appreciate a ride back to town. Now." Scooping up the remnants of their lunch, Hailey Beth stood, spinning neatly away from the table to toss the trash into a nearby bin. Her pretty dress floated out, then resettled around those incredible legs.

Stunned and shaken, all Ben could do was watch — but his heart, he realized too late, now lodged in his throat.

Lord, help him. What had he just done?

A couple days later, Ben sat across from

Aaron at a window-side table inside Sundae Afternoon, recapping his disastrous lunch date with Hailey Beth. Patronage of Mila's shop, they both figured, would be a nice boon and gesture to the absentee owner, presently enjoying a honeymoon trip to the Caribbean. Indulging in perfectly crafted burgers and piping-hot fries had absolutely nothing to do with it.

"Serves me right for ever opening my mouth. I know better. Situations like this are why I tend to stay quiet and learn the lay of the land before I speak. I played my cards and lost the bet." Ben paused to wolf down a few bites of his burger before continuing. "I tried, Aaron. I want her with me, so I asked her to join me on the mission. I laid my feelings on the line, but she shot me down. Even yelled some nonsense about me being pulled toward her only because *I'm* the one afraid of leaving my life behind." Now, his generally calm and unfettered psyche conducted a dance of turmoil that tied his stomach into knots. Loving her the way he did, how could he leave? By the same token, how could he stay?

"Once the dust settled, did it occur to you that she might not have been saying no to *you*? Sounds to me as if she said no to *leaving*. She said no to a sudden and probably unexpected proposal to vacate her present life . . . from someone who's beyond important to her."

"Yes, that occurred to me." Ben shrugged broadly. "After all, *I'm* doing it, and I told her as much."

"Giving her the perfect excuse to push things right back on you and say *you're* the one who's actually the scaredy-cat." Aaron snorted. "Lord, you two are a pair."

"Thanks." Ben filled his tone with plenty of snark.

"Look, Ben, you ambushed her, bro. You came at her unexpected. You've had time to make the decision, adjust to the ramifications."

"OK. So . . . ?"

Aaron groaned. "So . . . has she? No matter how much she loves you, she's got a lot to live for here in Antioch. Leaving would take miles of guts, not to mention a plan."

"Same as me."

"Not quite. You've had time to work out the details, right?"

Hmm. Aaron had a point.

"Has HB had the same luxury? Has she had the chance to discuss any of this with her family and friends? Has she had the time and opportunity to think this over on her own terms? To pray about it?"

Ben stared at Aaron in a hard, contemplative silence. "Well, doesn't this just beat all?"

"What's that?"

"You, being the logical, well-reasoned member of the tribe. I thought that was Phillip's gig."

Aaron tossed back some fries. Shrugged. "Since he's out of town, I'm acting in absentia. Don't get used to it."

Ben resumed his meal, smiling wryly. "I won't."

"Do you really want my advice?"

"Yeah."

Aaron studied Ben with that trademark level of intensity that belonged to him and him alone. "Talk to her father."

Huh? "Byron? Byron Thomas?"

Aaron arched a brow, and reiterate slowly, "Talk. To. Her. Father."

Suddenly, dots connected, forming what might be a pathway toward the mission, as well as a pathway toward something even bigger, even more daunting: the wholeness of his heart.

13

Ben had never been so nervous. A couple unsteady weeks had passed as he absorbed Aaron's advice and formulated a plan. Despite the first cooling days of early autumn, his palms left sweat marks against the leather steering wheel while he navigated the short drive to town, to the Thomas family home. Hailey Beth would be at the store, but Byron Thomas expected him in just a few minutes, and he was right on time.

No way would he be late for this meeting.

His heart thundered against his ribcage. He fought to steady his breathing. This would be OK. He had a plan. He had goals. Still, the entirety of his heart, and future, was on the line.

Corinne Thomas answered his summons when he knocked at the front door. Following a hug, and a brief exchange of post-wedding family updates, she led him into the main living area, where Byron waited.

He stood from the leather chair where he sat once Ben entered the room. Hailey Beth's father welcomed him with a warm smile and firm handshake.

"It's good to see you, Ben. Glad to have a chance to spend some time with you before you leave."

"Same here, sir. Weddings are a lot of fun, but not really conducive to many one-on-one conversations."

"I second that, for sure. Have a seat." Ben accepted the gestured invitation to occupy a black leather chair next to the one Byron had occupied. The Thomas family were generations-old merchants. Their home was well styled, reflecting a sense of affluence, but no pretense. He'd always been a bit intimidated by the power and status of the Thomas family, not because they were rich, or arrogant, but because they represented the opposite side of his life and upbringing. The Fisher family earned its livelihood from the land, from raw, physical work. The Thomas family earned its livelihood from book smarts and a sense of well-heeled confidence.

"You holding up OK? Last-minute details coming together? If there's anything you need, just shout, y'hear?"

"I do, and thank you for that. I appreciate

it, sir. We're set, though, far as I can tell. We're in the process of organizing supplies to be packed and hauled, then there will be the convoy of volunteers and a second round of supplies to be coordinated — mostly perishables and such. We appreciate your donation to that effort, by the way. The food staples and produce mean a lot."

"My pleasure."

Enough groundwork had been laid, Ben figured. It was now or never. He dipped his head for a moment, closed his eyes to find stillness and peace. Both descended upon him at once, soothing his nerves. *Thank you, Jesus. Take it from here. Please.* "I called because I wanted to talk to you about an idea I have. About the mission, and about me, and Hailey Beth."

"What's on your mind?"

"Well . . ." Another deep breath, and he dove into the deep waters. "I'd like Hailey Beth to come with me. To Arkansas."

"Come again?"

Oh, her father was beyond surprised alright, and not inclined to hide the fact. That was expected, and respected. Only full-bore openness would take this proposal where Ben hoped it might go.

"Sir, I think, if she were able, she'd come with me. Not for the whole year, but for

441

most of it. She could still receive training and be brought up to speed with respect to our objectives for the mission, but she'd only do so under a very specific set of conditions."

"Such as?"

"After the wedding, we talked about the idea of her joining me. Not surprisingly, she said she won't go. She won't even entertain the idea of joining me if the store isn't tended to in the manner she feels is best. Mila's an obvious candidate, but Mila's already got her hands full with Sundae Afternoon, and her marriage, and maybe even a family before too long, so —"

Byron's brows shot up. "Do you know something I don't know?"

Ben released a nervous chuckle. The moment of levity was just what he needed. He enjoyed the teasing glint in Byron's eyes. "Only a week past the wedding? No, I don't. But it stands to reason kids would be in their future."

"I'm hoping."

They shared smiles.

"So, I guess I'm here to ask for two things from you today."

Byron nodded agreeably, waiting.

"First and foremost, I am asking for your permission to marry Hailey Beth, if she'll have me." Ben stopped there, gauging, waiting a couple beats for any discernable reaction. Nothing came to him, though, except a smooth blink, a nod. Byron had always been a cool, collected man.

"And what's number two?

"Number two is a question I have about the store. A proposal, if you will."

"Which is?"

Byron's eyes sharpened, going narrow. A fire came alive — protection and passion for the business his family had created generations ago. That was precisely what Ben counted on. After all, Thomas's Grocery was Byron's flagship, his legacy.

Leaning forward, Ben propped his elbows on his knees and faced Hailey Beth's father in a moment of truth. "Sir, would you be willing to come out of retirement, for just under a year, so she would be free to either accept or decline my offer to join me in the mission based on her own wishes, her own heart, rather than the interests of the store and her family ties?"

"Neither one of which should ever be taken lightly." The words were gently spoken, but carried an undercurrent of warning.

"I couldn't agree with you more. I'm living proof of that truth. I know what I'm doing puts my family on the line. We treasure our heritage, just as you do, but the thing is, they're in support of what I want to do as a person above and beyond the world they've built. I'm grateful for that latitude, because you're right, it doesn't come easy. Or without risk. I want to know the farm will be OK without me. I care about it, and have since birth."

Byron leaned back, studying Ben anew.

Ben continued. "I know you have managers you trust implicitly, that HB trusts implicitly as well. But she'll never surrender her hold to anyone but family. Really, to anyone but you, the one who delivered management to her to begin with. And I don't blame her at all."

"What if you decide to continue?"

"We'd figure it out. Together. Maybe part-time mission work could be mixed into a schedule we could all live with. I thought the idea might be worth exploring, because, between HB, the people already in place, and you, of course, there are a lot of people standing ready to be sure everything continues on the way it should."

It took some time for Byron to mull over the pros and cons. In the silence that followed, Ben was pretty sure he could see cogs spinning away within an agile mind.

The coin flip he had initiated spun through the air. Heads. Tails. Heads. Tails.

"I'm on board, and you can tell Hailey Beth as much, but the decision to stay or to leave has to come from her."

"Absolutely, and that's all I want, sir. A chance to give her a level offer. I thank you. Truly I do." Ben shifted, uncomfortable as silence returned. He didn't want to have to ask for her hand again, but he would if necessary. Nothing would keep him from pursuing her with all the power he possessed.

"About marriage." Byron resumed their conversation.

Ben's chest rose and fell on a sigh of relief that was probably palpable, because Hailey Beth's father smiled warmly, with what Ben could have sworn was a sea of nostalgia rippling through his gaze. "Long ago, if someone had told me I'd have not one but two daughters married to sons of Jonathan and Anna Fisher, I never would have believed it possible. I love and respect your mother and father and your brothers. But we have a lot of history. Most of it good, some of it . . . tense."

"I know we had some tough scraps over crop sales. There've been some hard-fought negotiations, but the respect is returned tenfold. So is the affection."

Once again, something mysterious flashed through Byron's eyes. "True enough, but it goes beyond that. Someday, have Hailey Beth tell you the story of me, your mom, and dad and our earlier days."

"I'll do that. And I want you to know, I'd be honored to join your family. I promise you, with all that I am, if she takes me on, I'll be good to her. I'll treasure her. Always."

"Ben, I feel the same, and I know you're a man of your word. I'd welcome you readily."

Ben stood, overwhelmed by gratitude.

A firm handshake became a quick, hard hug.

When he left the Thomas's home, driving back to the farm with a light heart and shoulders lifted of an invisible weight, a piece of Byron's wisdom played through his head.

The decision to stay or to leave had to come from her.

Hailey Beth spent days agonizing.

Blowing up at Ben was bad enough. Now, having the seeds and roots of his offer to join the mission sprout leaves and flourish, was too much to handle. Really. He was a lunatic. Certifiable. He knew she had a store to run. He knew she had family and friends. He knew she had a life in Antioch she would never surrender on impulse. Even if that impulse came from the man she loved beyond reason.

Ben had picked quite the moment to become verbal and intense. It was as if he had surrendered his old sense of self and embraced some of the characteristics of his older brothers — Phillip's ability to argue and negotiate coupled with Aaron's straightforward intensity.

What was up with the universe these days?

Hailey Beth stood sentinel in front of the coffee machine in the kitchen of her family home, waiting for a jumbo-sized mug to fill with her favorite brand of dark roast. Not even those tempting curls of java-steam could rouse her from a relentless funk.

"Hey, Hailey-girl." Dad strolled into the kitchen, newspaper tucked beneath his arm. Dad refused to give up the print edition of the Antioch Herald. "Something smells good."

"Toasting some banana bread and making some coffee. Interested?"

"I sure am, if it's not too much trouble."

"Not at all." Hailey Beth went to work, glad to serve and glad to be distracted from further introspection about a certain member of the Fisher family. Once breakfast was dished up, she delivered Dad's portion and joined him at the eat-in area tucked into a wide, sunny bay window. They bowed their heads and Dad offered a blessing.

"Going to be a pretty day." Dad spread a napkin across his lap.

The Bay window overlooked a wide patio area and a chunk of green grass bordered by fences that divided the neighboring lots. Their home fronted Washington Avenue, one of the offshoots of Main Street, but the back yard offered a measure of solitude and quiet. Hailey Beth enjoyed the view, buttering her bread, taking a bite. When she sipped from her coffee, thoughts of Ben intruded. Banana bread was his favorite . . .

"That was a heavy sigh. You OK, sweetheart?"

Hailey Beth hid a cringe at her father's interruption. Yep, she was officially losing it, casting laden sighs aloud without even realizing it. "I'm fine. Just waking up is all."

Dad tasted his coffee, but delivered a knowing look over the rim of his cup before setting it aside. "I'd love to believe you."

Oh, what was the sense in hiding?

"I'm feeling a little down, I suppose."

"What's wrong?" He set the newspaper aside, leaning forward, intent and focused.

Hailey Beth loved that about her dad. There was nothing halfway when it came to his kids.

"It's Ben. And it's me. And it's . . . just . . . *everything.*"

"Can you narrow things down a bit?" A gentle, teasing light came alive in his eyes.

Hailey Beth grinned at him, but the grin quickly faded. "Actually, I'm ashamed to admit it."

"Admit what, Hailey-girl?"

"That I'm scared."

From there, she explained the muddled set of circumstances between her and Ben. She wanted to be with him, and the more she considered it, the more intriguing the idea of service became. But, beyond that was the heritage she cared for with every fiber of her being each day she tended to Thomas's Grocery.

"You turned over the store to me a year after I graduated college, and no honor has ever meant more to me."

"I know that, and it shows in your actions. The store is in great hands with you, but it was never meant to come with shackles."

"It doesn't!" She spoke hard, fast, and from the heart, but she also knew, deep down inside, that she was using the mercantile to dodge an emotional and life-altering bullet . . .

"Hailey Beth, that's the fear talking." She wilted at the shoulders, and he reached across the table to give her hands a squeeze. "There's no shame in fear. Fear is a natural and helpful response to danger, and to the unknown. Trouble comes when you let fear paralyze you into hiding, or when it leads to misplaced complacency."

Hailey Beth watched him for a few minutes, absorbing the truth he shared. Talk about spot-on delivery. "So, I'm not faithless?"

His deep laugh rumbled. "No. Far from it."

"Still, I'm afraid. I'm afraid of leaving. I love my life here. I love what I do. I'm happy. It's all I've ever known, and it satisfies me. What Ben offers feels so . . . risky."

"All that's true." He paused meaningfully. "But, will you be happy when he's gone?"

No.

The answer filled her at once. Completely. Still, she couldn't deliver an immediate reply. Part of her wanted to continue to use fear as a shield. In the end, though, facts wouldn't be denied. "No, Dad. I won't."

"Then I think you know what you need to do. Don't let fear win. Don't shy away from a risk. We'll cover matters here in Antioch.

We've got lots of support. But all of that is secondary to the most important thing of all."

"What's that?"

"You. You, and Ben." She dissolved on the inside as her father stood and pulled her to her feet, and then into his arms, swaying a bit. "Ben gave me his word he'd take good care of you, and I trust him on that count."

Hailey Beth leaned back, staring at her father wide-eyed. "What? When? When did he do that?"

"Oh, I believe he should be the one to fill in the details. For now, I think you need to go see him. Don't you?"

"Yeah. I do." On a burst of loving energy, Hailey Beth squeezed him tight, kissed his cheek. "I love you, Dad."

"Back to you a million, Hailey-girl. Now, go make it right with Ben, OK?"

"I will."

After breakfast, Hailey Beth climbed the stairs, headed for her room, ready to kick-start her day with a shower, and then a bookkeeping session at the store. She'd slip into problem-solving mode and work through what should come next, because wise as her father was, she still needed to come to her own decision, live her life, and the call of her heart, on her own terms.

The sound of her cell phone vibrating against the surface of her dresser caught Hailey Beth's attention. She paused to check the alert and discovered a text message from Ben.

Need to c u. So much 2 say. Never meant 2 drive you away. Just the opposite. Can we talk? ASAP? I'll b @ the farm.

Hailey Beth stared at her phone, nipping at the inside of her cheek as her pulse rate skyrocketed. Whatever it was Ben wanted to discuss, she was on board. God had obviously taken a hand, so everything else could wait.

I can b there in about an hour.

14

Ben tromped from the farm toward the field, boots tracking mud, twigs, and bramble. He hunkered within a wool-lined jacket. The air was chilly and moist. This seemed to be a morning full of farewell. A knitted ski-cap rode low across his forehead and against his ears, protecting from a misty first-of-Autumn drizzle. A loose-limbed stride took him down an increasingly crowded aisle of the field. Not far away, the hulking metal frame of a resting combine was all that marred nature's fluid and undulating perfection.

Harvest season was on fast approach. Only yesterday he had performed routine checks and maintenance. The header of the combine was in great shape. The wide, forward facing cab of the vehicle is where Dad would sit, for a few hours anyway, seeing to the start of the harvest in a few weeks. The header would cut the plants to ground-

level. The plants would be separated —
soybeans from pods and stems — then collected into the holding tank at the rear of
the machine.

Everything was ready. Everything but his
heart. Everything but Hailey Beth, and the
yearning she inspired.

Once again, he had gone all-in with regard
to Hailey Beth. He loved her. He wouldn't
be happy without her. Ben checked the time
on his cell phone. She'd be arriving shortly.
Thankfully she had accepted his invitation.

Fat, laden clouds piled together and
skimmed across the sky, a gray/white
mash-up that lent additional drama to the
moment.

In the barn, Ben launched into a session
of work therapy designed to let his mind
sort out all the issues Hailey Beth presented
in a form of background analysis. While he
pondered, he worked on finishing a gift he
intended to give her. A gift meant to touch
her heart and literally nourish her.

And that wasn't the only surprise he had
planned for HB.

He had already honed a piece of treated
wood to silky perfection in the shape of a
tablespoon. A wooden tablespoon he hoped
she would use when satisfying her daily
cereal fix. Last night he had used a wood

burner to create a pretty, feminine scroll design on the handle. All that remained to be done was personalization.

Ben knew just how he wanted to finish the piece. Her initials. A special date, precious to them both.

But again, it was a gamble, as he had said to Aaron at lunch recently. And his last risk with HB hadn't worked out well at all.

Would today be different?

Rather than fret over the things he couldn't control, he clung to his faith, to the love he felt. Ben drew a deep breath and engraved the back of the handle just as he wished — just as he dreamed — and he sent up a prayer that the Lord would see this moment through to completion.

While he worked, Ben redirected his thoughts to the farm. He thought of the old, but still sturdy combine, his dad at the helm. Dad had missed being an active participant in last year's harvest due to health issues, but this year was different, praise God. Dad had not only regained physical strength since his surgery last year, he had reasserted himself as a farmer without equal. He loved the land. Fed off it in a literal and figurative sense. His renewed oversight of production and a bit of manual labor was something the entire family rejoiced in and embraced. With Phillip and Aaron running the financials and crop teams respectively, Dad's duties wouldn't be overwhelming.

Life was good. Ben was truly free to go. He could pursue his dream. Why, then, was he in misery? He finished up the dedication markings on Hailey Beth's spoon, anxiety mounting.

"Hey there."

Ben nearly dropped his woodburning pen when he heard Hailey Beth's voice. She stood in the entryway, and he scrambled to stash the spoon and the stencil he had been using in a nearby drawer, grateful his back had blocked her from seeing what he was doing.

"Hey."

Once he faced her, Hailey Beth's expression was openly curious. "You were expecting me, right?"

Ben laughed. "Yeah. Of course."

She smiled at him, sweet, and kind of coy. That tweaked his senses and warmed him through. "By the way, you beat me to the punch."

"Huh?"

She wiggled the cell phone she held in her hand. "Your message. I was going to hit you up for lunch. I've really wanted to talk, too."

OK, this was a hopeful start. A promising start.

Tentatively, Ben moved toward her. "Yeah? What did you want to say?" He framed the words gently. Softly. He took hold of her hands after she stashed her phone in her coat pocket. Her fingertips were chilled so he rubbed them gently with his thumbs.

Hailey Beth looked down, seeming to study their connection rather than the depths of his eyes. Coy and playful morphed into winsomely shy . . .

"I'm really sorry about the way I jumped down your throat, Ben. I shouldn't have done that. You certainly didn't deserve it. Not when you were being open, and loving. You want me with you." Her gaze lifted. "That means so much to me. More than you probably realize."

"HB, I definitely realize. Know why? Because I feel the same way. I can't picture myself . . . my life . . . without you in it."

"I'm not going anywhere. I'll be here."

"And so will I."

Her eyes went wide. "Ben, no! You're not quitting the mission. No! You can't!"

He loved her zealous response, misguided though it was. Tears sprang to her eyes. "I'm not quitting the mission, but you deserve better than to wait and see what the future holds, without knowing my every intention." He gestured toward a hay bale. "Have a seat for a second, OK?"

She complied, studying him in open curiosity, but she hugged her arms around her midsection, as though warding off tremors. Ben returned to the work bench, the spot where he had completed her wooden spoon just before her arrival. He pulled it from inside the drawer, then reached into the pocket of his coat, fingers closing around gift number two.

And he prayed. *Jesus. Be with us.*

"I hope you like this." Ben handed her the spoon and Hailey Beth covered her lips, eyes moist, breathing shallow. "As often as you eat cereal is how often I want you to think of me."

"Ben, this is beautiful!" She studied the piece, glossed reverent fingertips along the front of the handle. Then, she turned it over. "Wait a second. You put . . ." She openly puzzled now; sentimental tears dried as confusion set in. "You put today's date, and our initials on the back."

"Because . . ." He sat next to her, wrapped an arm snug around her shoulders. "I had a talk with your father."

"Oh. Oh, my." He felt her nerves kick in. She trembled against him, her eyes never once straying from his.

"I asked him two questions."

"Yeah."

"The first was to ask him if he'd be agreeable to watching over the store while you took a few months, or however long you'd like, to join me in Arkansas, as a volunteer."

"What'd he say?"

"He's on board, and he'd have plenty of help from good people." Hailey Beth nodded, still shell-shocked, still trembling. "The second thing I asked him is, if I promised to take good care of you, to love you forever, if he'd allow me the honor of marrying you."

He didn't have time to extract gift number two from his pocket. Hailey Beth released an exclamation, and burst into tears, catapulting into his arms with as much fervor and joyful abandon as Ben could've ever dreamed — and he'd dreamed about her plenty of late.

"He better have said yes!" She laughed, cried, joked, swished her fingertips beneath her lashes to wipe away the trails of happy moisture.

"He did. But only if you're willing to say yes as well. Only if you're willing to take me on." He paused, pulled a black velvet ring box from the pocket of his coat, and flipped open the lid. The diamond inside was modest, but vibrant, throwing rainbow sparks even in the dim light of the barn where so much of their childhood, their lives, and the advent of their love affair had taken place.

Ben knelt, took her left hand in his. "Will you marry me, HB? I won't promise you easy, but I will promise you good. I can promise you love. I can promise that I'll treat you like a treasure, and always look for God's hand in all that we do, no matter what you decide about the mission."

"Ben, it's always been you. Always."

The simple words resonated, filling him.

Hailey Beth continued. "I could never hope or pray for more than you've just offered, and more than you've already given me. Yes. A million times, yes." They shared a long, tight hug. Hailey Beth leaned back in his arms.

Ben moved just far enough away to place the ring on her finger. For a moment, they silently admired the view of gold and a winking, captivating diamond.

Hailey Beth concluded matters with a decisive nod. "Let's do this. I'm on board. I want to get started on that future of ours just as soon as you can get me ready for Arkansas."

Ben could breathe again. He rested in an ordained sense of fulfillment. "There are people there who need us, HB."

"Amen, Ben. Amen."

ABOUT THE AUTHOR

Marianne Evans is an award-winning author of Christian romance and fiction. Her hope is to spread the faith-affirming message of God's love through the stories He prompts her to create. Her Christian women's fiction debut, *Devotion*, earned the prestigious Bookseller's Best Award as well as the Heart of Excellence Award. *Hearts Communion* earned a win for Best Romance from the Christian Small Publisher's Association. She is also a two-timer recipient of the Selah Award for her books *Then & Now* and *Finding Home*. Marianne is a lifelong resident of Michigan and an active member of Romance Writers of America, most notably the Greater Detroit Chapter where she served two terms as President.

The employees of Thorndike Press hope you have enjoyed this Large Print book. All our Thorndike, Wheeler, and Kennebec Large Print titles are designed for easy reading, and all our books are made to last. Other Thorndike Press Large Print books are available at your library, through selected bookstores, or directly from us.

For information about titles, please call:
    (800) 223-1244

or visit our website at:
    gale.com/thorndike

To share your comments, please write:
    Publisher
    Thorndike Press
    10 Water St., Suite 310
    Waterville, ME 04901